WIFE SWAP

'You want to kiss me?' Anne sounded hesitant.

Lisa nodded. Her features were inscrutable and Anne had no way of knowing if the woman was teasing or serious.

They were sitting on opposite sides of the four-seater table. Anne stood up to respond to the challenge, walked with forced casualness past her husband and stood at Lisa's side. Lisa turned to face her, her lips parted expectantly. Mark and Johnny watched, both feigning no more than the mildest interest, yet neither of them eating or moving as they waited for Lisa and Anne to act.

Aside from the music, the room was as silent as a held breath. The two women regarded each patiently. Anne's grin was uncertain, Lisa's mischievous.

'I've never kissed a girl before,' Anne croaked.

'I'm not a girl,' Lisa corrected. 'Bring your lips closer and you'll find out I'm all woman.'

The atmosphere crackled with electricity. Anne felt light-headed with anticipation. Johnny and Mark watched intently as the two women moved closer.

Anne licked her lips, desperately trying to fight the threat of nerves. Lisa reached up for her as she approached. Her fingers slipped inside the open front of Anne's shirt. And then their lips met.

Other titles available in the Nexus Enthusiast series:

LEG LOVER
DERRIÈRE
BUSTY
UNDER MY MASTER'S WINGS
THE SECRET SELF
OVER THE KNEE

WIFE SWAP

Amber Leigh

The LAST
WORD *in*
FETISH

enthusiast

This book is a work of fiction.
In real life, make sure you practise safe, sane and consensual sex.

First published in 2007 by
Nexus Enthusiast
Nexus
Thames Wharf Studios
Rainville Rd
London W6 9HA

www.nexus-books.co.uk

Typeset by TW Typesetting, Plymouth, Devon
Printed in the UK by CPI Bookmarque, Croydon, CR0 4TD

ISBN 978 0 352 34097 9

1

After The Party

Lisa used her thumb to roll the wedding band around her finger.

The diamond-cut facets danced in the glow of the overhead lights. Sparkling in so many different ways – needles of gold, glimmers of pure white, and devilish tinges of orange – Johnny couldn't help but think the ring reflected her personality. He snatched his gaze briefly from the road and admired her perfection in the nanosecond that his eyes were away from the motorway. He shook his head and grinned. 'You're an insatiable bitch.'

'What have I done now?' Her tone was shocked, injured and defensive, but he could hear the underlying smile.

'Didn't you get enough action at Becky's party?'

'I got plenty of action at Becky's party,' Lisa allowed.

She shifted position and he could hear the squeak and kiss of her short leather skirt against the Volvo's seat. From the periphery of his vision he saw her unfold her legs and realised that at some point in the evening, she had lost her stockings. It wasn't uncommon. He had lost a sock and his boxers in the course of the night. Her bare thighs disappeared and then reappeared repeatedly as the shadows of the road raced past. The dashboard clock told him it was a little after three in the morning.

The only vehicles sharing their route were an endless convoy of juggernauts in the slow lane, yet he didn't dare risk lowering his gaze to admire her properly.

She inched closer, snaking her hand across his thigh and reaching for the front of his pants. Lowering her voice to a sultry whisper Lisa said, 'I got plenty of action, but I'm not sure I got enough.' Her palm cupped the swell of his mounting interest, rubbing lightly as though she knew he would still feel sore. 'Would I sound like that greedy bastard Oliver if I said, *Please, Sir, can I have some more?*'

'Oliver wasn't a greedy bastard. He was just hungry.'

'I know that feeling. I'm hungry.' She curled her fingers around the thickness of his erection and squeezed. Her touch was perpetually light. The sensitivity of her hand was as delicate as a harpist trailing a shivering glissando.

Johnny kept his gaze fixed on the road. 'To the best of my recollection, Oliver wasn't hungry for cock.' He paused for a second and wondered if he should make some smutty remark about Dickens, and then decided the joke wasn't worth the effort.

'Don't be evasive,' she purred. 'Answer my question: *Please, Sir, can I have some more?*'

Johnny drew a deep breath and flicked his gaze from the incessant stream of traffic on his left to the illuminated traffic signs beyond them. With a heroic effort, and more regret than he could contemplate, Johnny reached for her wrist and gently lifted her hand away. 'You're breaking the rules, Lisa.'

'I'm only asking for a little more. It was a good party.' She paused reflectively and then decided, 'It was a *great* party, even if Becky did host it. I'm just in the mood for a little extra.'

'Breaking the rules.'

She moved on the seat and he fought not to notice her. In the light and shadows of the overhead lights her skin was bleached and then hidden in blackness. Her raven hair shone silver during the brightest moments before vanishing to impenetrable dark. Her porcelain complexion – sapphire eyes, pouting lips and sculpted cheekbones – was gloriously illuminated, then snatched into shadows. The cycle looked set to repeat itself until they arrived home. It was maddening to see her in such enticing glimpses.

'Which rule am I breaking?'

'You can't touch me while I'm driving. It's dangerous.'

'I was only touching your cock. You're not using that to drive, are you?'

'The rules are the rules, Lisa. We agreed on them months ago, after I nearly rear-ended that Toyota. You can't touch me while I'm driving.'

'Fine!'

It was the petulant declaration he expected.

'I didn't want to touch your stupid cock anyway. I wouldn't touch it now if you begged me.' She wriggled on her seat. While he thought she was going to simply fold her arms – turn away and maybe sleep – he was surprised to notice she was struggling with her clothes. The bolero jacket came off first, exposing her naked shoulders and chest. Her bare breasts swayed enticingly in the constant change from dark to light.

'Lisa!'

Instead of responding, she made an ungainly arc on the seat and released the fastener at the back of her skirt. Wriggling her hips, sliding the leather down over her thighs, she settled calmly in the passenger seat without any clothes. If he had wrenched his gaze from the road (and Johnny was desperate to tear his gaze from the road) he knew his beautiful wife would be sitting beside him in all her naked glory. From the corner of his eye he could make out her coltish legs, the smooth flesh of her shaved pussy and the awesome swell of her breasts. The hardness between his legs was so rigid it hurt.

Through clenched teeth he hissed, 'You're not wearing any clothes, Lisa.'

'Is that against the rules?'

'It's not against the rules but—'

'Then I'll stay without my clothes.'

She spoke with a finality that he had never challenged, but Johnny still tried to press his argument. 'Someone might see.'

'On a motorway? In the dark? At three in the morning?'

Inclining his head slightly to the left, never shifting his gaze from the road ahead, he said, 'One of those truckers might see.'

She shrugged. 'Let 'em look.' Adjusting her position, flexing her smile again, she asked, 'Did you enjoy the party?'

He sighed. 'It was a good party.'

'Do you think mine will be better?'

'I don't *think* yours will be better. I *know* yours will be better.'

'What did you get up to?'

He clutched the steering wheel tight. For an insane moment he could picture losing his concentration and swerving the vehicle into mayhem and carnage. Shaking his head, adamant he wouldn't be drawn into the exchange Lisa wanted, Johnny said, 'You're breaking the rules again.'

'Am not.'

'You know you are.'

'What rules am I breaking? Tell me? What rules?'

'We don't talk about any event until we're home and safe in bed. You know that's safest. You bloody well agreed when we set these rules.'

Her gaze flashed with that characteristic impatience he so loved and loathed. He could feel antipathy rolling from her in palpable waves and guessed she would find her jacket, curl herself into it and not talk to him for the remainder of their journey. She surprised him by stretching and saying, 'Every inch of me aches.'

'You're OK, aren't you?' Concern made him snatch his gaze briefly from the road. He saw she was using her thumb to twist the wedding band around her finger. Sighing pointedly, his fears for her well-being vanquished, he asked, 'Do you genuinely ache, or are you trying to tell me that parts of you are sore?'

She released a throaty chuckle. 'Becky was nibbling on my nipples. She can be a vicious bitch when she sets her mind to it. They feel really sensitive now. It hurts just to touch them.'

She paused and he guessed Lisa was studying, and maybe even stroking, her bare breasts. He gripped the steering wheel tightly enough to bleed the colour from his knuckles. His gaze remained focused on the road ahead.

'Is that a bruise she's left behind, or a smear of her lipstick?' Lisa pondered.

He heard the slurp of her tongue – knew without looking that she was lapping at herself – and then sighed when she said, 'Relief. It's just lipstick.'

'Lisa!' he warned.

'Did you have the pleasure of the hostess? I barely saw you all evening.'

The memory was too fresh to avoid. Becky was a Titian redhead with a sandy complexion blemished by light freckles. She had recognised him from those other parties he and Lisa had attended and made a special point of welcoming him. Conducting her hostess duties in a faux-dominatrix outfit – looking resplendent in thigh-length boots, a revealing waistcoat and a peaked cap – she had pressed herself against him and teased his length from his pants. Maintaining eye contact, never once letting her gaze slip from his, she had lowered herself to her knees and lapped at the end of his shaft.

5

Through wire-thin lips Johnny said, 'No talking about any event until after we've got back. That's the rule.'

'I was only asking.' She sniffed, as though appalled by his rudeness, and then fell back sulking into her seat. With a swiftness of mood change that was as fast as the motorway's shift from shadow to light, she sat brightly forward and said, 'I finally got to meet up with that guy they call Donkey.' Her laughter was sudden and infectious. 'Shit! I was worried he was going to split me in two. Have you seen how big his cock is?'

'Lisa!'

The mental image she conjured was unbearable. Johnny had seen the guy they called Donkey – conversation at parties never missed the two favourite topics of which woman had the biggest tits and which guy had the biggest cock – and he could easily picture the monstrous length sliding between his wife's legs. The thought of her having him, the concept of that mammoth shaft ploughing into her delicate hole, was enough to turn his palms slick against the steering wheel.

The car veered lightly to the right and he immediately compensated. His foot inched off the accelerator and he slowed a little. But his mind couldn't shake the glorious image of Lisa and the guy they called Donkey. He could almost hear her sighs of enjoyment and, with an empathy he believed that no other couple in the world could possibly share, he felt an echo of the pleasure she had enjoyed. In his mind's eye he pictured the guy called Donkey pulling out of her and leaving Lisa's hole lush and dark and open.

'He's certainly got some staying power,' Lisa said with a grin. 'He must have ridden me for a good half an hour.' She paused, giggled and then said, 'No. It wasn't a *good* half hour: it was a *great* half hour.'

'Rules, Lisa. You're breaking the rules.'

She ignored him. 'I feel so beautifully stretched and used. I'd be a lot sorer if that snooty wife of his hadn't gone down on me after. That girl with the designer specs helped her. Do you know the one I mean? Her head's not much to look at but she has that supermodel body with an almost perfectly flat chest?'

'Tara.'

'That's her. She's hot. I could do her again. You should have tried her.'

'I did.'

This was why he didn't like talking about events on the journey home. Instead of concentrating on the negligible traffic and focusing on the mechanics of driving at a steady seventy through the night, he was more involved in the memory of what he had just done. Tara's waiflike figure had been gloriously insubstantial to embrace. Her flat chest, although unimposing, made her spectacularly responsive. Flicking his tongue against her tiny, delicate nipples had inspired the woman to thrash and buck hungrily against him. When he slid between her legs, the tightness of her hole had been a splendid reward. The memory was still so rich he could taste the flavour of the woman's kiss.

'Really?' There was genuine enthusiasm and arousal in Lisa's voice. 'You got to screw Tara? Is she tight? Was she any good? Would you do her again?'

He made the decision in an instant. A turnoff loomed to his right, he could see a gap between the trucks that was almost large enough for the Volvo, and he flicked the indicator as he squeezed through the space.

A thunderous horn bellowed angrily behind them. Headlamps flashed like a bolt of halogen lightning. And then he was scaling the exit road and pulling into a parking strip at the side of the off-road.

'Johnny?'

He yanked the handbrake before popping his seat belt and then reached for her. Lisa escaped his grip and slipped out of the car. Johnny climbed across her seat after her. The thought that she was naked and out in the open air was exciting, but he knew it wasn't the source of his arousal. Her talk of what she had done and who she had done it with – their exchange of experiences – was always the thing that thrilled him most. It never failed to turn him on when they were anticipating each party; it constantly kept him aroused when they were attending one; and it always made him hard and in need of her when the party was over.

He caught up with her just outside the car door.

Her warm body was a divine contrast to the chill night around them. His fingers found her breasts, and then moved down to her waist. As he pulled her into his embrace his hands moved up and he revelled in the tactile bliss of her bare back. Her breasts pressed against him, her mouth found his, and then he was lost in her thrall.

It was almost magical the way she possessed him like no other woman.

He reflected that he was returning home from a party of excess and gratuitous sex. Naked flesh had been apparent in every direction. Easy conquests had fallen beneath him with a hunger that matched his own boundless appetite. Every detail of the evening was embedded in his memory and each passionate, exciting moment would stay with him forever as a treasured experience.

But being with Lisa was better.

'I've had six cocks inside me this evening,' she told him.

Her words rang musically above the whisper of the nearby motorway traffic. Distance and a hedging of trees muted the thunder of juggernauts. Aside from the glimmer of moonlight above, they were alone in a lightless void. But the scent of her body, the warmth of her words and the flavour of her arousal were all he needed.

She breathed, 'Do you want to be the lucky seventh?'

He pulled his shaft from his pants and pushed it toward her.

She leant back over the bonnet of the car, parting her thighs and guiding him between her legs. While her body felt warm, and her kisses were hotter, the inside of her sex was scalding. His length had been sheathed in condoms throughout the party and the contrast of sensations was phenomenal. From the smooth and almost impersonal penetrations, this was the warm wet haven he could always return to. The velvet sheath of her sex gripped him tight and the tremor of her muscles sucked against him. Breathing deeply, drinking in every detail, he plunged deeper as Lisa squeezed around him and pulled closer.

'Hard,' she muttered. 'I want it hard.'

He was tempted to taunt her – make a joke that it was already hard – but he could sense she was in no mood for frivolous banter. Knowing her needs as well as his own, intuitive to her desires and drives, he put one hand under her bottom and the other in the centre of her back. Making sure his hold on her was adequate, treating her with his characteristic blend of tenderness and control, Johnny began to ride his length vigorously in and out.

She groaned.

Her pussy tried to grip tightly around him but her wetness made the hold intangible. He could hear the slick squelch of each thrust and smell the rich flavour of their mingled scents. Traffic continued to drone past on the motorway beneath but the blackness of the desert surrounding them remained unbroken. His thoughts were fixed only on the pleasure of being buried inside his wife and sharing the bliss of release. When he heard her begin to gasp – a series of sudden, snatched breaths – he knew the orgasm was almost upon her. Delighted by her receptiveness, overjoyed that she could still respond to him the way he always responded to her,

9

Johnny continued to thrust until she shrieked with euphoria. Her body stiffened in his embrace, her cry whispered musically through the darkness and her inner muscles convulsed around him. He continued to slide back and forth, basking in the sensation of her pussy hungrily devouring him, trembling with a rush of emotions that were almost as strong as their physical symptoms.

'Now I've had seven cocks tonight,' she breathed. Her voice was drunk from the remnants of satisfaction. 'That huge guy called Donkey was one of them. Yet you're still the best lay of them all.'

Johnny came.

He couldn't resist the flattery of her words or the thrill of her confession. Shivering with the climax, he bucked harshly into her as his seed erupted. Through a haze of delight he heard Lisa cry out again, and then they were hugging and holding and giggling against each other. She kissed his mouth, passion spent but gratitude obvious. The sweetness of the exchange made Johnny want to melt into her again, even though his flailing shaft was already slipping from her hole.

In the last moments of their shared embrace they trembled together.

'That was what I needed to complete the evening,' Lisa whispered. 'Thanks.'

He shrugged off the seriousness of her voice, tucked himself back into his pants and gallantly helped Lisa into the passenger seat. As he took his place behind the wheel he said, 'You can thank me properly by declining our dinner invitation with the Kents.'

Lisa pursed her lips and her brow wrinkled. 'You were good just then. But you weren't *that* good. We're still going to dinner with the Kents tomorrow night. No way are we crying off.'

Johnny groaned. He tugged the car away from the side of the road and drove back onto the motorway.

Feigning weariness he sighed and said, 'I'm not looking forward to four interminable hours with that grinning tit and his jailbait bride. Is he going to bore me some more with his talk of urban legends? Maybe he knows why her hair changes colour so bloody often.'

'Stop being Mr Grumpy. Be nice about our new neighbours.' She had found her jacket and placed it over her shoulders for warmth rather than modesty. Curled on the passenger seat, and with her eyes half-closed, her voice was already shrouded with a gossamer veil of sleep. Slurring words together she said, 'They seem like good people and they're making the effort to be friendly. Besides, I like Mark's smile.'

Johnny sniffed. 'That's not a smile. It's a rictus.'

Lisa yawned. 'Change the subject, Johnny. I don't want to bicker.'

'Fair enough. How about you tell me what you want for your birthday?'

'Oh! That's easy.' She yawned again.

Knowing her as he did – knowing her more intimately than he believed any man had ever known a partner – Johnny felt sure she would be asleep within moments. He idly wondered if she would be able to complete her sentence before consciousness slipped from her grasp.

'I've already decided what I want for my birthday,' she mumbled. 'I want your secretary.'

Johnny clutched the steering wheel tighter.

2

Neighbours

Lisa had expected Johnny's prediction would be right –
dinner with the Kents promised to be deadly dull – but
she was pleasantly surprised by the geniality the pair
exuded. As well as being cordial hosts they were an
attractive couple. Mark was tall and broad and, although his face was too plain to be called handsome, his
constant smile was genuine and infectious and it made
him likeable. Lisa decided Johnny had been unfair in
dismissing him as a grinning tit and she suspected her
husband would revise his opinion by the end of the
evening.

Mark's huge build dwarfed his pretty wife, Anne, but
her petite stature suited her sprightly character and
made her easy company. She had already told them she
was a freelance writer by profession and, in her caffeinated manner, had insisted Lisa should read an article
she was composing. While Lisa knew the woman's
frenetic pace could have been irritating under other
circumstances, she thought Anne managed to carry it off
as an engaging and almost winsome character trait. This
evening her hair was a dark plum colour, a contrast
from the blonde it had been when they moved in but not
that dissimilar from the raven she had worn the week
after. On her pageboy crop the colour looked vibrant
and rich.

Lisa thought the only thing threatening to spoil the bonhomie of the evening was Johnny and his distracted mood. She passed him a subtle frown, trying to indicate that his lack of interest was obvious and rude, but he was lost in a world of his own thoughts.

'I've got a special wine for this evening,' Mark announced. 'I thought I'd crack it open before we eat, just in case it tastes like piss.'

Warming to his honesty, Lisa laughed.

Anne patiently admonished her husband.

Johnny flexed a terse smile.

They stood in a quartet in the centre of Mark's kitchen. It was a pleasant room, with polished chrome fittings on a black and white décor, but homely enough to feel comfortable and not sterile. A brimming fruit bowl, an open bottle of cooking sherry and the general clutter of a room in use made it tolerably informal. The flavour of a spicy marinade peppered the air. Above the sounds of boiling pans and bubbling sauces a CD player mumbled its way through Elvis's greatest hits.

'Special wine?' Lisa asked. 'What's so special about it?'

Mark plucked the bottle from an ice bucket and studied the label. 'It's a Le Montrachet chardonnay,' he explained. 'A Grand Cru no less.'

Lost with the subject of wine, and never daring enough to bluff knowledge when she had none, Lisa asked again, 'What's so special about it?'

'It cost five hundred quid. I guess that should make it pretty special.'

Her reaction was instantaneous. 'You're not opening that for us.'

'We bloody well are,' Anne argued. 'It's not like Mark paid for it with his own money. He bought that from unscrupulous winnings.'

Johnny raised an eyebrow. 'You're a gambler, Mark?'

'I'm not a gambler. I'm a salesman.'

13

'OK,' said Lisa with a chuckle. 'That's intriguing. Would you care to explain? Or are you going to remain a man of mystery for the rest of the evening?'

Mark glanced from Lisa to Johnny, his ever-present grin briefly widening. 'I was at a sales conference last week. On the last day there were half a dozen high-rollers sitting in the hotel lobby arguing about which of them stood the best chance with a redhead they'd seen at the bar. Most of them were drunk. All of them were puffed up with the bluster of being the best salesman in the world. So I bet them each two grand I could talk her out of her knickers.'

Lisa surprised herself by laughing.

Anne took the bottle of wine from her husband. She wore the tight smile of a woman who had heard the anecdote before but was content to listen through it again. With no regard for the chardonnay's age or expense, she discreetly popped the cork and filled four crystal flutes while Mark continued.

'There was twelve grand sitting on the table,' he explained. 'And I had half a dozen drunken reps telling me they'd rescind their title as best salesman in the world if I could get the redhead out of her knickers.'

Lisa accepted her glass from Anne with a polite nod. Anxious to hear the rest of Mark's story she held his gaze and asked, 'What did you do?'

'I stepped politely over to the redhead and introduced myself. Before I'd had a chance to buy her a drink she'd pulled up her skirt and wriggled out of her knickers. She gave the sales reps a quick flash of her bare arse and then she thrust the pants into my hand.' He chuckled and said, 'It was the easiest twelve grand I ever made.'

'You must be one hell of a salesman,' Johnny muttered.

'He is,' Anne agreed. 'He's gifted with a silver tongue.'

Lisa considered him carefully. She wondered if Mark had offered a percentage of his winnings to the redhead,

14

or if he really was the most gifted salesman she had ever met. Not sure which explanation was most likely, and unable to contain her curiosity, she finally asked, 'How the hell did you manage to get her to take off her pants so quickly?'

Anne said, 'It was easy enough for him.' She patted her plum crop and said, 'I happened to be a redhead that week.' Handing out the remainder of the drinks, and then stepping dutifully back to her husband's side, she added, 'But I've always had a superstitious thing about money that's been won with those sorts of bets.' Shivering, she added, 'It makes me worry that bad karma's going to come back at us if we use it for anything other than frivolous stuff. That's why Mark gave a big chunk of it to some animal charity and we blew the rest on a couple of new outfits and this bottle of plonk.'

Lisa shook her head, bewildered and amazed by this unexpected facet of their new neighbours. She glanced at Johnny and was pleased to see that some of his earlier stiffness had evaporated. He didn't look exactly like his usual affable self – it was clear that something was still worrying him – but he didn't seem as distracted as before. Knowing there was no opportunity to ask what was troubling him, wishing she had cancelled their dinner engagement with the Kents so they could discuss the cause of his consternation, she reluctantly dragged her attention from her husband when Mark proposed the toast.

'To neighbours,' he declared.

Johnny and Lisa raised their glasses and repeated the words.

Anne took the first sip of the chardonnay and grimaced. Wrinkling her nose and dancing daintily backwards, she gasped, 'It's fucking awful. It tastes like piss.'

Within moments all four of them were laughing together.

* * *

15

'You OK, Johnny?'

He blinked himself back to the room and realised how rude his silence must have seemed. Anne had dragged Lisa upstairs to get her opinion on the article she was writing. Johnny and Mark had remained in the kitchen and, at some point when the host began to muse about an urban legend that dealt with a choking rottweiler, Johnny had found his thoughts drifting.

'I'm so sorry. I was miles away.'

'You seem a little quiet. Anne and I aren't making you uncomfortable, are we?'

'No. Nothing like that. I'm just ...' He flexed an apologetic grin and said, 'Between you and me, I'm trying to think how I can get the birthday present Lisa wants.'

'What's she after?'

For an instant Johnny almost blurted the truth. *'She's asked to have my secretary for a night.'* He could feel the words brimming behind his lips and it was only when he thought how his host might respond that he stopped himself from speaking. Shaking his head, grinning broadly as he prepared to skate around the subject, he said, 'I'll fret about it tomorrow when I'm back in the office. At least that way I'll be salaried and unhappy. What were we talking about?'

Mark turned his attention back to the marinade. He moved smoothly and efficiently around the kitchen and Johnny watched with quiet admiration. His own skills in the kitchen didn't go much further than the kettle and the microwave and he was always willing to applaud those people with abilities he didn't possess.

'Is that your recipe for a successful marriage?' Mark asked as he stirred something in a large pot. He replaced its lid, wiped his hands on a dishcloth and then tossed it to one side. 'Do you recommend making sure your lady gets exactly what she wants?'

Johnny sipped at his chardonnay. He didn't think the drink was as terrible as Anne had declared but he couldn't imagine it was worth the price Mark had paid. 'Do you know a better way to keep a marriage successful?'

'No. And with a partner as attractive as your Lisa, I can understand why you put the effort into keeping her happy.' His ceaseless grin widened as he added, 'She's a very attractive lady.'

Johnny glanced toward the back door and the windows that led to the rear garden. Pulling a cigar from his jacket pocket he asked, 'Am I OK to smoke one of these out there?'

'Sure. Either Anne or I will come out and join you in a minute. I need to keep an eye on my salmon and cilantro sauce.'

Wondering if he was misreading Mark's compliment, Johnny stepped outside the house and wished he had kept his thoughts focused on the evening. If he'd spent less time worrying about Lisa and his secretary, Debbie, and if he'd paid more attention to Mark's mannerisms and conversation, Johnny knew he would have a better idea of how to take the comment about Lisa. At a swinging party, or at any event with swappers, he knew the remark would have been a thinly veiled enquiry into Lisa's availability. Because this couple seemed so straight and normal (terminally normal was the expression that kept creeping to the forefront of his mind), Johnny felt sure he was seeing signs where they didn't really exist.

Tucking the cheroot in one corner of his mouth he sparked his Zippo with a flick of his thumb and wondered if there had been genuine indications about the couple's interest or if he was simply too tired and distracted to properly interpret events. Anne was dressed in jeans and a T-shirt but it was obvious that she was braless. He hadn't been able to miss the detail of her neat nipples jutting stiffly against the cotton. And Mark's anecdote, innocent enough on the surface, implied that the couple didn't mind deceiving other people and showed that Anne had no issues about removing her pants in public or wriggling her bare backside at strangers.

He felt the familiar stirrings of arousal in the front of his pants and shuffled uncomfortably from one foot to the other before telling himself he was wrong. Taking in the splendour of the suburban garden, admiring the nicely landscaped touches the Kents had added since moving in, he drew on his cigar and decided he was thinking too much. Sipping again at his chardonnay, finding it grew more palatable with each mouthful, he almost laughed at the ridiculous idea of Mark and Anne being swingers or swappers.

Through an open window from the kitchen he heard Mark's baritone voice. 'Anne? Honey?' he called. 'Can I borrow you down here in the kitchen?' The simplicity of their affection, and their easy way with each other, was enough to convince Johnny that they weren't involved with any alternative lifestyle. Laughing at his own foolishness, he smoked a little more of his cigar and marvelled at the idiocy of thinking that Mark and Anne might be swingers.

When Lisa glanced up from the article she saw Anne had stepped out of her jeans and T-shirt. She wore a skimpy thong and its lack of substance accentuated her diminutive size. Braless, but with not much of a chest to speak of, she still managed to look like a powerfully sexual creature. Her suntanned skin was the colour of rose gold. Her minimal breasts were little more than pectoral muscles, tipped with mocha areolae and nipples. She made no attempt to cover herself – every nuance of her posture indicated a confidence in her nakedness – and she still seemed to buzz with the same furious energy Lisa had noticed earlier.

'Mark prefers me not to wear jeans when we're entertaining,' Anne said by way of explanation. She bent down, picked up the discarded clothes and tossed them into a convenient laundry basket. 'He says it's more appropriate for entertaining if I look like a woman.'

'You certainly look like a woman in that outfit,' Lisa said dryly. 'Are you going down to dinner like that?'

Anne giggled, a pretty and musical sound. 'I don't think Mark would object. What would your Johnny say?'

She stood on tiptoes and did a dainty pirouette to display her back. The rear of the thong disappeared between her taut buttocks. Drinking in every detail, Lisa could see the shadow of dark curls that was neatly crushed inside the gusset of the thong. Every inch of her golden skin looked surprisingly inviting. As Lisa studied the woman's back and buttocks, and then her breasts, she realised her breathing had dropped to an expectant hush. The heady atmosphere of anticipation made her momentarily queasy and – still sitting at the computer keyboard, with Anne's article on the screen before her – she pressed her thighs together.

'Johnny wouldn't raise any objections.'

'Is he not comfortable here tonight? He seems a little distant.'

Lisa shrugged. Although she was worried about Johnny she was more concerned with why Anne had suddenly and unexpectedly undressed. Nudity didn't trouble her – she figured it would have made for some rather uneasy swinging parties if it had – but she couldn't equate Anne's nakedness with what she expected from this evening with their new neighbours. 'We had a late night last night,' Lisa said eventually. 'I think he's just a little tired.'

'Poor boy,' Anne said. 'What can we do to pep him up?'

'Again,' said Lisa with a sour grin, 'you going downstairs like that wouldn't spoil his night.'

Anne waved a dismissive hand, finally blushing. 'I can't see Johnny being interested in me when he's married to you. You're gorgeous, with bosoms and height and beauty. I'm just flat-chested and plain.'

Lisa had heard false praise before – and she recognised the difference between self-deprecation and fishing for compliments – but she didn't think Anne's comments fell under any of those labels. Considering the woman's body language – the well-set shoulders, the proud gaze and her genuine and honest tone of voice – Lisa got the impression that Anne's appreciation was honest. She stood up, reached out to place a reassuring hand on her arm, and said, 'Trust me. You'd make Johnny's evening if he saw you like that.'

It was the moment when they touched that Lisa expected something to happen. If the couple were genuinely interested in swapping, Lisa believed Anne would do something daring and outrageous. Running down the stairs to the kitchen, flashing herself at Johnny and then scampering madly upstairs would have been Lisa's first guess. Her second would have been that the woman would ask a coy question (*Do you think Johnny would really want to see me like this?*) and slyly solicit Lisa's permission to flaunt herself in front of him.

Instead of doing anything so obvious, Anne glanced at Lisa's chest and asked, 'Are those real?'

Lisa hesitated before replying. Confused by Anne's whirlwind approach to conversations, feeling a little dizzy from trying to keep track of where things were heading and what motivated this question or that action, Lisa composed her thoughts before giving a response. Anne's article had been an argument about the pros and cons of breast enhancement. Her enquiry about Lisa's breasts seemed to be within the context of that subject and polite conversation. But Lisa had also heard the line used as a tried and tested come-on within those circles of swingers and swappers where she and

Johnny mingled. Her heart hammered with the familiar thrill of anticipation. She steeled herself to appear daring.

'Do they look real?'

'What I can see of them. Yeah. They look real.'

'Do you want to touch and see if they feel real?'

Anne's eyes widened. She flicked her gaze from Lisa's face to her breasts. Her grin broadened and a bright pink blush rouged her cheeks. Although she made no move to step closer her fingers flexed with obvious eagerness. 'Wouldn't you be embarrassed? Wouldn't you think I was some kind of pervert or something?'

Lisa shrugged back her shoulders and stood up. She was taller and knew her clothes gave her the confidence to dominate the situation but she was reluctant to make herself appear too eager or draw the impetus away from Anne. Teasing open the top three buttons on her blouse, exposing an indecent amount of cleavage, she took hold of Anne's right hand and lifted it to her left breast.

The crackle of arousal that spat between them was impossible to ignore.

It struck Lisa like an electric charge and she noticed that they both gasped. Anne's hand, small, fragile and delicate, only lay against the upper half of Lisa's breast. The heel of her palm rested against the arc of lace on her bra and the weight pressed against Lisa's nipple. The hard bud of flesh was stiffening and Lisa could feel the tingle of fluid warmth rippling through her sex. She wanted to glance at Anne's breasts and see if the woman was suffering the same obvious symptoms of excitement but she couldn't drag her gaze from Anne's large hazel eyes. The intensity of her stare was both thrilling and disquieting. It was as stimulating an aphrodisiac as the sensation that came when the woman's fingers lightly kneaded Lisa's breast. Her touch was gentle and delicate. The contact between them remained constant and unbroken, and Lisa could feel herself responding to the

21

caress while still being unsure if such a reaction was appropriate in these circumstances.

'Do they feel real?' she asked eventually. The words came out as a croak. Her mouth was so parched she would have chanced another glass of the chardonnay to moisten her throat and lips. Maintaining eye contact with Anne, she reached for the right cup of her bra and eased the fabric down. With her breast fully exposed, the rigid cherry nipple openly displayed, she continued to hold Anne's stare as she said, 'Hold it properly. You'll be able to make a more informed decision.'

Anne opened her mouth to say something but before she could reply Mark's voice boomed up the stairs. 'Anne? Honey?' he called. 'Can I borrow you down here in the kitchen?'

'Mark said you were hiding out here.'

She had crept behind him so quietly that Johnny almost shrieked when Anne's words announced her presence. He didn't know how long he had been standing in the garden but half his cigar had already disappeared and the light was fading as the sun slipped further beyond the horizon. He mumbled a brief apology, took a moment to admire the smooth contours of the clinging black dress she now wore and made a gesture with his cigar. 'I wouldn't call it hiding. I'm just being the rudest houseguest you've ever entertained. I'm sorry.'

'You're not the rudest house guest we've ever entertained. You haven't suggested my Elvis CDs are crap, or told Mark his cilantro sauce has too much garlic.'

Her voice was quick-fire and she rattled off words with a haste that made him feel his own speech was the lumbering conversation of someone with a learning difficulty. On anyone else he would have thought the habit pinpointed her as nervous but Anne had a deportment that made him think she was quietly confident. 'You're just outside enjoying the evening and a smoke. I can't blame you. It's a lovely night. We should have organised an intimate barbecue out here rather than dinner inside. Mark said the weather was too unpredictable, though, and he does have a point.' She nodded at Johnny's cigar and added, 'May I?'

He blinked and silently passed the cheroot to her.

Their fingers touched briefly. The warmth of her hands surprised him and he was startled that the momentary contact made him realise that she looked extremely desirable in the slinky black frock. Considering the way the smooth curves followed her body he guessed she was still not wearing a bra and wondered if she was either wearing a thong under the frock or simply nothing at all. Shifting uncomfortably to hide the bulge of his growing excitement, he let her take the cigar.

Trying not to stare, but fascinated by something about Anne, Johnny watched her place the end of the cigar between her lips. The twist of tobacco leaves pressed against the plum-coloured lipstick and he noticed a wisp of white smoke trailing against her tongue before she closed her mouth. When she sucked on the end her cheeks briefly dimpled and the tip of the cigar glowed a furious orange.

'I take it you're married to a non-smoker too.'

She nodded, savouring the cigar before replying. 'I quit to make Mark's life more bearable,' she explained. 'But I enjoy the occasional indulgence now and again. Doesn't Lisa smoke?'

'Never has and never will. I try and keep it out of the house at home.'

'It seems like we have a lot in common.' As she said the words she handed the cigar back to him. Again he was struck by the warmth of her touch and, watching the way the smoke slipped past her lips as she breathed out, he was stung by the yearning need to kiss her. Unwilling to make such a bold move with the new

23

neighbours, still uncertain that he was reading the signs correctly, Johnny drew on the cigar and then passed it back.

'I used to smoke,' Anne said reflectively. She toyed with the length between her slender fingers, rolling it back and forth, her hypnotic gaze lingering on the smouldering tip. 'It was one of the many bad habits I picked up at school.' She laughed and asked, 'Did you smoke back then? Did you ever *share* cigarettes?'

The peculiar emphasis she placed on the word made him hesitate. 'Share in what way?'

Her giggle was shrill but not unpleasant. When she glanced up at him her eyes were bright with vital enthusiasm. 'It probably sounds like a filthy habit, but no filthier than smoking itself. Fags were expensive when I went to school, way beyond the reach of the pocket money I got, and we always used to share the smoke. I don't mean passing a fag round like it was a joint. What we'd do is, someone would take a draw from their cigarette, and they wouldn't exhale until they were kissing someone.' Her eager grin sparkled with the prospect of mischief.

'I remember doing that on a couple of occasions,' Johnny said with a laugh. The memory startled him into relaxing a little more. 'God! I'd forgotten some of the horrible habits I had when I was a kid. Weren't we disgusting children?'

'Do you still remember how to do it?' Anne asked. 'Do you want to try it now?' Without waiting for a response, she took a long draw from the cigar and then lifted her mouth so her lips were inches from his.

'There you are.'

Lisa glanced up on hearing the cheery boom of Mark's voice and returned his smile. 'Here I am,' she agreed. She was sitting in front of the monitor in Anne's makeshift office, alternating her attention between the article on screen and the décor on the walls and the desk. A life-sized poster of Elvis dominated the wall beside the office door. Framed articles, clipped from magazines, and a handful of university certificates hid a lot of the bland wallpaper. The desk was cluttered with pens, CDs, papers and empty chocolate wrappers. A fluffy pink bunny rabbit, holding a heart that was inscribed with the words 'I WUV YOU', sat beside the monitor.

'Anne's outside, and probably sharing a cigar with your husband,' he explained as he mounted the last step on the landing. 'I didn't want you to feel as though we were ignoring you so I came up here to drag you back downstairs.'

'You haven't been ignoring me. I was rereading Anne's article.'

His bulk filled the doorway of Anne's makeshift office. His massive breadth managed to make the life-sized poster of Elvis seem petite. Glancing at the monitor he asked, 'Does it make sense to you? I've read through it but I'm not the expert on women's breasts that I'd like to be. She's been looking forward to you and Johnny coming over so she could get another woman's perspective on the piece before she submits it to her editor.'

Lisa nodded. 'It reads well. It gave me pause for thought.' Easing away from the computer screen she stood and asked, 'Can I help you in the kitchen?'

He shook his head. 'The kitchen is my domain. I turn ugly and violent when anyone interferes with my creations.'

She laughed at the idea of Mark turning violent. His constant smile and obvious gentleness made it impossible to think of him as being unpleasant under any circumstances. 'How about I set the table?'

'Anne's already taken care of that. The best crockery is laid out in the dining room. You can come and chat with me in the kitchen if you like. Ask me nicely and I might even pour you another glass of that godawful chardonnay.'

'Do you have anything that tastes less like vinegar?'

He glanced at her chest and, in the moment that his gaze fell from her face, Lisa realised she hadn't fastened the buttons on her blouse. She had tucked her right breast back inside her bra but, in the haste to help Anne slip into her slinky black dress and hurry down the stairs, she had forgotten to deal with her own clothing. The indecent amount of cleavage was there for Mark to see and her breasts, encased in the lacy cups of her bra, seemed to swell under his attention.

'Do you know your blouse is open?'

'I'm sorry.' Blushing lightly at the indiscretion, she reached for the buttons. Her fingers were shaking and she stammered to think of a response that would sound light and unconcerned. 'Anne and I were—'

'Don't hide them on my account,' Mark joked. 'That's a view I could admire all evening.'

'We got to talking about breasts,' Lisa explained hurriedly. The buttons were refusing to slide into their holes as her shaking hands let them slip from her grasp. She kept her face lowered, staring at herself and the blouse and anything else that helped her avoid Mark's eyes. 'Anne asked if mine were real or not,' she babbled. 'And, because of the article . . .'

'They look very real to me.'

She stopped trying to fasten the buttons and came to a sudden decision. Holding the blouse open, boldly raising her head so her gaze met his, she asked, 'Do you think you'd be able to tell if they're real?'

Kissing Anne made Johnny instantly hard.

Her slight body pressed against him as she pushed her mouth over his. The caress of her lips was a glorious exchange and, as she allowed the fragrant smoke to trail over his tongue, he shivered. Through the thin fabrics of his shirt and her dress he could feel their bodies yearning to touch. Her nipples were stiff beneath the slinky fabric of her frock. His erection throbbed with a sudden and unarguable need for her.

When she placed a hand against his back, he realised he was caught in her light embrace. A moment of panic threatened to quell his arousal as he wondered how Mark might respond if he found Johnny kissing his wife, then he decided the woman was merely trying to maintain her balance as she stood on tiptoe. He didn't know why such a consideration should assuage his fears but, somehow, it seemed to make the idea of adultery less of a complication.

Anne broke away from him with a giggle. Her eyes shone with a devilish glee that made his erection hurt. 'Isn't that just the nastiest thing to share?' She passed the cigar back to him and Johnny took a light draw on the end.

He was grinning with her and had to nod his head in agreement. 'Absolutely ghastly,' he declared. Holding her gaze, savouring the sparkle that made her hazel eyes so enchanting, he asked, 'Do you want to try it again?'

The mirth vanished from her expression at once. Snatching the cigar from his fingers she said, 'OK.' Taking a quick draw from the cheroot – making the action seem like an afterthought rather than the supposed real reason for their kiss – she pressed against him again and the pout of her lips inched closer to his mouth.

'Are you two ready to come inside?' Mark called. His voice trailed through the open kitchen window behind them. Whatever spell had been between them was lost as soon his cry reached their ears. 'I'm just about to serve dinner.'

'I'll get rid of this,' Johnny said, taking the cigar from Anne's fingers.

Her gaze was lowered as she nodded agreement. She started towards the door, moving with the brisk pace that he had noticed in her all evening, and then she paused. Glancing back at him, regarding him with eyes that were hypnotic and exciting, she asked, 'Have you got any more of those, so we could maybe share one after dinner?'

Lisa thought it was a fantastic meal.

Mark and Anne described themselves as DINKYs, and then explained it was an acronym for Double Income No Kids Yet. Although he'd called himself a salesman earlier, Mark's job description turned out to be an understatement when Anne explained he was the sales director of a fledgling software company. Her passion for Elvis echoed throughout the meal, as the King's music provided a soundtrack for the evening. She confessed that she was saving the money from her writing to make a pilgrimage to Gracelands. Johnny discussed his own work at the accountancy practice, modestly brushing over his importance with the firm, while Lisa described herself as 'a lady of leisure.' The boys discussed the merits and drawbacks of Johnny's Volvo and Mark's BMW while Lisa and Anne cheerfully debated the virtues of Prada and Versace. The banter was as light as the salmon and as friendly as the Californian white that Mark found to replace the chardonnay. The prospect of a blossoming friendship was as sweet as the crème brulée their host served for dessert.

And yet, throughout the evening, Lisa couldn't shake the idea that there was sexual tension in the air. Squirming lazily in her chair, enjoying the heady thrill of trying to guess if Mark and Anne shared their interest in swinging, she kept her concentration fixed on the conversation for fear of missing any telltale clues.

'Which magazine is your article for?'

'It's one of the smaller glossies,' Anne said, finishing off the last of her dessert. 'They commission me to do various things that are sex-related. Last month I had to give them a special feature on toys: jackrabbits, rockets and that kind of thing. This month it's breast enhancement. Next month they want to run a feature on partner swapping. Apparently it's something that nearly every couple considers during the course of their relationship.'

Lisa felt a knifeblade of arousal twist in her stomach. Struggling to keep her voice steady she said, 'That doesn't surprise me. I'd imagine it's a popular fantasy.'

'Have you two ever considered swapping?'

As soon as Anne said the words, Lisa could feel the tension thicken the air. She noticed Johnny stiffen in his seat and, although Mark hadn't asked the question, she could see he was waiting attentively for a response, his usual grin briefly replaced by an expression of serious concern. Lisa could see the pair had spent the entire evening building to this moment. Her heartbeat lurched at a phenomenal pace.

Because she had been in their situation and suffered the gamut of this experience Lisa understood the worry and unease that they would both be feeling. A mischievous part of her was tempted to heighten their anxiety and change the subject. But she couldn't bring herself to be so cruel. 'Swapping?' Lisa breathed coolly. 'Been there. Done that. Bought the T-shirt.'

Mark's eyes grew large. His smile returned and was broader than ever. 'You two have swapped? When? Where? Who with and what was it like?'

'Do you want me to explain?' Lisa held his gaze. 'Or would you like to find out firsthand?'

'Christ! Yes!' Anne blurted. She dropped her fork as she reached across the table to excitedly clasp her husband's hand. The clatter was deafening in the tense atmosphere of the dining room but, despite their shared tension, no one flinched. Glancing from Lisa to Johnny,

Anne said, 'We'd love to find out what it's like. Are you two up for it?'

'No,' Johnny said flatly. 'Not tonight.'

3

The Romano

Johnny could understand why Lisa wanted Debbie as a birthday present. At six foot tall (six foot three in the heels she wore for the office) Debbie was blessed with Nordic good looks from her platinum hair down to the toes of her black leather ankle boots. Her cheekbones were sculpted to an austere beauty that could make her appear cool and diffident but didn't stop her from being striking. Her regal deportment – every step measured to show off her long, shapely legs and every jacket tailored to proudly display her full, firm breasts – made heads turn to admire Debbie wherever she went. She could type at 120 wpm, speak three languages fluently and was impressively qualified in office administration. In Johnny's opinion her only fault was her absolute lack of sexual adventure.

'I want to suck your cock,' Debbie whispered. She put the fork down beside her plate with quiet authority. Half her salad had been eaten, her glass of wine was three-quarters finished and the impatience in her eyes was impossible to ignore. 'I want to do it here. And I want to do it now, while we're sitting in the restaurant. I want to suck your cock.'

He glanced around the faceless diners at neighbouring tables. He and Debbie sat in their regular booth, enjoying the secrecy of the restaurant's shaded corner.

Her suggestion was exciting and made the flesh inside his pants strain with arousal. 'Are you sure you want to do that?'

She leaned across the table so their noses almost touched. He could smell the scent of wine and vinaigrette on her pale lips. 'I want to suck you off now, here in this public place,' she breathed. He could see her tremble as she whispered the words. 'Then, while I can still taste your come on my lips, I'm going to go to the bathroom and rub myself off.'

He kissed her.

Debbie wasn't as graceful a kisser as Lisa but that didn't stop him from enjoying the moment. Her breathy promise of what she wanted, and the excitement of her own lascivious intent, made him respond with a hunger that matched her enthusiasm. Her tongue probed and plundered his mouth. She reached one hand to the back of his neck so she could hold him in place whilst she devoured him.

'I'm going to suck you dry,' she whispered.

And then she was gone.

He was surprised by the speed with which she disappeared beneath the table, and madly wondered if it was a skill she might have been practising. The stupidity of that notion was brushed aside when he felt her move between his knees and stroke down the zip of his trousers.

Because he couldn't see her, and because he was trying to appear calm and composed as he sat on the periphery of a busy restaurant, the experience struck him as something delightful and new. Ordinarily, when Johnny and Debbie spent their lunch time together, they visited her nearby flat and fucked each other vigorously. Because of her striking good looks she was a pleasure to behold and he always savoured the enjoyment of admiring her nudity or watching his length slide into the velvety folds of her sex. On those occasions when they visited the Romano, Johnny usually got as much enjoyment from her company as he did from savouring the envious glances of the restaurant's other male diners. He smiled grimly when he realised how envious they would be if his dinner partner and her activities were visible rather than being hidden beneath a floor-length tablecloth.

Debbie's slender, chilly fingers snaked inside his open trousers. Her cool touch was icy against the heat of his erection but he didn't contemplate flinching away. Drawing steady breaths, trying to appear as though he was concentrating on his wine glass and the remains of his steak, Johnny remained immobile as Debbie released his length from his pants.

She held him gently. The warmth of her mouth hovered close to his shaft. And then the velvet muscle of her tongue slid against him. From beneath the table he heard Debbie sigh with satisfaction. If not for the danger of being overheard by the other diners, Johnny would have echoed her. Ripe lips, soft, moist and inviting, welcomed him into her mouth. Her tongue, working slowly but with such dextrous skill, lapped at his length and teased him to full erection. Debbie's icy cold fingers pressed tight around the base of his shaft.

He drew a shuddering breath and steeled himself against the threat of too swift a release. One of the joys of his liaisons with Debbie – one of the many joys – was that Lisa knew every detail of their relationship. Sitting in the corner booth of the Romano, basking in the pleasure of the Nordic beauty's lips kissing magic into his length, Johnny knew he would recount the entire incident of this lunch to his wife later in the day. Knowing how much pleasure she would get from the anecdote, knowing she would beg him to repeat parts and insist on clarification and extra detail, he could almost forget about the secretary sucking his shaft and lose himself in the idea of Lisa's responses.

33

'Was everything all right with your meal, Mr West?'

The waitress's voice made him suddenly uneasy. He glanced up and saw she had a pin over her right breast that said: CALL ME MANDY. It took every effort not to start in surprise. Struggling to appear nonchalant, flexing a smile that felt slick and false and greasy, he raised a fork and nodded at his unfinished steak. 'It's very satisfying, thank you, Mandy.' Silently he prayed that the waitress would scurry away and leave him to discreetly enjoy the bliss of having Debbie's mouth around his cock.

'Has your companion gone?'

'She's just . . .' He floundered for a moment, wondering if he dared make some sly joke but not trusting himself to deliver it properly. *'I think she was having difficulty swallowing something . . .'* Sweating beneath the waitress's innocent smile, he stammered, 'She went to powder her nose.' He could see Mandy wanted something more from him but, with his concentration fixed on delaying his climax, he couldn't work out what it was he should be saying.

Her smile glinted with private knowledge and her gaze hovered over the table as though she could see through the cloth and the surface and gaze directly at Debbie as the secretary slid her face up and down his erection. Nodding eventually, tightening her smile for him, Mandy started away as she said, 'Enjoy your meal, Mr West.'

He thanked her again and, once she was far enough away, released a sigh.

'Who were you talking to?'

Debbie's words trailed from beneath the table but he could also feel them shudder through his length. The tremor of each syllable was as arousing as the languid way she held him inside the tight ring of her lips.

'The waitress wanted to know if everything was OK.'

'Did you tell her the vinaigrette was too acidic?'

'Yes,' Johnny growled softly. 'I'm sitting in a public place, enjoying a blowjob from my secretary and running the risk of an indecency charge, and I took the time to tell the waitress that the vinaigrette tastes of vinegar.'

The sarcastic remark made him feel like a bastard. It crossed his mind that Lisa would giggle hysterically when he told her but that didn't stop him from feeling as though he was abusing Debbie and doing her an injustice as she pleasured him. Wishing he could retract the words, and fretting that someone would notice if he started apologising to the table, he could only sit in silence as she continued to suck and lick at his shaft.

The pleasure quickly banished his feelings of guilt. Her lips were shockingly warm against his skin. The sweetness of each kiss made him gasp for breath and steel himself against the table. He thumped one hand down too heavily, and then cursed the movement when it made his cutlery clatter and caused a couple of heads to turn briefly in his direction.

'Go on,' Debbie urged from beneath the table. 'Let it go. Let me drink you.'

He wondered if she had received a thrill from the harsh tone of his sarcasm. She made no secret of the fact that she had a fascination for rough sex, coarse language and the pleasure of feeling a hand smack against her backside when she was being ridden from behind. Her public denouncement of anal sex and her private obsession with the act made her character seem tantalisingly complex. But he told himself those interests didn't excuse his own rudeness as he fought to stave off his impending release.

'Go on,' Debbie insisted. Her voice was deliberately low, partly muted by the length in her mouth and partly kept quiet so they remained discreet. Each time her lips and tongue moved to shape a word Johnny could feel the sensation before he heard the sound. 'I want you to

35

spurt in my mouth. I want to drink every drop you can shoot into me.'

Unable to resist any longer, sweating from the effort of holding back, Johnny relaxed in his chair and allowed the seed to pulse from his length. Debbie's responses were almost deafening to his ears but he noticed that none of the other diners even glanced in his direction. He could hear her muffled exclamation of delight; her sigh of contentment and each noisy swallow she released as she drank down his ejaculate. She kept her mouth around him as he continued to come and she dutifully sucked as the release throbbed through his length.

He was trembling when she finally returned his spent shaft to his pants.

They shared a knowing grin when she emerged from beneath the table, looking flushed but otherwise as composed and desirable as ever. Leaning across the table she kissed him hungrily on the mouth so he could taste the tang of his own semen on her tongue and lips.

'That was quite unexpected,' he mumbled.

'It's something I've always wanted to do. Public places turn me on. And I figured you were shameless enough to let me.'

He ignored the slight of her backhanded compliment. Concentrating on his own agenda, figuring this would be the best time to ask Debbie about sharing Lisa's bed, he asked, 'Is there anything else you've ever fancied trying that's equally daring? Had you ever thought about sleeping with another woman? Because, if you have—'

'Christ! No!' she gasped. 'That's disgusting.' She stood up and backed away from the table, adding, 'I'm just off to the ladies.' Lowering her voice and making a circular gesture with her finger, she added, 'I might be a few minutes.'

He watched her go, marvelling that she thought nothing of giving oral sex in a public restaurant, or

36

completing her lunch break by having a wank in a toilet, but sneered with disdain at the simple idea of having sex with a woman. Her stark refusal meant it would be difficult to persuade her to be Lisa's birthday present, but he was determined to try every available method of coercion before admitting failure. Drawing a deep breath, shaking the sensation of unreality from his mind as he tried to convince himself he really had just had his cock sucked, he lifted his fork and prepared to tackle the remainder of his steak.

'Johnny!'

He glanced up to find Mark by his shoulder. His neighbour's presence was massive and, because he was dressed in a formal business suit, somehow ominous. But Johnny grinned at the man and momentarily forgot about the problems of Debbie and her irrational dislikes.

'A Welsh girl at your office said I'd catch you here.'

'Were you looking for me?'

'Damned right I was. I wanted to make sure you were OK after last night.'

Johnny paused and frowned and tried to think why he might not have been OK. 'The salmon was delicious,' he said, puzzled. 'Lisa wanted the recipe for your cilantro sauce, although I doubt she'll ever use it.' His frown intensified as he added, 'It's not brought you or Anne down with the shits, has it? You're not suggesting I should take a couple of those stomach tablets—'

'Damn it, Johnny,' Mark snapped. 'I'm not a violent person but I could pop you one right now. Last night you insulted my wife. Today you insult my cilantro sauce and—'

'Hold on a second,' Johnny broke in quickly. He gestured for Mark to take Debbie's seat. Heads were turning among the neighbouring diners as they tried to spy on the cause of the raised voices and heated words. Johnny's heart pounded with adrenalin and he wished

37

Debbie had let him book a seat in the smoking section so he could calm his excitement with a cigar. His fingers nervously drummed the table as he said hastily, 'Let's rewind this and play it again. When did I insult Anne? What did I do or say that's upset her? Whatever it was, it wasn't intentional.'

Mark began to speak and then glanced around the restaurant and closed his mouth. His brow was knitted into an unfamiliar frown and his cheeks were rouged by high spots of anger. 'You wouldn't fuck her,' he hissed.

Johnny wanted to laugh. Although he worried that the response might worsen Mark's anger, he couldn't restrain a smirk. Shaking his head, unable to suppress the mirth any longer, he finally released a long guffaw. Unable to continue with the meal, he pushed his plate aside and drained the remnants of his wine.

'My wife's upset is amusing?' Mark growled.

'No,' Johnny told him. 'What's amusing is that you're pissed at me because I *wouldn't* fuck your wife. Some people would say that goes beyond amusing and heads directly toward hilarious.'

For a moment he didn't think Mark was going to see the funny side of the situation. It was only when the huge man's face broke into his usual smile that Johnny could feel the tension easing out of the moment.

The head waiter stumbled past their table and asked if everything was all right. Mandy lurked in the background, watching the pair with obvious consternation as she rocked an empty tray against her stomach. Her gaze flitted between Mark and Johnny as though she expected a fight to break out at any moment. Johnny assured the head waiter that there was no problem and took the opportunity to order Mark a cappuccino. Mandy brought the drink with unseemly haste and, as soon as he had taken the first sip, Mark stared levelly at Johnny.

'What was the problem last night? You were awfully quick to refuse our hospitality. Is there something about

Anne that you don't like? The poor girl is tearing herself up at the moment.'

Johnny winced, uncomfortable that he was responsible for Anne's angst. He remembered how sweet her kisses had been and the arousal she had awoken. Quietly he cursed himself for his insensitivity. 'Part of it was me,' he began. His voice was discreetly low. 'You noticed my mind was elsewhere. You had me so comfortable I came close to telling you the real deal on that particular issue and, for a private person like myself, that's quite an accomplishment on your part. But the main reason I said no was because of you two. You're new to this, aren't you?'

Mark took another sip of the cappuccino. His upper lip was daubed with a moustache of froth and the comical appearance made him seem less formidable. The anger he had brought to the table was no longer apparent and Johnny breathed a sigh of relief, thankful that particular storm had passed without incident.

'We're kind of inexperienced,' Mark allowed. 'Does that trouble you?'

'Have you thought about what you want?'

'We want to swap.'

Johnny nodded. 'That's not very illuminating,' he said sharply. 'That's like going into a shoe shop and saying you want something for your feet.'

Mark's plain features looked puzzled.

Exhaling through his nostrils, keeping his impatience concealed, Johnny asked quickly, 'Did you want to see Anne going with Lisa?'

'That would have worked.'

'Did you want to go to bed with me?'

'Fuck! No!' Mark jolted back in his chair, almost spilling his drink as he cast a nervous glance around the other diners. He looked as though he was fearful of causing a scene and Johnny admired that: it indicated a natural tendency to discretion. He was warming more to

Mark each time he met the man. He gave him his most disarming grin.

'I've got nothing against gays,' Mark hissed. 'But I'm not into guys.'

Johnny could see Debbie returning to their table. Her cheeks remained flushed and her normally faultless appearance looked beautifully strained. He was briefly struck by the image of her squatting on a lavatory seat, her short skirt hitched up around her hips as she rubbed and fingered herself to a blistering climax. In his mind's eye he viewed the contrast of grubby squalor and the perfection of her Nordic beauty. Stirrings of fresh interest began to tingle in his loins. Shutting those thoughts from his mind, Johnny held up a hand, indicating that she should give him five more minutes with Mark. Pouting, and clearly unhappy with the way she was being dismissed, Debbie turned her back and returned to the ladies' toilet.

Mark glanced at her and his brow briefly furrowed. He raised a finger, wafted it in Debbie's direction and looked set to ask a question, but Johnny spoke first.

'The term "swapping" is a pretty generic catchall.'

Mark lowered his finger. 'I see where you're going with this.'

Johnny was annoyed that he hadn't explained himself more eloquently the previous evening. Mark was friendly and likeable and pissing him off wasn't on Johnny's agenda. Similarly, Anne was sexy and fun and the idea that he had caused her any upset made him feel like a wretch. Raking fingers through his hair, he said, 'I was knackered and distracted last night. I made for lousy company and I would have made for a lousy lay.'

'Fair enough but—'

'You two were clearly up for it. So was Lisa. But I don't think you and Anne had a proper idea of what you were up for. Did you want us all fucking in the same room? So we could swap and change as the mood best pleased us?'

40

'I—'

'Or did you want Lisa to take you back to our house while Anne and I got it together in yours?' He could hear his words rattling off at a speed that reminded him of Anne's quick-fire, caffeinated conversation. It was a habit he knew only came to the surface when he was impatient and he tried to tell himself to behave with greater composure.

'That could have been—' Mark started. He got no further.

'Would you have been content to screw your lovely wife while Lisa and I simply watched and maybe mirrored what you were doing? And did you see our get-together as being a one-off affair? Or would you want us to meet up and swap and share on a regular basis? How would you feel if you came back from the office one day and found Anne in bed with Lisa and me while you'd been busting your balls peddling software? Would the idea turn you on? Or would you be pissed that you weren't a part of the action that day?'

'Jesus! John! I hadn't thought that far ahead. We were just . . .'

'I was knackered and distracted,' Johnny said crisply. 'If I appeared rude I'll apologise again, just like I apologised last night. But if Lisa and I are going to get into a swap with our neighbours I want it to be meticulously planned and without any risk of turning sour.'

Mark sat back and sipped at his cappuccino. 'Lisa said you weren't exactly Mr Spontaneity,' he grunted. 'That lady knows how to make an understatement.'

Johnny grinned sourly. 'Too many people carry too many issues out of the bedroom. I love my wife. I like my home. And I'm happy with my lifestyle. I don't want to find that six months from now I'm driving twice round the block so I don't have to face you before going into my house. I'm sure you don't want to have a great

41

night in bed with Lisa and then discover that Anne's upset or jealous and decides to either divorce you or just become some sort of bunny-boiler.'

'You've made your point,' Mark said softly. 'And I ought to thank you for being so considerate.' He studied Johnny carefully and asked, 'Do you worry to this level of detail all the time? How the hell do you sleep at night?'

'Anne's sexy and I'm aching to have her,' Johnny said quietly. 'Lisa's hot for you and it's apparent that you feel the same way. If I seem like I'm over-thinking things, that's just my way. But I'm never going to change and I'm never going to put my wife in a situation that could result in her being embarrassed or hurt.'

Debbie appeared at the table and Johnny made curt introductions between his secretary and his neighbour. He could see Mark studying his secretary with something more than polite interest and he quietly wondered how Mark and Anne had avoided swinging for so long.

Mark finished his cappuccino. Apologising for intruding, he stood quickly, widened his smile for Debbie and bade her farewell. 'Are we going to finish this discussion tonight at your house?' he asked Johnny.

'I'd prefer if we met at yours,' Johnny said honestly. 'I'll always favour the cooking of any man prepared to fight over an insult to his cilantro sauce.' Mark's broad grin vanished briefly but, when he began to chuckle, Johnny understood he had made himself a new and trustworthy friend. And, although he had enjoyed having Debbie suck his cock, he believed the prospect of that friendship was the best thing to happen to him throughout the lunch.

4

Phone Sex

Becky's ringtone played a version of Tom Jones's 'Sex Bomb'. The volume was set high and, even from the bottom of her handbag, the gutsy melody sounded loudly around the tax office. Her husband, Alec, had told her the opening bars to Bach's Toccata and Fugue in D Minor might better suit her menacing presence, and added that the confrontational themes from Prokofiev's 'Montagues and Capulets' might also be appropriate for someone with her personality. Because the conversation had occurred at a party, some cruel wag had suggested she should use Darth Vader's march. The comment had provoked a barrage of hurtful laughter with Alec's chuckles sounding loudest. But she had settled on 'Sex Bomb' because it reminded everyone within earshot that she was, first and foremost, sexy.

'I'll have to put you on hold,' she snapped into her land line. Without waiting for a response from the caller she pressed the letter H on her telephone keypad and reached for her bag. While her line manager was away, Becky found the tax office was fairly lenient about her accepting personal calls during working hours. She appreciated that it wasn't encouraged to put callers on hold in favour of her private life but, because the majority of people she dealt with through work were scroungers, thieves or miscreants who had been caught in the act of dodging what they rightfully owed, she believed it didn't matter that she caused them a minor inconvenience. After rummaging through her copious handbag, finding the phone and checking the caller display, she flipped open the Nokia and cooed, 'Hiya, Tara. How are you, hon?'

'I'm wet,' Tara breathed. 'And I'm naked. And I'm thinking of how many times I came while you were eating my pussy last week.'

Becky glanced around the office. She was a natural redhead and, although it wasn't in her nature to be shocked, whenever blushes did come to her freckled cheeks they turned her skin the colour of ripe strawberries. The office was an open-plan arrangement, with three dozen operators working together. She was touched by the paranoid fear that they had all heard Tara's sultry greeting and seen her own blushes. A murmur of general chatter continued to drone through the air, occasionally interrupted by the musical chime of email arriving or a telephone ringing. Those few faces she could see were half-hidden from her as her colleagues continued with their work and conversations. Assuring herself that she wasn't being overheard, Becky turned her back on the office and asked, 'Are those lips of yours still pouting?'

'No. You're the only one who's ever made them pout. Remember?'

Closing her eyes, Becky could remember that detail all too easily. Tara's sex was a smoothly shaved cleft. The lips were contained in the perfectly neat split of flesh between her legs. Her skin was soft and perfectly flawless. Becky's tongue had slipped against it as though she was licking a marble statue. At the party, mesmerised by the perfection of Tara's body, Becky had taken it as a personal challenge to lap at the woman's pussy lips until she made the labia swell and protrude from their haven. It had been a fun evening and the party had been a great success, but it was the delicious ordeal of coaxing a physical response from Tara that lingered with her: that, and the memory of Tara's triumphant screams each time she climaxed. Picturing the details of those flushed lips, and still able to savour the taste of the woman's musk, Becky could feel her own body responding to the memory of arousal. Her voice dropped to a husky drawl. 'I remember very well, hon.'

'I've got a finger inside myself,' Tara confided. 'I'm rubbing my thumb against my clit. And I'm thinking about how well you tongued me.'

'Wish I was there to lick it for you, hon.'

'I wish that too. You looked so damned hot in your domination outfit. I could have you round here, dressed up like that, telling me what to do for you.' There was a pause before she added, 'I'd follow any instruction you cared to give me. I'd be your willing, pliant and obedient sex slave.'

Becky squirmed against her chair. Her sex was suddenly fluid. Inside her bra her nipples tingled with heightened sensitivity. She felt a familiar wrench in her stomach, a sensation that was at once painful and delightful. Easing her legs slightly apart, daring to snake one hand beneath the desk and press the heel of her palm against the crotch of her suit's trousers, Becky cast another nervous glance around the office and then whispered, 'I'd start by telling you to get a vibrator.'

'Way ahead of you,' Tara said with a giggle.

Beyond the woman's voice, Becky could hear the faraway drone of a distant vibrator. The buzzing was sufficiently high-pitched to tell her that it was on its fastest setting. She wanted to groan with frustration. The knowledge that Tara was on the other end of the line, able to play with herself, willing to be devoured again, made Becky sick with jealousy, arousal and longing. She closed her eyes, picturing the vibrator pushing between Tara's sex lips and spreading her open as it slid easily inside. The mental image was so vivid she could almost smell the perfume of the slender woman's sex. Her heartbeat quickened and, without realising she was doing it, Becky pressed the heel of her hand more firmly against her crotch.

'I'm glad you're thinking ahead,' she said coolly. 'Although I trust you've not put that thing anywhere near your pussy.'

She was relieved to hear a tremor of hesitancy in Tara's tone. Becky thought Tara was a rare find from a swinging party. Facially she was plain, bordering on ugly. Unflattering spectacles and an angular face with a prominent nose and buck teeth accumulated to make her features geeky and unappealing. But, although her face was nothing special, she possessed the body of a supermodel and the sexual appetite of a nymphomaniac on Viagra. Her lack of inhibitions had startled Becky and her greed for sexual satisfaction had caused something of a stir at the party. As a bonus, Becky had discovered Tara had an unexploited submissive streak and a strong affection for other women. Delighted to have found such a willing plaything, Becky had happily given the woman her mobile number with the invitation that Tara should call 'any time she felt particularly horny'. Although when she made the offer Becky hadn't reckoned on Tara calling and expecting phone sex while she was working.

Dismissing that detail as a triviality, and deciding the office almost certainly owed her a ten-minute diversion, she hunched her shoulders, drew a deep breath and repeated, 'You haven't put that thing anywhere near your pussy, have you?'

'I . . . I was going to,' Tara stammered.

'No, no, no, honey,' Becky purred. Her voice was low. She kept darting an occasional glance around the office to confirm no one was listening but her attention was focused on the conversation with Tara. Staring blindly at the monitor that dominated her desk she was absorbed with the image of a naked Tara brandishing a vibrator. 'There's no sense in using that on your pussy, now, is there, hon? Didn't we just agree that I'm the only one in the world who can properly stimulate those bashful little lips of yours?'

Tara moaned.

Becky could picture the woman sliding a finger over her clitoris. She remembered the nub of flesh was not just tiny, it was also tightly hidden by the folds of her outer labia. Properly locating Tara's clit had been a delightful chore that cost Becky some time at the party. But, when her tongue had eventually landed against its slippery surface, she remembered Tara had howled with satisfaction.

'Where are you going to put that vibrator?' Becky asked.

'Wherever you tell me.'

Becky squirmed against her seat.

The flashing red light on her land line's keypad reminded her that she still had a caller on hold. But that consideration was low on her list of priorities. She cast another furtive glance around the office, smiled with smug satisfaction when she realised her colleagues were oblivious to the fun she was having, then breathed, 'I want you to slide it up your arse.'

'Becky!'

'No,' she murmured. 'Don't say my name. Don't say anything, except for describing how that feels as it enters you.'

Tara whimpered. There was the wet sound of her tongue gliding over her lips before she whispered, 'OK. If that's what you want me to do.'

'Is it lubricated?'

'Yes.'

'Are you pressing the end against your anus?'

47

A pause. And then, 'Yes.'

'Tell me about it. Tell me how much of it you've forced inside. Tell me how it feels. Tell me how much it hurts. And tell me how much you're enjoying it. Tell me all of those things and, the next time we meet, I'll fuck you with a strap-on.'

Tara groaned.

Over the mobile Becky heard the drone of the vibrator grow softer and then slow. Tara snatched breaths, grunting and gasping. She managed the occasional whimper that sounded somewhere between a sob and a scream. 'I wish you were here to help me do this.'

'That makes two of us.'

'I want you kneeling over me, shoving your pussy in my face. I want to lick you and taste you while I do this. I want to be your obedient slave.'

Becky glanced around the office. Her palm was slick with sweat. The nagging excitement between her legs had risen to an insatiable demand and she had to drag her hand back to the desk before the temptation to do more grew too strong. She knew she couldn't finger herself in the office. That sort of thing only happened in novels and false fantasies from magazines and would be far more daring than she would ever risk. But the urge was almost irresistible. Shaking with need and trying desperately to contain her excitement, she asked, 'Has it started to slide inside yet?'

'It's too big, Becky. It's stretching me too wide.'

'Force it, hon.'

Tara groaned.

Becky felt her stomach lurch as she pictured the quivering length of the vibrator pressing against Tara's anus. She had spent so long between the woman's legs she knew the terrain intimately. She could imagine the flushed muscle protesting against the intruder, straining as it fought not to yield, and then slowly giving way. The thought made the inner muscles of her sex quiver with their own need for satisfaction. She bit her lower lip so as not to moan in sympathy with Tara's plight.

'Have you forced it inside yet, hon?'

'It's far too big,' Tara complained. 'And my arse is too tight.'

'I know just how tight your arse is,' Becky mumbled. 'I could barely fit a finger through that naughty little muscle of yours.'

Tara's moan faltered to a whimper.

'Ease it inside, honey,' Becky urged. 'You want to be ready for me when I fuck you with my strap-on, don't you?'

This time Tara's groan was a shriek.

She wasn't obeying Becky's instruction to describe the scene, but her wordless cries conjured up a delicious picture of the naked woman suffering the ordeal of having a huge vibrator plugging her backside. Becky didn't know how a scream could conjure up such a picture but there was no doubt in her mind that she was hearing the sound effect for that very scene. Her pulse raced and she stroked her tongue across her lips. 'Deeper,' she demanded. 'Take it all the way inside, hon.'

When Tara eventually replied her voice shook with emotion. 'Have you really got a strap-on, Becky?'

'Is the vibrator inside?'

'I've got the head inside.' She sounded close to tears. 'I'm trying to get the rest of it in there now. Have you really got a strap-on?'

'It's twelve inches long and as thick as your wrist.'

Tara whimpered. 'Will you bring it to Lisa's party?'

Becky was still smiling agreement until she realised she hadn't properly understood the question. 'Will I bring it to whose party?'

'Lisa. She and her husband Johnny were at—'

'I know who Lisa is,' Becky broke in. The sweetness of her tone had gone as though it was never there.

Thoughts of arousal were instantly banished as she tried to process this unexpected development. 'I know exactly who Lisa is,' she growled. 'But I didn't know the bitch was trying to organise a party. What the fuck does she think she's doing?'

'Shit! I don't know. What's the problem with her organising a party? Won't it take some of the pressure off you if she's in charge of the event? Won't it give you and I more time to—'

'Fuck the pressure. I like the pressure. I like being known as the woman in charge.'

'I'm sorry, Becky. I didn't mean to be the bearer of bad news.'

'I'll call you back,' Becky growled. She severed the connection without sparing a thought for Tara's arousal. Then she broke into the holding line on her desk. 'I'm still trying to reconcile an error on your account,' she said primly. 'Are you all right to hold for a moment longer?'

'I've been holding for—'

Becky didn't allow him to finish. She pressed the H key on her telephone pad and then used her mobile to call Alec. As she waited for him to pick up she glared at the telephone on her desk and quietly cursed the caller and the charity that he represented. Her gaze scanned the computer screen and she saw there were a couple of anomalies on the account that might be awkward for the man to explain. But even that discovery didn't help to lighten her mood.

'Did you know about Lisa's party?' Becky snapped.

'And hello to you, darling,' Alec said coolly. 'How's your day going?'

'I've just found out that Lisa is throwing a party.'

'A swingers' party?'

'No. A fucking chimps' tea party. Of course I mean a swingers' party.' She managed to drop her voice and lower the last two words to hissed sibilants.

50

'Well, it's news to me.'

Becky didn't know if she believed him or not, and, after a moment's consideration, she decided it didn't matter. 'I want it stopped,' she snapped.

'Stopped? Why would I do that? More importantly, how could I do that?'

'The how is a detail we'll work out tonight,' Becky growled. 'But the answer to why is simple enough. You'll stop the party because your wife wants it stopped.'

She hung up, picked up the call on the land line and said, 'There are a number of serious errors on your account that I can't reconcile. If you'll hold the line a moment longer I'm just passing you over to our Fraud Investigation Team.' And, as she pressed another key on the telephone pad, a smile finally stretched across her lips.

5

Frisky

Johnny passed her the gift-wrapped box. 'It's an apology,' he explained. 'Mark told me that my refusal last night upset you. This is my way of saying sorry.'

'Mark shouldn't have said anything. He has a big mouth.'

They sat outside, reclining in wooden chairs that overlooked a pristine garden. The neat lawn, edged by pink and lilac frills of petunias, spread out before them. The grass had been mown in lines that were ruler-straight. A rockery in the northwest corner was set with stones that were painfully bright and clean and unsullied by dirt or soil. Anne quietly reflected that this garden had been the feature that won her into wanting the house yet, now it was hers, she no longer found it quite as appealing. An occasional breeze, providing welcome respite from the evening's balmy heat, wafted the scent of the flowers in their direction.

Anne had chosen jet-black denims and a matching shirt this evening to complement her freshly coloured raven hair. The black ensemble was dramatic but she thought it suited her despondent mood. From inside the house they could hear the strains of Glenn Miller. The languid melodies were not the Elvis she preferred but, whenever she felt low, Anne found the distinctive strains of the big-band sound were something of a comfort blanket. They engendered an urge to dance that could occasionally prove strong enough to lift her plummeting mood. But, although her toe was tapping time to 'Pennsylvania 6–5000', she didn't yet feel any compulsion to dance the jitterbug. Reluctantly accepting the box, mildly curious as to what the gift might be, she regarded Johnny through long lashes.

'Mark shouldn't have said anything.'

Johnny shook his head. 'He didn't just call on me to say I'd hurt your feelings. He was trying to flog me some of that dodgy software he's peddling.'

Anne laughed and started to relax. 'I can see three things wrong with that statement, the first being that Mark is the company's sales director, so he no longer "peddles dodgy software" to customers.'

Johnny raised an eyebrow, encouraging her to continue.

Anne toyed with the box as she settled back in her seat. 'Second,' she added, 'Mark's company is a leading provider of bespoke solution providers. The software he "peddles" is not dodgy.'

'And third?' Johnny asked, grinning for her.

'And third,' she echoed, 'if Mark had tried to sell anything to you, you would have bought it. He's better than good. He could sell laptops to the Amish.'

They fell silent for a moment. Anne fingered the box she had been given, her curiosity to know what was inside growing stronger with each passing moment. Her short, bitten nails scratched lightly against the shiny silver wrapping paper. The box itself was roughly the shape and size of a videocassette. Surprising herself with her show of restraint, she didn't pull the bow open. Instead, she kept it pressed against one thigh as she tried to figure out what might be inside.

'You love Mark very much,' Johnny observed.

She shrugged. 'Of course.'

'Aren't you worried you might jeopardise that love if you two start swinging?'

She shrugged again. Instead of looking at Johnny she kept her gaze fixed on the complex silver ribbon around the box. It was professional enough to look as if it had been bought from a shop but she suspected that the meticulous Johnny had tied it himself.

'Has swinging jeopardised your relationship with Lisa?'

'No. But it could have done.'

'Yet you still went ahead and did it.'

'Yes,' he agreed. 'And, ordinarily, I would have pounced on your bones last night and spent a lovely evening humping you rigid.'

She fluttered her eyelashes and glanced up. 'You smooth-talking bastard,' she murmured. 'I bet no girl's ever refused a chat-up line like that, have they?'

Johnny chuckled. 'But,' he continued, 'because you're my neighbour, I thought it would be prudent to let you take a night to make sure this was what you really wanted.'

'Maybe I've changed my mind now?' Anne said quickly.

'Then, if that's the case, I was clearly right to give you the time to think things over.'

'Damn!' She scowled. 'Lisa said you have an answer for everything. Doesn't it get tiresome being infallible?'

'The most tiresome part of being infallible is constantly having to say, "I told you so." ' He flexed a terse grin and added, 'And I do say that quite a lot.'

She glanced at the box in her hands. 'Can I open this now?'

'I'd be offended if you didn't.'

Anne wrenched off the ribbon and quickly tore open the wrapping paper. She considered the contents warily, not sure what to make of the gift. Her heart began to beat a little faster as she realised the implications of what she held in her hands. Glancing shyly at Johnny she asked, 'Are these cigars for you or me?'

'If you've forgiven me, I thought we might be able to share one tonight.'

Anne didn't hesitate before replying. Her bleak mood had already begun to evaporate, as though dispelled by the heat of her swelling arousal. Glenn Miller continued to drift out from the kitchen but the idea of dancing was suddenly far removed from what she really wanted to do. Extending a hand to Johnny, willing herself not to look too eager, she said, 'Pass me your lighter.' With a wicked grin she added, 'I might even try to make you feel like a president before the night's over.'

'How's that?' Lisa asked.

'Wow!' Mark gasped. 'Not only is that impressive, it's also completely pointless. You've excelled yourself.'

Lisa stuck out her tongue.

He looked surprised to see her offering the label to him and he blinked with obvious uncertainty. As Johnny and Anne shared a cigar in the garden, Lisa sat in Mark's kitchen rolling the wedding band around her finger. They had been chatting easily as he went through the final preparations of their meal, Mark dominating the conversation as he regaled her with an urban legend about opera tickets and a stolen Daimler. Whilst talking, Mark had found them each a bottle of pleasantly chilled lager from his vast stainless-steel fridge. Lisa had been happy to listen to him as she busied herself with removing the label from the bottle. The scent of a plum marinade sweetened the kitchen's air and gave the atmosphere a rich and fruity perfume. The strains of Glenn Miller were loud and unfamiliar to Lisa as they poured out into the garden but she found herself liking the upbeat rhythm and the old-fashioned style of the music. Through the slits of the Venetian blinds she could see Johnny and Anne in their chairs, their body language suggesting a greater distance than that which separated them. However, although she couldn't hear what they were saying, Lisa had seen the smile of delight when Anne unwrapped her box of cigars. She figured the pair would soon have bridged the potential rift that had threatened their blossoming friendship.

'Why are you giving this to me?' Mark asked. 'I already have one.' He waggled his lager and added, 'I keep mine attached to the bottle.'

Lisa held out the yellow and green Holsten Pils label for him and grinned at her own achievement. Trying to keep her tone matter-of-fact, she said simply, 'I thought you might want it.'

The expression of uncertainty was transformed into his usual smile. She had already come to suspect that Mark grinned at everything regardless of whether he understood or approved. His automatic reaction of good-natured amusement was one of the reasons she found him so appealing. It was the exact opposite of what she expected from her cynical husband.

'Sure,' said Mark with a laugh. 'It's just what I've always wanted. Gosh! Lisa! You really know how to show a guy a good time. The label from a beer bottle! Will you let me give you some of the carrot peelings, as my way of saying thank you?'

'The sarcasm pills are working nicely,' she remarked dryly. 'I thought you were the expert on urban legends? I thought you would have known immediately what a complete and untorn lager label meant. Don't tell me I know more about this one than you do?'

He hesitated for an instant and she could almost hear the whirr of his thought processes as he tried to retrieve some near-forgotten memory. Lisa watched, sipping daintily from her unlabelled bottle as she saw understanding wash over his face. If she hadn't been trying to play a cool hand she would have matched his triumphant smile with a grin of her own.

'It wasn't beer labels when I first heard that legend,' he started hesitantly. 'It was the ring pulls from cans of

56

pop.' His voice became more animated as his enthusi-asm increased. 'The rewards varied depending on how much of the unbroken tab you were able to retain. The ring on its own was only worth a kiss. If you got the ring with the little triangle of metal attached it was, purportedly, redeemable for sex. A BJ at the very least.'

Lisa nodded. 'I think it started off as ring pulls from cans of pop when I was at school,' she admitted. 'It moved on to tins of beer when I was around fifteen and able to get served at the off-licence. Then it shifted to the labels when everyone went all posh and started to drink their lager from bottles.'

Mark sighed happily. 'The development of an urban legend.' He studied the label with grudging affection and chuckled. 'That one always struck me as particularly ludicrous. Do you think anyone has ever claimed sexual favours for either a beer label or a ring pull?'

Lisa shrugged and sipped at her bottle. 'I don't know,' she admitted. Staring poignantly at the label in Mark's hand, then lifting her gaze to meet his eyes, she added, 'I'm still waiting to find out what you're going to give me in exchange for that one.'

The kiss lingered for an age.

Anne had suggested it would be easier to share the cigar if she straddled Johnny's lap. Her Levis were tight against her crotch and she could feel his swelling erection pressing urgently up to meet her. Her sex lips were crushed by the seam of denim and his hardness. The knowledge that mere layers of fabric hindered a fuller intimacy increased her excitement. When their mouths eventually broke apart she glanced toward the kitchen window, wondering if Mark had seen them. The idea of her husband watching as she kissed the hand-some neighbour from next door was more thrilling than the kiss. Venetian blinds at the window prevented her from knowing if he had witnessed what happened. He was nothing more than a shadowy blur in the faraway kitchen. She couldn't even tell if he was watching now as Johnny's hand slipped under her denim shirt and cupped her small breast.

Johnny's fingers gripped tight around her nipple. The plump bead of flesh was hard for him and that was the thought that made her arousal escalate. Her nipple wasn't hard for Mark, as it had been since she got married: *it was hard for another man*. More than that: *it was being touched by another man*.

She trembled against Johnny and almost dropped the cigar she held. With his free hand – the hand that wasn't holding her breast, she thought hotly – he stole the cigar from her and took a lazy draw on its end. The tip glowed orange and she was close enough to hear the crackle of dried tobacco leaves as they burnt.

'Are you OK?'

'It's a good cigar,' she said with forced nonchalance. He was still squeezing her nipple. His finger and thumb had caught her in a firm grip and she was stung by another flurry of excitement. Struggling to remain cool she said, 'The smoke must have gone to my head.'

'It must,' Johnny agreed. His confident smile said far more.

He passed the cigar back to her and then slipped his free hand under her shirt. He cupped both breasts, casually arousing her and effortlessly urging Anne to a level of excitement she didn't usually encounter until she reached the brink of orgasm. Her chest rose and fell, as though her body was forcing her small breasts to fill his large hands. The end of the cigar trembled as she tried to place it between her lips.

'Wouldn't you just love for Mark to see you now?' Johnny asked.

Anne groaned and tossed the cigar aside. She cast a final glance at the kitchen window, hoping to meet her husband's gaze and see his smile of approval. But, because he wasn't there, she simply lowered her mouth to Johnny's lips and kissed him again. As his tongue slipped against hers, and his hands squeezed more firmly at her breasts, the thrill of the moment took her closer to the climax her body now craved. Deliberately, she rolled her hips and pressed her sex against him.

She was so involved in the exchange that she couldn't even say she was disappointed that she hadn't seen Mark. She had only been able to see Lisa and, being honest, she had thought there was something attractive about the way Johnny's wife lounged back in her chair in the kitchen as she listened to Mark. The little thought Anne did give to that glimpsed image suggested that the woman seemed to be having her own sexual experience.

'Mark!' Lisa gasped. 'When Anne told me you had a silver tongue I didn't think she meant you could do that!' She lay back in the chair, holding her naked beer bottle but no longer bothering to drink from it, as Mark pressed his head between her open thighs. His tongue stroked firmly against the moist split of her sex, teasing a path through her outer labia and then her inner. Stroking upwards each time, ending each leisurely lap by trilling his tongue against her clitoris, Mark easily brought Lisa to a giddy haze of euphoria.

Lisa had thought things might develop with the neighbours this evening and she had dressed accordingly. Her skirt was short, her blouse was tight and revealing, and her knickers were at home. As soon as Mark had asked her what she would like in exchange for the Holsten Pils label, Lisa had parted her thighs, raised the hem of her skirt and opened her legs to expose her bare sex. 'Use your imagination,' she challenged.

Mark had looked towards the kitchen window and Lisa saw he was glancing at his wife, straddling Johnny while holding a cigar between her trembling fingers. His eyes had flashed with good-natured appreciation and then he had fallen to his knees, so quickly that Lisa briefly feared he might hurt himself on the kitchen's hard, tiled floor. That consideration was brushed from her mind as soon as he began to kiss the tops of her thighs. By the time his tongue stroked the shaved flesh of her pussy, all other thoughts were brushed from her mind and Lisa was enjoying a delicious rush of arousal.

Taking a hefty swig from her bottle of beer, she looked out into the garden and watched Anne pull her shirt open. The woman's bared breasts were hidden from Lisa's view because Johnny's head was in the way. And, although the angle didn't lend itself to revealing what was happening, she knew from the concentration on Anne's face that her husband was proving his skills at nipple sucking just as capably as Mark was showing off how gifted he was with his silver tongue.

She sighed, enjoying the moment and quietly anticipating the pleasures that were still to come. Running her fingers through Mark's hair, encouraging him to lick deeper, shuffling on the seat so her pussy was more accessible, Lisa basked in the pleasure of his attention and the excitement happening outside. Her stomach was bludgeoned by the familiar thrills of pleasure and delicious jealousy, which weighed like lead inside her, and she didn't doubt the evening was going to be a complete success. As Mark trilled his tongue against her clit again, her response was a confirmation of every high hope she had for the evening.

She quietly told herself that this was what swinging was all about. She was enjoying the thrill of being intimate with their neighbour, she could casually watch her husband doing similar things to the petite and curiously attractive Anne, and the only consequence they had to worry about was which of them would be obliged to host the next encounter.

'You're certainly giving me full value for my beer label,' she reflected idly.

Mark pulled himself away from her, gasping. His usual smile glistened with her musk but she could also see a tinge of regret in his expression. 'I intend to give you a damned sight more before the night's over,' he began. 'But I'm going to have to check on the pork before I continue.'

She nodded and eased herself off the chair. Arousal made it difficult for her to stand steadily but she struggled to look coordinated and composed. 'Do you need a hand with anything in here?'

'It's my kitchen,' he said firmly. He sounded gruffer than when they had spoken before and she guessed he was tormented by the same need for release that now tortured her. Reaching for a pair of oven mitts, then adjusting dials on the oven and hob, he added, 'Guests are only allowed in here on the condition they don't touch anything.'

She gave him a soft kiss on the cheek, a perfunctory thank-you for the foreplay. 'I'll go outside and watch your wife seduce my husband,' she murmured. 'It should make for an interesting distraction before to-night's main event.'

Mark glanced through the kitchen window.

Johnny and Anne were joined at the lips. The view from the kitchen wasn't particularly revealing. They could both see that Anne was straddling him, her shirt looked to be open and her hips rolled against Johnny in a lascivious motion. But it was impossible to tell if they were watching a passionate kiss or something far more intimate.

'It looks like Johnny's fighting her advances,' Mark said dryly.

Lisa nodded agreement. 'Any minute now he's going to stop sucking her nipples and tell her that he's not that kind of boy.'

Mark placed an arm around her waist and pulled Lisa closer. His lips hovered inches from hers and she could detect the scent of her own juices on his smile. The perfume of her fresh wetness was an aphrodisiac that never failed to make Lisa tremble. 'If you are going out there,' he began, 'can you tell them my tenderloin and honey plum sauce will be served in five minutes, regardless of whether or not they've finished?'

Lisa pressed herself close against him, teasing the shape of his erection with her thigh. He felt large, hard and eager for her and she grudgingly admired his restraint in pulling away from her before their intimacy had become too involved. She didn't know many men who would have been able to show such self-control. 'Your loin doesn't feel that tender to me,' she murmured, sliding her thigh against him. 'Do you want me to tell them that too?'

He shivered and finally found the strength to break their embrace. 'I've worked for three hours on this pork and the sauce,' he replied. 'And I have the distinct feeling that the meal will be the least memorable aspect of this evening.'

Lisa paused in the kitchen doorway. 'I'm looking forward to sampling your plum sauce.' She managed the words with only a hint of a giggle in her tone and was relieved to see he understood she was making a lewd joke. Stepping out of the room she said, 'I'll just go and make sure that Johnny and Anne don't have any objections to my swallowing it.'

It took twenty minutes before they were all gathered around the table and, as Mark had predicted, his cooking was virtually forgotten while the foursome exchanged kisses, caresses, glances and lewd suggestions. Anne found a bottle of red wine to accompany the meal and, even though her hands shook, she replenished everyone's glasses as they ate and talked.

The CD player worked its way through more Glenn Miller music, the old-fashioned melodies and rhythms bubbling pleasantly in the background, and the air was thick with anticipation. Anne hadn't bothered to fasten her shirt after returning from the garden and, each time she shifted position, her bare breasts were revealed to them all. She realised she was forgetting her responsibilities as hostess. Breaking away from Johnny, glancing guiltily at Mark and smiling indulgently at Lisa, she made a hurried attempt to address the oversight.

'You never told us, Lisa,' she began. 'What is it you look for in a couple that you're going to swing with?'

Lisa moved her hand from Mark's thigh. 'Are you asking out of polite curiosity or personal interest, or is this for the article you're writing?'

Anne didn't hesitate. 'Yes,' she said simply.

Mark and Lisa laughed.

'Ask the question again,' Johnny said encouragingly. 'I think your reporter's voice is one hell of a turn-on.'

She blushed. Her fingers moved to the front of her shirt – an automatic reaction, she guessed – and then she placed her hands firmly on the table. She was enjoying the evening and adamant that her usual modesty wasn't going to spoil the fun. Staring solemnly at Johnny she dropped her voice to a husky whisper and breathed, 'What is it you look for in a couple that you're going to swing with?'

'Tits,' he said quickly. 'That's what I look for.'

This time Mark's laughter made the table shake. Anne's grin was almost coy as she lowered her gaze and then glanced at him through fluttering eyelashes.

Lisa nudged her husband and placed a hand over his. To Anne it looked as if the pair understood each other sufficiently for him to know she wanted to respond. She quietly admired their obvious connection and wondered if it was as total as the one she shared with Mark.

'What do we look for in swingers?' Lisa repeated thoughtfully. 'If the question is for those three reasons, it deserves three answers. Tell your readers that I look for hot, well-hung guys and Johnny looks for something vaguely feminine with a pulse.'

Mark said his own standards weren't quite so discerning.

Johnny squeezed his wife's hand and asked her if she'd like a saucer of milk.

Lisa ignored them both. She continued to stare at Anne as though they were the only ones involved in the exchange. 'If you were asking out of polite interest, I'd have to tell you that we look for attractive couples who share our seriousness in most matters but can also balance it with a playful attitude towards sex.' She paused and sipped at her wine, allowing the moment to linger as the four of them bonded in the silence.

'And if you were answering to satisfy my personal curiosity?' Anne eventually prompted. It was a struggle to keep her voice level and steady. She had always thought that the sex life she enjoyed with Mark was wonderful and beyond improvement. But this evening was proving more stimulating than any she could ever recall. Arousal had made the crotch of her pants sodden. The thrill of knowing that something might happen – most likely *would* happen – kept her constantly in the throes of a bubbling excitement. 'What would you say if you were answering to satisfy my personal curiosity?'

'I'd want a kiss before I answered,' Lisa replied.

'Oh! Yes!' Mark exclaimed.

Johnny grinned at him.

Lisa and Anne were lost in their own intimate exchange of gazes.

'You want to kiss me?' Anne sounded hesitant.

Lisa nodded. Her features were inscrutable and Anne had no way of knowing if the woman was teasing or serious. 'You kiss Mark all the time,' Lisa pointed out. 'You've spent most of the evening kissing Johnny. Unless you're able to kiss yourself – and I can only think of one way you could make that interesting – I think it's my turn to get a kiss.'

They were sitting on opposite sides of the four-seater table. Anne stood up to respond to the challenge, she walked with forced casualness past her husband and stood at Lisa's side. Lisa turned to face her, her lips parted expectantly. Mark and Johnny watched, both feigning no more than the mildest interest, yet neither of them eating or moving as they waited for Lisa and Anne to act.

Aside from the music, the room was as silent as a held breath. The two women regarded each patiently. Anne's grin was uncertain, Lisa's mischievous.

'I've never kissed a girl before,' Anne croaked.

'I'm not a girl,' Lisa corrected. 'Bring your lips closer and you'll find out I'm all woman.'

The atmosphere crackled with electricity. Anne felt light-headed with anticipation. Johnny and Mark watched intently as the two women moved closer.

Anne licked her lips, desperately trying to fight the threat of nerves. Lisa reached up for her as she approached. Her fingers slipped inside the open front of Anne's shirt. And then their lips met.

'The true answer is that we swing because it's fun,' Lisa admitted. 'We both like sex. Neither of us has any hang-ups about jealousy or other such issues. We enjoy the parties, and the occasional guy, girl or couple that we find through the internet or in the classifieds.' She glanced back over her shoulder at Johnny and waited for him to nod before she continued. The lightheartedness was gone from her tone as she said, 'What we're ultimately looking for is a couple with whom we can become friends as well as lovers. That's really why we swing.'

Her remark had made the mood serious, and the four of them ate in a stilted silence. The air of sexual excitement remained heavy and foreboding, like an impenetrable fog, but no one seemed eager or able to take the next step and move things forward.

'What about you two?' Johnny asked eventually. It was difficult to concentrate on the conversation because the excitement of watching Anne and Lisa kiss had left him with a large and uncomfortable erection. The need for satisfaction was at the forefront of his thoughts but he tried to think past that urge and behave like a rational adult. He glanced from Anne to Mark and asked, 'What was it that you two wanted from swinging?'

'Cock,' Anne said quickly.

Her quip burst a bubble of nervous laughter.

'Touché,' Johnny acknowledged.

She blushed and turned to glance at her husband.

'We're open to new experiences,' Mark said eventually. 'We've got a good sex life but we both worry that it's going to become repetitive if we don't try and build on what we've got.'

Anne nodded agreement. She sipped quickly at her wine and her large, dark eyes flitted round the table, constantly assessing the others. Outside, dusk had fallen. The only light in the room came from the swaying candle flames in the centre of the table. The encroaching shadows wrapped around the four of them like a large and comfortable blanket. Johnny could feel that, regardless of whether any of them wanted it, they were all drawing closer together.

'I get that,' Johnny agreed. He squeezed his wife's hand and said, 'I don't think sex with Lisa could ever get tiresome. But I don't want to take the risk that it will.' He sipped the last of his wine and watched Anne hurriedly refill his glass. 'But what is it, specifically, that you fancy trying? Are you both looking to swap? Do you want to share? Or are you after a foursome? What is it – in explicit and graphic detail, if you like – that you fancy trying?'

66

Anne looked set to answer when the CD player fell silent. Her cheeks were blushed to a high colour that gave her appearance a freshness she hadn't worn at the start of the evening. She opened her mouth, clearly ready to give an honest response to Johnny's question, when the CD started up again with 'In the Mood'. A smile flooded across her face as the horns sounded from hidden speakers. She leapt out of her chair.

'This is what I've always wanted,' she said, laughing. She hit the light switch. The room was flooded with brightness, breaking the spell that had held them. 'This is what I've always wanted,' she repeated earnestly. Jitterbugging in time to the music, dancing to the unconcealed amusement of her husband and their new friends, she showed no embarrassment that her shirt was repeatedly flashing open and exposing her bare breasts. Her movements were exuberant, fluid and perfectly synchronised to the music. Her obvious enjoyment made the performance a delight to watch. Johnny thought he would have found it no less engaging if Anne hadn't been exposing her chest with each staccato punctuation of the horns.

'This is what you've always wanted?' Lisa said, laughing.

Anne beckoned to her to come to her side and join the dance. With only the briefest show of reluctance, Lisa stood up and gingerly followed Anne's lead. The steps looked comparatively simple and, within moments of standing by her side, Lisa was doing a passable jitterbug. She stayed a half a step behind Anne and Johnny admired his wife's restraint in not stealing the other woman's limelight.

'I can be pretty shy around new people,' Anne explained. She raised her voice to include all three of them in the conversation. 'I've always wanted to do something bold like dancing near-naked in front of a group of strangers.' She managed an impressive flourish

67

step before saying once again, 'This is what I've always wanted to do.'

'So we're strangers now?' Lisa taunted her lightly. 'You've tongue wrestled everyone in this room, and still you describe us as strangers?'

Still dancing, and still trying to show Lisa the steps of the jitterbug, Anne simply stuck out her tongue.

Johnny marvelled that the two women, who were so dissimilar in so many ways, could share the same easy solution to ending an argument. 'Perhaps you should get Anne to dance like this for your forthcoming party?' he suggested. 'If she wants to dance naked in front of strangers that would be the ideal place, don't you think?'

Lisa's eyes grew wide and her smile turned eager.

Anne was shaking her head, an expression of horror replacing her smile. She stopped dancing immediately. 'I couldn't do it in front of genuine strangers,' she confessed. 'It was a struggle plucking up the courage to do this much in front of you guys.'

Lisa continued to dance, clearly enjoying the experience and the exercise. She used each move to turn the steps into something more provocative than they had originally been. Raising her skirt so the hem sat high on her thighs, she went on to roll her shoulders and emphasise her cleavage. Although her blouse remained fastened, the shape of her breasts and stiff nipples pressed obviously at the front. Mark's gaze remained on her and Johnny felt the familiar thrill of seeing someone admiring his wife.

'I wouldn't be asking you to do much,' Lisa teased. She was so involved in the music she almost sang the words to the tune. 'Just dance the jitterbug naked, in front of a hundred or so swingers. You could do that, couldn't you?'

Anne glanced at Lisa as she continued dancing. Her unease had clearly lessened as she muttered, 'I doubt I could do it as well as you.'

Lisa immediately stopped. Grabbing hold of Anne's hand, pulling her from the room, she said, 'We'll talk about this upstairs as we pretty ourselves up. Pour me another glass of wine Johnny. We'll be back soon.'

Alone with Mark, listening to the faraway giggles of his wife and Anne, Johnny turned to Mark and raised his glass in a mock salute. 'It seems like we're going to have a good evening.'

Mark raised his own glass in return and sipped a little of the wine. 'I take it you resolved the problem that was troubling you last night?'

Johnny blinked before remembering the reason for his angst the previous evening. He didn't want to brood on the problem of Debbie – not now that events looked as if they were becoming interesting. 'I haven't resolved the problem,' he admitted. 'I've just not let myself worry about it.'

'Anything I can help with?'

Shaking his head, and deciding he could openly confide in his new friend, Johnny lowered his voice and said, 'I'm having trouble arranging Lisa's birthday present.'

'You mentioned that last night. When is Lisa's birthday?'

'Friday.'

'I'll bake a cake,' Mark decided. 'Unless you've got something planned, you must both come round here. I've been wanting to do something fancy with royal icing for ages now.'

Johnny grunted and drained his glass. 'Wow! I didn't realise there'd be benefits to having such a macho-man living next door.'

Mark's grin faded. 'Do you want me to bake the fucking cake?'

'Christ! Yes. If it tastes as good as the rest of the stuff that comes from your kitchen I'd be delighted.'

'Then don't take the piss,' Mark said flatly. 'I'll sort out the details and an appropriate message tomorrow.

For now, why don't you just tell me about the present you're having difficulty acquiring.'

There was a moment's silence. 'It's my secretary,' Johnny said eventually. 'You met her this afternoon. Debbie.'

'The blonde ice maiden?'

'She's not that icy.'

'And you want to give her to Lisa as a birthday present?'

'No.' Johnny struggled not to sound scathing. The nuisance of the situation wasn't Mark's fault. 'I want to go to a shop and buy something that Lisa can return if she doesn't like it. It was Lisa who said she wanted Debbie for her birthday.'

Mark nodded solemnly. 'And, since it's what Lisa wants, and since I can't imagine you having a problem with the arrangement, I take it that Debbie is throwing a spanner in the works.'

Johnny nodded. 'You've got to admire the diversity of the woman's mind, haven't you? Debbie thinks nothing of going down on me in a restaurant at lunchtime. And her need for anal borders on being more than I can accommodate. But ask her if she'd like to eat a little pussy and she reacts as though you've just suggested she should watch Richard and Judy.'

Mark grunted. His usual smile was missing and Johnny could see that he was thinking something through. 'Do you want me to sort that for you too?'

'As well as the cake? If this is an 'either or' arrangement, I want the cake as my first choice.'

'I'll rephrase the question. Would it hurt the progress you've made if I took a shot at persuading Debbie to spend a night with Lisa?'

'It couldn't hurt the progress I've made, because I haven't made any progress. But do you really think you can do it? I mean, Anne keeps telling me you're a great salesman –'

'The best,' Mark interrupted. He said the words without arrogance, as though he was merely stating a fact.

'– but are you really that good?'

'I'll sort it tomorrow,' Mark promised. He looked set to say more but the sound of Lisa and Anne descending the stairs broke the moment.

'Anne and I have come to a decision,' Lisa declared.

Anne stood by Lisa's side, her thoughts and emotions in turmoil. The rush upstairs had been followed by Lisa rummaging through Anne's wardrobe and lingerie drawers. Lisa selected something more appropriate for the evening than the black denims Anne had been wearing and she insisted that Anne change immediately. Her choice of stockings, suspender belt, thong and matching bra was predictable and more exhibitionist than Anne would have risked. But, once her new friend had told her what she thought they should do, Anne decided the choice was appropriate. Even so, as she stood by Lisa's side with Mark and Johnny staring at her, she felt vulnerable and underdressed.

'It's been fun watching Anne dance,' Lisa continued. 'And Mark's cooking, as always, has been outstanding.'

Mark bowed.

'But the time has come for us to get frisky.'

Anne squirmed. If Lisa hadn't been holding her hand she knew she would have fled from the room to find some clothes that were less revealing. Arousal still governed her body's reactions. Her nipples were hard inside her bra. The crotch of her thong was already filmed with a layer of warm moisture. But she wasn't sure those responses would be enough to keep her from screaming with terror at the enormity of what she and Lisa were preparing to do. Her heart thudded so loud inside her chest that she felt certain the others could hear every pounding beat.

'And,' Lisa went on, 'because my husband is doing his usual irritating trick of waiting for someone else to make a decision for him, and because Mark is too thick to know his own mind, Anne and I have decided that we'll start the ball rolling this evening with our own demonstration of friskiness.'

Anne glanced up and saw that neither of the men had been insulted by Lisa's brusque assessment. Mark watched with lurid eagerness and Johnny was clearly anxious to see how events would unfold.

'May we watch?' Johnny asked, pouring wine for himself and Mark.

'It's not a demonstration unless someone is watching,' Lisa said tartly. 'You can watch. You can applaud.' She flitted her gaze from Johnny to Mark before saying, 'You might even be invited to participate if you're really good boys. Now pass me my wine and allow Anne and me a little space here.'

Anne watched the woman drain her full glass with one quick, effortless gulp. She wished she had thought to take a drink before they started, because she felt sure her nerves could do with an anaesthetically settling glass of red. But with Lisa beckoning her to a seat at the table, and events hurrying along faster than she had expected, Anne had had no chance of grabbing a drink.

She slumped into in the chair.

Lisa straddled her, sliding one long leg over Anne's pair and then resting lightly on her lap. They were face to face, Lisa's body obscenely close to Anne's naked flesh, and the promise of intimacy had never been more blatant. Anne remembered that she and Johnny had been in a similar position earlier in the evening. The memory ignited another rush of swelling excitement as she realised she had now been physically close to both her neighbours. Later, when she and Mark were alone and in bed together, Anne knew that telling him about her emotions during these experiences would be enough to make him climax. The thought swathed her body with perspiration.

'Relax,' Lisa whispered. 'You're in control here. Whatever you want will happen. Whatever you don't want stops immediately. Do you understand?'

'I understand,' Anne murmured.

'And isn't this exactly what you wanted?' Lisa asked.

Anne frowned, not sure this had ever been on her agenda and anxious for Lisa to explain. Lisa's thighs pressed tight against her own. The woman's skirt had risen high enough for Anne to see that her neighbour was not wearing panties, and the discovery made her feel ill with fresh anticipation. The buttons on Lisa's blouse had fallen open at some point since they left her bedroom. Anne could see the swell of the woman's bare breasts and the mesmerising tips of her nipples. The naked skin was unbearably close. Her need to touch, explore and discover grew with each tentative breath. But she lifted her gaze to meet Lisa's eyes and begged her to explain. She knew she had been coy about her requirements from swinging. Her impromptu jitterbug, while it had been the fulfilment of a crazy ambition, had been little more than a displacement activity to delay what she knew was coming. And, because Johnny and Lisa both seemed so comfortable with their swinging, she wanted to show the same sense of cool control. 'What makes you think this is *exactly* what I've wanted?'

'You're the centre of attention in this room.' Lisa lowered her voice to a whisper and placed her lips close to Anne's ear. The movement made her breasts press against Anne's. 'Johnny's struggling with a hard-on that you've caused. Mark is bursting with pride and arousal because everyone here is so excited by the sauciness of his wife. I'm pretty turned on by you myself, and we haven't even begun to get frisky yet. Isn't this exactly what you wanted?'

73

It was all the encouragement Anne needed. She pressed herself into returning Lisa's kiss, devouring the woman's mouth and tasting the remaining flavour of the wine that Lisa had sipped. Arousal surged through her with fresh abandon and, laughing giddily as she revelled in the moment, Anne threw herself into enjoying Lisa. Her hands slipped under the woman's open blouse and she thrilled to the novelty of touching feminine skin. Her fingers trailed against the slenderness of Lisa's waist and the smoothness of her back, then she moved her hands to the woman's chest and cupped the large, round shapes of Lisa's breasts.

The stiff nipples pressed urgently against the palms of her hands.

Mark and Johnny released appreciative grunts.

Lisa groaned with obvious pleasure.

And Anne knew, after this experience, the night was only going to get more and more enjoyable. The thought was confirmed when Lisa slipped from her lap and peeled the thong away from Anne's hips. Totally exposed to Johnny and Mark, and allowing Lisa to lower her head to the warm split of her sex, Anne felt certain the night was going to rank as the most memorable one she and Mark had ever enjoyed.

A warm tongue slipped against the dewy folds of flesh.

She groaned.

It was tempting to lie back, close her eyes and bask in the pleasure being given. But with her eyes open she could watch Johnny's approving smile and see the obvious desire that tainted her husband's grin. She could also glance down her own body and see the upper half of Lisa's face, bearded by the trim of her pubic hairs. Lisa kissed her again and the moment threatened Anne with sensory overload. So much was happening so fast. She had never thought it would be possible to be *too* aroused. But she had never imagined that any scenario could be so charged with sexual excitement. Unable to control her responses, screaming as the orgasm bubbled through, she lifted her pelvis to meet Lisa's face and let the climax shudder through her body.

6

Debbie

'Don't say a word,' Debbie insisted.

Obligingly, Johnny remained silent. He watched Debbie enter his office, close the door behind her and twist the key in the lock. He guessed she had already turned the sign outside his door, to display the words CONFERENCE IN PROGRESS, and figured they would remain undisturbed until she left. His office window overlooked a nearby park. It was one of the more prestigious views afforded by the building and an occasional reminder that he was an important member of the management team. Debbie simply drew the blinds without admiring the picturesque greenery.

The daylight that filtered through left the room as dim and hazy as Johnny's memories of the previous evening. Inwardly he smiled, pleased that those recollections were already wrapped in a warm fog of amnesia. The night had been exciting and satisfying. If its poignancy hadn't started to fade Johnny knew he would have spent the day in the thrall of a constant and uncomfortable arousal.

'Don't say a word,' Debbie repeated. 'Let me do the talking.'

Johnny had just been on the verge of asking Debbie why she was locking his door and closing the blinds. The actions reminded him of the covert precautions that were needed six months earlier when everyone in the company had grown paranoid because of a rumour about a takeover from a Japanese conglomerate. But, because this was Debbie, Johnny suspected her actions were governed more by salacious needs than by a fear of corporate subterfuge. His grin grew broader as he remembered that Debbie was one of the few people in the building who possessed a more voracious sexual appetite than his own. Their relationship often provided a satisfying diversion from the daily grind of the insurance company. Admittedly, Johnny knew that he and Debbie were grist for the mill of the office gossips. But because they both acted as though they were above such rumours, the stories struggled to generate interest or effectiveness.

Debbie stepped to the front of his desk. She stood with her hands on her hips and her shoulders thrown back. 'You've not got any appointments for the next hour.'

The remark was what he thought of as a *questment*, a combination of question and statement. He glanced at the wall clock above the door behind her. The hands were creeping towards eleven o'clock. 'No,' he agreed. 'No appointments. Why? Was there something you wanted to discuss?'

Her smile was broad and etched with the promise of wicked pleasures. Behind her heavy-framed spectacles her ice-blue eyes twinkled. In her stylish suit – skirt above the knees and jacket tailored to accentuate her breasts – Johnny thought she looked less like a secretary than like an elegant model posing as a businesswoman. He could almost imagine her as the cover girl for some seedy photo magazine with the title *Dominant Boss*. Admiring her curves and statuesque height, he thought she would be guaranteed the centre page spread.

'I can't make our lunch date today,' Debbie began.

'Damn! I was looking forward to that.'

She nodded, her expression indifferent enough to show she didn't really care. Her perfectly shaped lips were painted the colour of ripe cherries and they made no suggestion of a frown. Glancing at him over the top of her spectacles she said, 'Because I knew you were looking forward to it, I thought you and I could move our lunch date up an hour.' She shrugged the jacket from her shoulders and immediately started to work on the buttons of her blouse. Studying him, she asked, 'You don't have any objections to that, do you?'

He remained seated behind his desk. 'It depends what you fancied doing,' he started guardedly. 'If you think I'm going to make do with a cheese roll from the dirty sandwich man, then you're seriously mistaken.'

Her brow creased with obvious impatience. 'I'll have that Welsh tart from reception fetch you a burger from McDonalds.'

'Gee! Thanks. Now I can eat like a successful executive.'

Debbie made no response as she slipped out of her skirt and stepped to his side of the desk. Now she looked like a model from a lingerie catalogue, her silver-white bra complemented by matching panties, stockings, suspenders and heels. More than any woman he knew, Johnny thought, Debbie always looked as though she had dressed for glamorous sex. Even at the swingers' parties he attended with Lisa, Johnny had never met any woman who appeared as resplendent in only her underwear. His erection, although still sore from overuse at Mark and Anne's, was instantly hard.

'What I fancy doing is having your cock up my arse,' Debbie breathed.

She squeezed between Johnny and his desk, bending over so that her backside pushed into his face. The triangle of silver-white panties sat taut against her smooth backside. The fabric only bunched slightly as it disappeared between the tops of her thighs. Automatically he reached for her hips and stroked the smooth skin. Her flesh was silky-soft beneath his fingertips and he could feel the caress was a two-way avenue of mutual excitement. She sighed hungrily while he drew a long and satisfied breath. A part of him yearned to wrench the panties down, expose her holes and take her vigorously over the desk. But for Johnny the greatest pleasures in any sexual encounter seldom came from the act itself. Most of his satisfaction came when he later confided each detail to Lisa. In a leisurely manner he continued to smooth his hands against the perfection of Debbie's backside.

'You're a tease,' she panted.

He grunted agreement. 'I'm a tease who's going to fuck your arse.'

Debbie trembled. As the shiver coursed through her body her buttocks quivered under his touch. Slowly, Johnny eased his thumbs beneath the waistband of her panties.

Debbie stiffened.

He drew them down slowly, allowing the silver-white fabric to caress her skin as it was drawn away. Inch by inch he revealed the cleft between her buttocks, the tight pink ring of her anus, the dewy folds of her shaved labia. The flesh was smooth and inviting. Her musk was a subtle perfume that heightened the aching in his loins. And suddenly he could understand why Lisa so desperately wanted to experience Debbie. Licking his lips, trying not to make the words sound like a tried and tested line, he said, 'I can't believe you've never been with a woman.'

She trembled again. Johnny wondered if the response was a shiver of interest or a shudder of distaste. He only had to wait until she spoke to discover the truth.

'Not that again, Johnny,' Debbie complained. 'It spoils my mood.'

His fingers smoothed the soft centre of her skin. Mumbling an apology he said, 'I wasn't trying to spoil your mood. I was just stating a fact. I know a couple of women who would long to kiss your pussy.'

Again Debbie shivered. And again, he couldn't tell whether the tremor suggested arousal or revulsion. Even when she spoke Johnny still wasn't certain that she was repulsed by the idea. 'No more talk of my screwing women,' she insisted. She didn't turn around to face him. Instead she remained bent over the desk with her backside poised provocatively in front of his face. 'It doesn't do it for me, Johnny. *It's dirty*. Would it do anything for you if I told you I knew guys who would love to spend some private time with that tight arse of yours?'

The question caused his scrotum to shrivel. He considered congratulating her for making the point so eloquently. Rather than continue trying to persuade her, he raised his finger to her cleft and stroked the length of her labia. The smooth flesh suckled him. They both sighed and he knew, regardless of how much he wanted Debbie to consider spending a night with Lisa, he wouldn't be able to make it happen. Clutching her buttocks, pushing the skin apart until her labia pouted and her anus was briefly open, Johnny lowered his tongue between her cheeks and licked the stretched flesh of her sex.

'Oh! Yes!' she moaned. 'That's more like it.'

Hungering to have her, Johnny could have easily echoed that sentiment. He smothered her sex lips with kisses, wetting her hole and tasting the source of the delicious fragrance that now perfumed his office. Her clitoris pulsed beneath its hood and, as he trailed his tongue against its throb, he was rewarded by Debbie's growing sighs of excitement.

'Up my arse, Johnny,' she insisted. 'I want you up my arse.'

'All in good time,' he assured her. He nuzzled the tight ring of her anus before flicking his tongue against the centre of the hole.

Debbie gasped.

He chuckled and said again, 'All in good time.'

It occurred to him that this would possibly be his last chance of enjoying sex with Debbie. Because she showed no interest in doing anything with Lisa he didn't think it fair to carry on seeing her. He didn't suppose Lisa would have any objections to him continuing the relationship: there were men she occasionally met who didn't fully meet with his approval. But seeing Debbie when she didn't reciprocate Lisa's interest struck him as inappropriate behaviour for a good husband. Not letting the decision spoil his arousal, savouring the taste of her pussy and her anus and revelling in the thrill of her mounting excitement, Johnny kept his thoughts fixed on pleasing Debbie. All the time his mind catalogued each detail so he could share it with his wife at the end of the day.

'Stop teasing,' Debbie insisted. 'I want you up my arse.'

'You're desperate for it, aren't you?'

'You know I am.'

'Tell me how desperate you are.'

'Johnny! Don't make me beg. It's humiliating.'

He placed his finger over the centre of her anus and tested its resistance. He had plundered the muscle several times before and was always delighted by her paradoxical display of eager reluctance. Sliding the wet digit through the ring of her sphincter, waiting until she had caught her breath and sighed with a blend of surprise and contentment, he said again, 'Tell me how desperate you are. Beg for it, Debbie.'

'I want your cock,' she breathed.

'Tell me where,' he insisted. His finger squirmed deeper. The gossamer walls of her anus contracted against him as he pushed a knuckle inside. 'Tell me exactly where you want my cock.'

'Up my arse.' Her words came out in an animal growl. She had presented an image of office chic before, but now he thought her true nature had been uncovered. Debbie was a wanton creature with sexual demands that needed satisfying. She was a horny bitch who knew exactly what she wanted and how to get it. She had been reduced to a craven slut with only one goal that could sate her lust. 'Up my arse, Johnny. Please.' Her tone was close to tears as she begged and he knew, if he persisted with his torment, she would forget to keep her voice low enough to maintain their discretion. 'Please, Johnny,' she insisted, 'put it up my arse.'

He stood up and took the erection from his pants. Searching inside his jacket pocket, quietly congratulating his own foresight in keeping a couple of condoms for just such an eventuality, he found one, tore the wrapper open with his teeth and unrolled the sheath down his erection. Prudence made him glance toward the locked office door. But, because he knew that Debbie guarded her privacy as securely as he looked after his own, he felt sure their liaison would be safe and uninterrupted.

'Please, Johnny,' Debbie begged. 'Don't make me wait for it. I want it now. I need it now.'

He smoothed the cheeks of her backside apart and rested the end of his shaft against her anus. Debbie moaned and strained against him. Releasing his hold on her rear with one hand, using it to steady his length as he prepared to ease inside, he urged his hips forward and told her not to move.

'Yes,' she insisted. Although she was promising not to move, her pelvis wriggled as she urged herself closer to him. Her words came in a low and breathless gasp that barely veiled her desperation. 'Right up my arse.'

He pushed gently against her.

Debbie whimpered.

Her sphincter resisted at first, as though it shared his delight at drawing out her torment. And then he had squeezed past that first barrier. He heard Debbie struggle to contain a scream as her ring of muscle fought against him. Johnny waited until her involuntary spasm had passed and then returned his hands to her hips. The head of his sheathed length was settled into her rear and he savoured every glorious sensation that gripped his shaft. Holding her tight, keeping her still so she didn't move too quickly, Johnny plunged into her.

'Fuck! Yes!' Debbie spat.

Her inner muscles convulsed around him. She raised her hand, as though ready to hammer it against the desk, and then it fell gently down as though she understood such a noise might draw unwanted attention from outside the office. Urging himself deeper, revelling in the pleasure of her tight hole gripping his erection, Johnny pulled on her hips and coaxed her buttocks forward to meet him.

Debbie groaned. She bit her tongue and lips to mute her cries. Her entire body vibrated and Johnny wondered how close she was to orgasm. Her responsiveness always amazed him and he had often wondered if she climaxed so quickly because he was a great lover or she possessed an easily sated libido. He hoped it was the former while accepting it was most likely the latter.

'That's it,' he said, forcing the last of himself inside. The torrid heat of her rectum engulfed his shaft. He stood rigid for fear of prematurely exploding. The rush of sensation tortured his erection. Her buttocks tickled the short hairs at his scrotum. He stared down at the Nordic beauty of Debbie's back and buttocks and marvelled at the sight of his own length buried in her anus. 'That's all you're getting from me,' he growled. 'Because that's all that I've got.'

Debbie shivered. 'Call me a dirty bitch,' she hissed. 'I want you to tell me I'm a filthy and depraved slut.'

He slapped his hand once against her right buttock. The sharp retort was little more than a muted cough against the walls of the office. They both knew the

83

sound wouldn't go any further. But they both started as though the noise had drawn the interest of the entire floor.

Pleased with the effect, Johnny slapped her buttock again. Debbie moaned. She clutched her muscles tight around him and they both trembled excitedly.

'You're a dirty little bitch,' Johnny growled. Her sphincter renewed its grip. Instead of being simply tight, the pressure on his shaft was almost unbearable. 'You're a dirty little bitch who loves to have her arse fucked,' he grunted. 'You're a filthy slut who loves to gobble cock in restaurants.'

Debbie's guttural roar reverberated through her body. Her hands gripped at his desk and her buttocks trembled with exertion as he quickened his pace. Her sphincter shifted around his sheathed length and the muscle stretched and strained as he rocked back and forth.

'You're a dirty little bitch who wants to finger herself while I fuck her arse,' he said quickly. 'That's how filthy you are, isn't it?'

She nodded. 'Oh! Yes!' she gasped. 'Please, let me do that.'

He mumbled acquiescence. She was so eager to obey, and so anxious to do anything that could be described as depraved, he considered exploiting that foible. He reasoned that, if she thought anal sex was dirty – yet was doing it and loving it – she might apply the same twisted logic to having sex with a woman.

'Harder,' Debbie demanded. 'Harder and deeper. And call me a dirty bitch again. I love it when you call me a dirty bitch.'

He slapped her backside again and rode her with more vigour. 'You filthy little slut,' he grunted. 'Grab my cock tighter and squeeze until I come.' He opened his mouth to say more, perhaps suggest that she should be eating pussy while they did this, and then realised that sort of coercion would be beneath him. He enjoyed recreational sex, he loved having sex with different partners and then vicariously sharing the experience with his wife, but he didn't like the idea of exploiting anyone. Debbie had said she didn't want to have sex with a woman and Johnny wasn't going to push the issue. Even if it did seem like a good idea to broach the subject while she was wallowing in her most depraved desires, even though he felt sure she would get off on the idea while her agreement would only be part of some masochistic fantasy, he knew it would be an act of exploitation.

'That's it,' Debbie insisted.

Her hands had moved from his desk and now squirmed between her legs. She had lifted her buttocks high so she could touch her pussy as he slipped in and out of her anus. The shift in position made her sphincter clutch him with a tighter hold. As she stroked and teased at her sex her knuckles brushed lightly against his balls. The added stimulation was almost more than he could bear.

Gritting his teeth, and willing every muscle in his loins to stave the impending release, he increased the force of each thrust as he hammered into her. Continuing to berate Debbie, using every insult that seemed appropriate, he lurched into her with a series of long, penetrating lunges.

'Fuck! Yes!' she gasped. Her fingers scrabbled madly at her wetness. He could tell she was making a concerted effort to keep her voice from rising to a shriek. 'Fuck! Yes. That's perfect.'

He knew her orgasm was close. His own had already built to a point where it was only being contained by an effort of willpower. Holding his breath and steeling himself against the swell of pleasure, he rolled his hips back and forth as he strove to take her to the point of climax.

'I want it deeper, Johnny,' she insisted. 'I want it much deeper.'

He made each thrust as forceful as a punch. Burying himself all the way inside, squashing his sac against the taut flesh of her backside, he grimaced with the effort of containing his climax.

'That's it,' she gasped. 'That's just what I need.' The words came out in a garbled blur. Her knuckles brushed at him with an urgent speed. He knew she was frantically rubbing at herself as he pushed into her rear. But he couldn't tell if Debbie's climax was being inspired by her own touch or his skilful technique. And, as they basked in the pleasure of a mutual orgasm, he realised that it didn't matter.

Debbie growled with satisfaction, but she was careful to keep her cries contained. Her body was wracked by a series of shivers and it was that as much as anything else that sucked the orgasm from Johnny's body. He plunged deep inside, pressed against her rear, and relished the sensation of her body shuddering around him. The climax was strong – he briefly feared it would be powerful enough to break the gossamer sheath of the condom – and then they wrenched their bodies apart as he and Debbie separately savoured their satisfaction.

She writhed against the desk, still touching her sex as she struggled to contain her cries and inspire more. Johnny collapsed back into his chair, breathing deeply and allowing himself to relax and relish the moment. When his shaft had finished pulsing he slipped off the used sheath, tied one end and wrapped it in a tissue from the box on his desk. Tucking his spent cock back in his pants he watched Debbie go through the final throes of her orgasm while gracing her with a smile that was somewhere between pleasure and regret. If it was the last time he and Debbie were going to do anything, he wished it could have been something more spectacular than just another bout of illicit anal sex.

'You're nasty,' she chortled as she eased away from the desk. Her spectacles had been nudged askew. She straightened them before retrieving her panties from the floor and checking for the location of her other clothes.

While Debbie went through her familiar rituals of cleaning herself, Johnny went to the cooler by his office door and poured two recyclable cartons of mineral water. He could hear handfuls of tissue being torn from the box on his desk and knew Debbie would be patting her sex lips and anus dry before dressing herself. He had never been able to understand why he could watch his own erection slide in and out of her sphincter, yet be disquieted by the sight of Debbie patting her cleft and sphincter with tissue paper. He didn't consider himself a prude yet there was something about the habit that struck him as vaguely lavatorial. Determined she wouldn't see his distaste, he kept his back discreetly turned until Debbie had finished dressing.

'Is that for me?' she asked, plucking the second carton of water from his hand.

He grinned. When he turned to face her she was the same resplendent businesswoman who had entered his office. Two familiar spots of colour darkened her cheeks and Johnny realised that was the closest Debbie was ever likely to come to blushing. She sipped at her water before speaking. 'I took a message for you before,' she said. 'With the excitement of deciding to do lunch early I forgot to pass it on.'

He shrugged. 'I'm sure it can't be that time-sensitive. What's the message?'

Her tone was apologetic. 'The owner of the Red Mill Hotel?'

Johnny nodded.

'He said there's been a problem with your booking. He can fit you in for the week after, if that suits you. But the party this Saturday can't happen.'

He groaned and put down his water as he headed back to his desk. 'When did the message come in?'

'This morning. About half an hour before you arrived. I meant to tell you earlier but, as I said . . .'

Lifting his phone, dialling Lisa's mobile, Johnny wasn't listening to the remainder of Debbie's excuse. His wife answered within two rings and he didn't bother with any of their usual niceties. 'I've just got word that the Red Mill has cancelled your booking.'

'Shit!' Lisa gasped. 'Why?'

He shrugged and knew, in the silence that was being transmitted, she would understand he was equally mystified. 'Because the manager is a twat?' he suggested.

'OK,' she sighed. 'I'll sort another location. Thanks for letting me know.'

Absently, they exchanged the words 'I love you' before ending the call.

'I'm sorry,' Debbie said quickly. 'I didn't realise it was important.'

He waved the matter aside. The worry that Debbie might start to ask questions about the booking, which would lead to questions about Lisa's party and result in a conversation about their swinging lifestyle, flashed through his mind in the blink of an eye. Determined to shift the topic away from such delicate subjects, he asked, 'So, how come you can't make our lunch date?'

Debbie grinned. 'I've had an invite from a mutual acquaintance,' she said. 'He interrupted our lunch yesterday. It's Mark Kent.'

'You know Mark?'

'He used to be a sales rep when I worked for Cox's.' The two spots of colour returned to her cheeks. 'I always had a bit of a crush on him,' she explained. 'The lunch invitation came this morning out of nowhere. That was probably the reason I forgot to pass on your message about the Red Mill.' She gave him an apologetic smile.

Johnny grinned. 'Don't hurry back,' he said generously.

She raised an eyebrow and looked suddenly defensive. 'I'm not planning to fuck him, if that's what you're suggesting.'

He shook his head. 'I wasn't suggesting that at all. I just know that Mark can go on and on for hours.' His mind briefly revisited a moment from the previous evening.

He and Lisa had been entwined on the floor of the Kents' dining room while their neighbours were similarly engaged on one of the dining chairs. Johnny had ridden his wife with a rhythm made sporadic as he teetered on the brink of a second climax. Thrusting too vigorously would push him beyond his ability to contain the orgasm. But he had watched as Mark slid in and out of Anne with an urgency that bordered on being demonic. While Johnny was measuring every thrust, Mark had gone on and on for hours. Listening to Anne groan beneath him, sure that Lisa would soon enjoy the same indescribable pleasure with their neighbour, Johnny had to slow his own pace for fear of peaking too soon.

He shook his head to clear the memories from his mind. 'When Mark gets started on the subject of urban legends,' Johnny told Debbie, 'he can go on and on and on.'

'I'll be sure to steer clear of the subject,' Debbie promised. Frowning as she made for the door, looking briefly pained, she said, 'I'm sorry I wasn't doing my job properly before. I hope I haven't caused problems by not getting that message to you sooner.'

Johnny shook his head. 'These things happen,' he said easily. 'And I'm sure Lisa will be able to organise an alternative venue.'

7

Location, Location, Location

'I'm never going to be able to organise an alternative venue,' Lisa complained. She stamped a Versace boot against the carpet to emphasise her anger. 'I could kill that bastard manager at the Red Mill. I could string him up by his bollocks.'

'Why not have the party here?' Anne suggested.

They had gathered in Anne's home office. Lisa sat in front of a spare desk, with a buzzing laptop before her. She did not consider herself a computer person and the strange symbols and stylish graphics on the screen only added to her confusion and feelings of helplessness. On the opposite side of the room Anne was dwarfed by the huge screen of the main PC. She said she was *googling* for an alternative location, although the term meant nothing to Lisa. Instead of asking for an explanation, sure it had something to do with the strange world of computer people, she simply nodded grateful encouragement.

'Would this place do?'

Lisa glanced toward her and saw that, instead of indicating something she had found on the internet, Anne was whirling a finger in the air to suggest she meant her house. 'I can't see Mark objecting,' Anne said hurriedly, 'and I'd love to attend a swingers' party. Especially if it was held in my house.'

Lisa shook her head. 'It's a kind offer but here is too small. And too risky. And too close to home.' With each reason for refusing she could feel the potential of the party slipping from her grasp. Frustration and anger threatened to drag her mood spiralling down. 'And I'm always more comfortable when parties are set a little bit out of the local area,' she added.

'There are other hotels you could use, aren't there?'

'No,' Lisa said sadly. 'There aren't many that are swinger-friendly. And, usually, hotels need at least a couple of weeks' advance notice. There won't be any hotels able to fit us in now.'

'Then it's time we got proactive.' Anne shifted in her seat, turning the swivel chair around and snatching a notebook and pen from beside her mouse. Aside from a beatific smile she appeared calm and composed and businesslike. 'Tell me: what exactly do you need for a venue?'

Despite the setback of losing her booking at the Red Mill, Lisa couldn't help but grin at Anne. She knew exactly what the young woman was going through and understood her emotions were currently scaling meteoric heights. After the first time she and Johnny had been with another couple, Lisa remembered she had spent the following week in a state of absolute euphoria. The discovery that such forbidden pleasures could be attained, shared and enjoyed was an epiphany. The memory of what she and her husband had done, and the knowledge that they could (and would) do it again, perpetually inspired new awe. During the years she and Johnny had been swinging, Lisa had seen other couples revel in the same blissful awakening. And, while Anne seemed to be handling the discovery with more composure than most, Lisa thought it was still sweet to see some of the woman's symptoms of delight.

'Earth to Lisa. Earth to Lisa. Are you receiving me? Over.'

Lisa shook her head. 'Sorry,' she mumbled. 'Daydreaming.'

'What do you need for a venue?' Anne repeated. She had the notebook on her lap and a pen poised over the blank page. 'Tell me everything that will make for the ideal location.'

'The Red Mill was the ideal location,' Lisa said sadly.

Anne tapped her notebook. 'That's not proactive. Tell me what makes for the perfect location. Let's see if we can do better than the Red Mill.'

Lisa paused, thought for a moment and drew a deep breath before beginning.

An hour later, as Anne drove them out of town, Lisa was still adding to the list. She had mentioned the important details – a venue that was large, clean, secure and discreet – and had simply continued and continued.

'Plenty of parking spaces. No chance of outdoor activities being overlooked by neighbours. A swimming pool is always good fun. Somewhere with a kitchen that can cater for veggies, carnivores and perverts. Also, ideally, somewhere with a well-stocked bar. And some place that has plenty of TV screens and doesn't mind showing lots of porn.'

Anne nodded and continued to drive. 'I had fun last night,' she murmured. The words were almost too soft to be heard. 'I had a lot of fun.'

Lisa glanced at her from the passenger seat and saw a blush rouging the visible side of Anne's face. Placing a hand on her new friend's thigh, lightly squeezing the leg beneath the short denim skirt, she said, 'We all had fun last night. Thank you.'

'Mark and I have talked about some stuff,' Anne began. She kept her gaze fixed through the windscreen as she spoke, studying the light flow of lunchtime traffic and the surrounding greenery. 'Mark and I have done some things that are a little bit more daring than most couples would risk. But we've never done anything like that.'

'You enjoyed yourself?'

Anne's blush deepened. She spoke as though making a confession. 'I licked your pussy.'

Lisa shivered. She remembered when her new neighbour pressed her tongue against her sex – the recollection was fresh enough for Lisa to relive the raw pleasure she had received – and she was stung by another tickle of arousal as Anne's words transported her back to that memory. Not for the first time that day, she realised the crotch of her panties was warm and damp.

'I can't believe I did that,' Anne whispered. 'I can't believe I went down on another woman. That's just not something I've ever thought of doing before. It's not something Mark and I have even discussed when we've been fantasising. It's just . . .'

'Did you enjoy doing it?'

Anne's blushes deepened. 'I think I did.'

'You only think you enjoyed it?'

'I know that I want to do it again,' Anne confided. She snatched her gaze away from the road, studied Lisa and said, 'I know I want to do it again soon.'

The sincerity in her large hazel eyes stung Lisa with a sharp pang of arousal. Shocked by the sudden excitement, and delighted they shared similar appetites, Lisa squeezed her leg again. 'If you want us to do it again, then we will.' She coughed, cleared her throat, and gestured to Anne to turn her attention back to the road ahead. Trying to take her thoughts away from the electric tension inside the car, and hoping neither of them suggested pulling into the next lay-by, she resumed the list of requirements that were needed for her ideal party venue. 'Did I mention there should be at least one large bedroom that can be converted into a playroom?'

'A playroom?'

'A playroom is the mainstay of a lot of parties. For some people that's the only reason they bother going.'

'What is a playroom?'

'That's where four or six double beds can be roped together so we can have a massive orgy of naked bodies writhing on the same bed.'

'Sounds like fun.'

'It is. And, ideally, the whole venue should have something distinctive that means it will stick in people's minds.' The huskiness was beginning to fall from her tone. Although her arousal remained intense, she was no longer worried that either she or Anne would not be able to contain their libido. 'The Red Mill had something distinctive with that big red windmill in front of the building. Almost every couple who's ever attended a party at the Red Mill has a picture of the wife standing naked beside the windmill.'

'Have you got one?'

Lisa laughed. 'I've got seven.'

'Lucky cow,' said Anne with a smile. She looked set to say more and then glanced at the road on her right. 'What about that place?' she asked, pointing to a forbidding-looking building by the side of the road. 'Would it work as a location if I could make an arrangement?'

It was a dark building, standing alone at the peak of a hill. With the sunlight behind it, the walls were trapped within their own black shadows. Lisa's first glance reminded her of the splendid and spooky buildings that always featured in haunted-house movies. She thought, if the Addams family had a UK holiday home, this was what it would look like. And yet, although there was something sinister about the building, she found it peculiarly appealing. Eventually Lisa shook her head. 'It's a thought,' she said kindly. 'But people just don't rent their homes to swingers. It doesn't work like that.'

'Would it work as a location if I could make an arrangement?' Anne pressed.

Lisa shrugged. 'I'd need to take a look around the place, make sure it had enough rooms and the right sort of ambience but, from what I can see . . .'

Anne was indicating to her right, guiding the car off the main road and driving towards a rough lane that led up to the house. With her fingers tapping at her mobile phone she struck Lisa as being a consummate professional, not the caffeinated airhead she and Johnny had first met three days earlier. It occurred to Lisa that Anne was making the transition to a swinging lifestyle a little too easily. Considering that the previous evening was supposedly the first time Anne and Mark had interacted with another couple, Anne seemed to be handling the experience like a woman revisiting familiar terrain.

Oblivious to her friend's thoughts, Anne drove down the dirt track leading to the house as she balanced the mobile between her shoulder and her ear. 'Tony Samuels,' she said. 'Can you tell him it's Anne Kent? I need him to call me back on this number. It's urgent. Thanks.'

Lisa opened her mouth to ask a question and then, as they passed a sign that read SAMUELS LETTING & BUYING, she realised she already knew the answer.

The kiss began without warning.

The silence that had fallen between them was amicable. They were parked in front of the large, ominous building with the heat from the summer sun warming them both. Dappled glints of light bounced against the car's roof. The conversation shifted to their likes and dislikes. Number one on Anne's list, now, was the things that had happened the previous evening.

'I was so turned on.'

'I noticed.'

Anne blushed. 'I wasn't too wet, was I?'

'Did you hear me complaining?'

'I'd never kissed a woman before.'

Lisa gazed at the deserted landscape surrounding them. They were outside an empty house on the top of a hill with a view that showed nothing but desolation and a faraway road beneath them. It was a discreet spot and she realised there was a chance to use that to their advantage. Grinning seductively for Anne, stroking her lips with her tongue, she asked, 'Do you want to try kissing a woman again?'

Anne's eyes grew wide. 'Here? Now?'

'Yes.'

Lisa leaned forward until their lips met.

The exchange was different from the night before but no less exciting. They were inside the claustrophobic confines of Anne's Mini, and it was daylight outside rather than the comforting security of nighttime. But those were only peripheral differences. For Lisa the main thing separating this kiss from the last one they shared was that neither of them had a husband watching. Rather than being done to show off and excite an audience, this kiss was being exchanged purely for the pleasure of becoming intimate.

Anne's lips were warm and responsive. The moment when their tongues met hinted at a hunger that equalled Lisa's mounting desire. They moved as close as the awkward confines of the Mini would allow, pressing their bodies together as each raised hands to touch and caress. Lisa found the swell of Anne's breast. She snatched a startled breath when the woman fondled her with the same languid urgency. The electricity between them had been a constant throughout the morning. As they talked about the forthcoming party, and plotted to find a way around the setback of losing their booking at the Red Mill, Lisa had noticed Anne studying her. She knew that they shared a healthy interest in each other and both of them were eager to continue from where they had left off the night before.

The kiss seemed like the first step on that road to discovery.

Lisa raised herself from the seat and placed a knee between Anne's legs.

Pushing against her, Anne groaned and thrust her tongue more fully into the exchange. It was no longer possible to decide who was touching where. As Lisa slid her fingers inside the waistband of Anne's denim skirt, Anne pushed her hands beneath Lisa's top. Cool fingers stroked warm flesh. Nipples were caught, stroked, aroused and teased. The Mini's interior was quickly fogged by condensation. Lisa wondered if they dared do anything more. The idea was tempting, adding fresh dampness to the crotch of her panties. She studied Anne's hazel eyes, sure the woman would be bold enough to go along with anything she suggested. But she couldn't bring herself to break the sweet contact of the kiss.

Even though Johnny wasn't there, Lisa knew she would share the details of this moment with him when he returned from work. She also suspected, having seen the closeness that bound them, that, Anne intended to confide her version of this exchange to Mark. The idea that perhaps they could confess to their partners together, so all four of them could share the excitement, filled Lisa's stomach with a fresh flurry of acid arousal.

But again, she couldn't bring herself to make any suggestion to Anne because she knew that would spoil the moment they were enjoying. Anne had released Lisa's breasts from the constraints of their bra. Her fingers massaged and kneaded the flesh, the palms of her hands maintaining constant contact with the stiff nubs of Lisa's nipples. Not wanting to be outdone, and relishing the discovery of Anne's inquisitive nature, Lisa pushed one hand inside Anne's skirt and found the dewy centre of her panties. Stroking her fingertip back and forth, exciting the lips that pressed against the thin veil of cotton fabric, Lisa eventually teased her nail against the crease of Anne's thigh and slipped her finger inside the underwear. When she managed to stroke the bare flesh of the other woman's labia they both groaned.

'You have to stop,' Anne muttered. 'I think someone's coming.'

'I think both of us might be coming soon,' Lisa giggled.

Anne laughed. But still she was making an effort to pull away. 'Look behind you,' she muttered. 'There's a car coming up the driveway. I think it's Tony.'

Panting, Lisa glanced down the steep incline. She wanted to do more with Anne. She needed to do more now that the arousal had been awoken in her loins. But she could see that wasn't going to happen on this occasion. A car was approaching, which meant their position was no longer as discreet as they needed. Groaning with frustration, wishing they had started this exchange back at Anne's house so they would have the comfort of a bedroom and the privacy of a closed door, she quietly cursed the events that had led her here, aroused and frustrated outside an empty house atop an open and exposed hill. As she straightened her clothes and made herself seem a little less dishevelled, she hoped Tony Samuels would be quick about his business so she and Anne could get back to what they had been doing.

Two hours later Tony Samuels was still talking and the chances of escaping him before sunset seemed remote. His banter had been relentless from the moment he stepped out of his car. Although he had shown them all the way round the beautiful property, and pointed out its many wonderful features, Lisa didn't think the dapper little gentleman would allow them to use the building for the purpose she wanted. The tour of the house had revealed a splendid find. It was in a good state of repair, more than adequate for the party Lisa

98

wanted to throw, and distinctive enough to make it the ideal setting. There was a light scent of must in the air, not surprising because the house hadn't been used during the past three months, but that was the only fault Lisa could find with the place. Its predominant position on the top of the hill meant it would be easy to locate. The lengthy driveway provided ample places for guests to park. And its remoteness lent the security of knowing that they would not be overlooked or give anyone any offence. Admittedly the building had a slightly forbidding appearance. But Lisa simply thought that added to its charm.

Yet she couldn't see Samuels allowing it to be used for a swingers' party.

It was frustrating because there were so many things about the house that made it a perfect location. Not only were there dozens of bedrooms, with only one being used to store old clothes, but the place had an elegance that she believed her party deserved. There was a hall with a galleried landing and the master bedroom was sumptuous in size and ideal for the massive playroom she wanted to offer to her guests. Seeing such a perfect location, and certain Samuels would refuse them, she couldn't bear to endure the upset of a denial. Discreetly pulling Anne to one side, pushing her mouth close to the other woman's ear, she whispered, 'This isn't going to work.'

'Is there a problem, Mrs West?'

Tony Samuels seemed like a pleasant fellow. Anne had introduced him by saying she had written promotional material for his company, and he had helped her and Mark to find their home next door to Lisa and Johnny.

But he was dressed in a very conservative suit and everything about his appearance told her he would be repulsed by the idea of a swingers' party. Lisa had seen his expression when his car approached the house and she knew he was not impressed to find the two women kissing each other while they waited. His attitude towards them had been professional but detached. Unlike the majority of men with whom she associated, he did not make any time to glance at her chest or respond to the invitation of her most seductive smile. She noticed a wedding ring on his left hand and decided he was either gay or devoutly monogamous, or she simply didn't do anything to excite his interest. Whatever the cause, Lisa felt sure it would mean they wouldn't get any favours from Tony Samuels.

Talking more to Anne than Tony, trying to convey the message without causing embarrassment, Lisa said again, 'This isn't going to work. We should thank Mr Samuels and then get back to either organising an alternative or cancelling the whole thing.'

Anne ignored her as she studied Tony. 'We need the house for three days,' she said brightly. 'Would that be possible?'

'Three days?'

'One to set up. One for the party. And one for the clean-up afterwards. Three days.'

'I'm not sure I could allow that, Anne,' he began. His smile was apologetic. 'We don't usually let properties for three days. Our contracts have a minimum letting period of six months.'

'Come on, Tony,' Anne pressed. 'I cut you a special deal with that advertising copy. And didn't that last sales letter score some interest?'

Tony's plain features tightened into a friendly grimace. Lisa could see he wanted to help a valued client but she didn't think he would be able to oblige Anne on this occasion. She watched his mind tick through options that would allow him to refuse and, with an infuriating stroke of bad luck, it seemed as if his first question was the one that would prove their undoing.

'What sort of party are you talking about?' he asked. 'If you're planning a rave it's absolutely out of the question.'

'My friend here is throwing a swingers' party,' Anne explained.

Lisa rolled her eyes and wished she had warned Anne to be more discreet about using the word 'swingers'. From previous experience she knew it was a phrase that won either immediate interest or instant loathing. Having already decided which reaction Tony would most likely give, she cringed at the thought of suffering his hostility as he stormed away from the building and told them they were perverts who had wasted his time.

'You two are swingers?' Tony gasped. The sparkle in his gaze was bright and lurid. His eager smile was quickly replaced by a flicker of uncertainty. 'What does that mean exactly?' He paused, licked his lips and added, 'Does that mean you're willing to negotiate for three nights' rental here?'

Lisa shook her head and pulled Anne to one side. In a heated whisper that she didn't try to keep confidential she said, 'I'm not going to fuck this guy for the privilege of renting this place. That's not swinging. That's prostitution. I might be a slut. But I'm not a whore.'

Anne laughed. Easing herself away from Lisa she sidled up to Tony and said, 'Let us have this place for three nights and we'll let you come to the party. How does that sound for a fair exchange?'

'You're asking a lot. If anyone found out I'd rented a building for a swingers' party it would kill my good name in this town.'

'You're an estate agent,' Anne observed. 'You don't have a good name.'

Lisa stiffened, shocked that Anne could deliver such a joke during this crucial point of the negotiations. She quietly marvelled at the petite woman's control of the situation and realised it was time to offer some support. 'It's going to be the best party I've ever thrown,' she told him. 'You can bring your partner if you like but, if you want to come alone, you'll be made very welcome.'

To show she and Anne were united in their appeal, Lisa placed a hand around her friend's waist. Anne grinned and pressed against her with an open display of affection. She lazily brushed stray hairs from Lisa's cheek and planted a soft, seductive kiss against the side of her face. Turning slowly to study Tony, regarding him with an easy, confident grin, she asked, 'What do you say?'

In that moment Lisa knew they had the house.

Tony shuffled from foot to foot, his gaze flitting between Lisa and Anne and his interest now drawn to the way they idly caressed each other. Although he had shown no sexual interest in them before, now his attention had been drawn to the fact that they were flaunting their relationship, his gaze couldn't be wrenched away. Lisa noticed he shifted his grip on his briefcase and held it defensively in front of his groin. Used to gauging people from their body language, she suspected he was trying to conceal a sudden erection.

Anne and Tony continued to dicker. The objections he raised were childishly surmountable. And the conversation was concluded as the two women remained in each other's embrace.

'You know this isn't some clever con to get the keys from you,' Anne assured him. 'We've done business before and you know I'm a responsible professional. We only want the place for three nights and, in exchange, you'll be receiving an invite to this year's hottest party and getting your property cleaned from top to bottom.' She shook her head, looking as though she was marvelling over some detail, before adding, 'I guess the question here isn't: *can we have the house for three days?* To me, it seems like the question should be: *why wouldn't you let us have it?*'

'I . . . I'd have to calculate the cost of three days' rental,' Tony stammered.

Anne shook her head. 'I've just told you what we're prepared to pay. You'll receive an invite to the party and, when we hand the keys back, the place will be cleaned and ready to rent.'

'Will you throw in some free advertising copy to sweeten the deal?'

Anne pushed out her hand. 'It won't be free,' she told him. 'But I'll make sure it's twice as effective as the last I wrote. And you'll get the same discounted rate this time.'

Tony grabbed her hand and shook it. 'Your husband has taught you to be a formidable saleswoman.'

Anne waved the comment away. She took the keys from Tony, promised they would be back with him by first thing on Monday morning, and then took his business card so she could contact him with his invitation. The formalities were concluded so quickly Lisa was still coming to terms with what had happened as Tony climbed back into his car and drove away.

Anne held up the house keys and dangled them in front of Lisa's face. 'Fancy going in there and continuing what we started in the Mini?' she asked cheerfully. Her eyes shone with a flush of satisfied excitement. 'We've got the entire place to ourselves and a couple of hours left before the afternoon's over.'

'Fuck! No!' Lisa replied. Speaking quickly to try and pacify the hurt she could see in Anne's expression, she said, 'You're on a roll, sweetheart. While you're negotiating this well I want you with me while we try and organise entertainment for the party.'

8

Duelling Dildos

The room was black. There was the hum of a hidden PA system and the soft clatter of heels against a wooden floor. Twin spotlights appeared from the ceiling overhead and pinpointed Trish and Amber. They stood resplendent against the darkness, bravely facing the audience with their hands behind their backs.

Trish was brunette and busty with impossibly long legs.

Amber was slightly fairer yet far from blonde. Her figure lacked the curves of her onstage partner. Nevertheless, there was something in her impish smile that suggested she would be the more daring of the two. Both women wore matching bras and thongs that had been cut from a cheerful gingham fabric.

The sound of a strummed banjo throbbed through the room. Trish moved her hands from behind her back and showed she was holding a thick black dildo. A second banjo – higher in tone, less metallic yet somehow slightly discordant – sounded from the speakers in response. Amber moved her hands from behind her back to show she also held a dildo. This one was flesh-coloured and longer than the length brandished by Trish.

As two more chords were played, the women exchanged glances and then made a show of twisting the bases of their dildos. The music was loud enough to cover the sound but it was clear to their modest audience that both instruments were now vibrating vigorously. From the depths of the shadows Rupert's rich dark voice announced, 'We call this number "The Duelling Dildos".'

The music resumed with its tentative opening bars and the melody alternated from one banjo to the other. Trish performed as the first played its challenge. Amber responded as the second echoed and improved on snatches of the same tune.

Trish stroked her dildo against one gingham-covered breast. Her grin was broad and appeared genuine. The shape of the dildo was difficult to see as it vibrated at a ridiculously high speed. She held the buzzing black length in place and clearly delighted in the thrill of having her nipple stimulated. Although the act was staged to look like a polished performance there was nothing artificial or fake about the glow that coloured her cheeks.

Amber responded by teasing her dildo inside the left cup of her gingham bra. The fleshy length was trapped between the tight fabric and her modest orb. Her grin grew broader as she threw her shoulders back and basked in the pleasure of having the dildo against her breast.

The first banjo responded with a quickly plucked arpeggio.

Trish twisted the clasp at the front of her bra and allowed both breasts to spill free. She shifted position on stage and glared a challenge in Amber's direction.

As the second banjo mimicked the first's arpeggio, Amber unfastened the clasp of her bra and then pulled the string that held her thong in place. Both garments fluttered to the floor, dancing in and out of the spotlight as they fell. Amber was revealed shamelessly naked.

When the first banjo picked up the tune Trish removed her panties and pushed the dildo against the shaved lips of her pussy. She stood for a moment with her eyes closed. An expression of salacious pleasure flooded over her face.

Both women looked glorious and confident standing naked on the stage. Rupert occasionally spoke over the music, encouraging handclapping, foot-stamping and cheering and telling the audience they could join in if they wanted. Amber and Trish exchanged mock confrontational glances as each strove to do something more daring than the other. The music quickened its tempo.

Amber slid the fleshy dildo inside her sex. She splayed the shaved lips of her pussy and stood so the audience could watch the slick penetration. Her mouth hung open as she pushed the length inside. By the time the dildo was fully inserted, her expression had creased into a broad grin. She chuckled softly as she basked in her own private joy and then glanced at Trish.

The first banjo plucked out a refrain reminiscent of 'Yankee Doodle Dandy'. While the music played, Trish followed Amber's lead by slipping the long black dildo into her own sex. Showing that she wasn't to be outdone, she made the penetration swift and easy and followed it with a lazy flick of her wrist to make the shaft plunge in and out.

In response, Amber used her dildo more vigorously.

The music had taken on a frantic speed, sounding like something that would have been appropriate as a movie soundtrack for a hillbilly car chase, and both Amber and Trish worked in unison as the banjos harmonised their staccato melodies into the same jaunty tune. They each found a convenient swivel chair that had been lurking in the shadows behind them.

Trish sat back, pushed her thighs over the arm of her chair and worked the dildo briskly in and out of her sex. Amber knelt in her chair, displaying her backside to the audience and allowing everyone to see the depths she was penetrating.

106

The music grew louder and faster.

Trish pushed her dildo in and out with increasing speed. Her mouth was agape and her pleasure was obvious. Stage show or not, she was clearly enjoying every moment of showing herself off and wanking in time to the music. Her nipples stood hard and the flush of colour that darkened her labia could not have been achieved by the trickeries of clever lighting or the greatest acting ability in the world.

Beside her, equally immersed in pleasure, Amber forced her dildo deep inside and wriggled her svelte buttocks in time to the music. She glanced over her shoulder at the unseen audience and made no attempt to disguise her arousal. Her cheeks were blushed with high colour and her eyes held the glazed expression of a woman hurtling to the brink of climax.

A third spotlight came on as Rupert appeared between them. He was tall and his black flesh glistened like liquid tar beneath the beam of the stage lights. Dressed only in a cowboy hat and a pair of tight leather pants, he posed so his well-honed six-pack was displayed to best effect. 'These are "The Duelling Dildos", ladies and gentlemen,' he called. The microphone amplified his voice to a thunderous roar. 'I want to hear some handclapping and foot-stomping to help these girls along.'

To encourage the audience's participation, or possibly to make the finale more spectacular, he grabbed the back of Trish's swivel chair and began to spin her around. As soon as she was turning in time to the music he set Amber's chair going in the opposite direction. Both women continued to rub and wank, pushing themselves closer to orgasm. The music was so fast it was little more than a blur. Rupert kept the chairs spinning whenever they began to slow down.

Amber screeched with ecstasy while Trish wailed on the brink of release. It was impossible to tell if the orgasms were faked or sincere but, in the splendour of the show's climax, that detail was immaterial. Rupert reached out and brought both chairs to a halt just as the music came to its abrupt conclusion.

Amber had collapsed over the back of her chair, the fleshy length hanging from her sex and an expression of obvious contentment plastered across her face. Trish was relaxed in her seat, one leg dragging on the floor and her hand concealing the black length that penetrated her sex. Both women looked fully and completely sated.

The stage lights went out.

'The Duelling Dildos,' Rupert boomed enthusiastically. His tone seemed excessive for the smattering of applause he received. The house lights came on, illuminating Rupert, Amber, Trish and their audience. The three performers were now holding hands in a line and they made a show of bowing. Both Amber and Trish looked a little unsteady on their legs, adding to the idea that they might genuinely have climaxed while performing. The dildos they had been using now rested on the chairs behind them.

'Let's have a big hand for Amber and Trish,' Rupert enthused. He spoke as though this was a genuine performance rather than a simple audition. Releasing his hold on their hands and motioning them to exit the stage on opposite sides, he said, 'That's Amber and Trish. The lucky ones amongst you will be seeing a lot more of them later in the evening. Thank you.'

One of the two women who had been watching the show stepped forward. 'That was perfect, Rupert,' she called. She applauded loudly and with obvious appreciation. 'Thank you, Amber. Thank you, Trish. We couldn't have picked better. I'd like to book you for Saturday night.'

On stage Rupert grinned. Behind him Trish's cheer of delight was drowned by Amber's groan of frustration.

'Shit! No! Not Saturday night.' Her cry sounded genuinely pained.

'Problem?'

'Yes, there is a problem. We can't make Saturday night. Only this afternoon we received a booking to play for a party being thrown by Lisa West. That is such bad luck. Would another night suit you better, Becky?'

'Lisa West has booked you for her party on Saturday night!' Becky exclaimed. 'Damn! I wish I'd known!' Even to her own ears, she thought the exclamation sounded theatrical and overstated. She paused a beat and then smiled. 'Saturday night is the only one that will work for me. I'll pay you double if you perform for me instead of her.'

There was no consultation. 'Double? Shit! Yes!' Rupert declared. He frowned and added, 'But Lisa's going to be really disappointed.'

Becky struggled to contain a wicked smile. 'We wouldn't want to disappoint Lisa,' she said with saccharine kindness. 'So, perhaps it's best if you don't tell her that you won't be appearing.'

Rupert's hesitation stretched out in the silence. Clearly uncomfortable, he said, 'If we cancel now and let her know, that will give her the chance to book another act. If we just don't turn up on the night, that could really spoil her party.'

'I'll pay you triple,' Becky told him.

'It's a deal,' Trish decided. She stepped forward to shake Becky's hand and confirm that they wouldn't be appearing at Lisa's party.

9

Lisa's Birthday

Johnny greeted the neighbours with a warm hug for Anne and a genuine smile for Mark. Knowing that he was considered to be aloof when away from his swinging lifestyle – he was aware the words 'distant', 'cold' and 'unapproachable' were often used – the honest enjoyment of welcoming the couple surprised him. 'It's good to see you both,' he said with a grin. 'Come on in. Make yourselves comfortable. Lisa will be down in a moment.'

Anne carried two prettily wrapped boxes. Mark held a cake tin as carefully as if it contained a life-support machine fashioned from eggshells. Johnny thought of teasing him about it but decided Mark deserved a little more respect for the effort and trouble he had invested in doing something nice for Lisa's birthday. 'Birthday cake?'

Mark nodded. 'Yes.'

'Take it through to the kitchen,' Johnny said, pointing down the hall. 'I'll escort your wife through to the lounge and start seducing her.'

Anne laughed and punched him playfully on the arm. Mark's ever-present smile widened as the door to the kitchen closed behind him. Johnny reflected that, as well as bringing gifts and cake, the couple had also brought a warm ambience to the house. It genuinely was a pleasure to see them again.

'You and Lisa have had a busy couple of days, haven't you?'

'We spent most of today up at the party house,' Anne enthused. 'It's looking glorious up there.' Her hair was a vibrant pink, the colour of seaside candyfloss. It complemented the electric magenta of her sleeveless T-shirt and matching jeans. Instead of wearing her hair in her usual bob, she had used styling gel to make it stand up in a punky fashion. It transformed her appearance into something completely different from what he had already grown used to seeing. This version of Anne looked impossibly youthful and incredibly exciting. A familiar shiver tingled in his loins.

'Lisa and I have to go down there tomorrow morning,' Anne continued. 'But only to sort out the final preparations. The place is as good as ready now. We've got a stage area cordoned off for when Rupert, Amber and Trish do their duelling dildo routine . . .'

'That sounds classy,' he teased.

Anne ignored the playful jibe. '. . . and I've been sewing together a few sheets so the playroom looks more hospitable. Did Lisa mention that we might need a pair of strong hands to help carry a couple of crates of wine into the bar?'

Johnny chuckled. Because he had followed Anne into the room he was able to clutch her from behind. His embrace allowed him to easily cup her breasts. Holding her lightly, barely pressing himself against her, he asked, 'Do you want to find out if my hands are strong enough? I can think of a way to prove that I'm the man for your job.'

'Another audition?' Anne giggled. She made no move to pull away from him. Still holding the presents she simply writhed her taut buttocks against his groin. 'I don't think I could handle another audition,' she laughed. 'I think I'm now in need of the real thing.'

He pushed his nose against her neck and inhaled her perfume. Immediately his length began to harden.

111

Instead of shying away from the erection, Anne pressed more forcefully against him. 'If it's the real thing you're after, then I can supply that too,' he murmured.

'Are you accosting my friend and fellow party host?' Lisa asked as she breezed into the room. She had dressed down this evening. A hint of makeup, paired with a light blouse and designer jeans, suggested casual elegance rather than anything artificial. After the long day she had spent labouring with Anne at the party house, Johnny could understand why she hadn't bothered spending any time preparing for their guests. And, as he smiled at her, he accepted that his wife was attractive enough to carry off the understated look.

Lisa pressed a kiss against Johnny's cheek and then a second against Anne's. With one hand she squeezed her husband's backside. The other stole lazily over Anne's stomach. It was a sultry welcome for both of them.

'I'm accosting your friend,' Johnny agreed. 'But only in a sexual way.'

Dropping lazily onto the settee Lisa said, 'Well, if you let go of her now, I can finish accosting Anne while you sort out drinks for this birthday girl.'

Johnny tightened his grip on Anne's breasts, savouring the moment, before finally releasing his hold. He went through to the kitchen as the two women casually embraced on the settee. The thought of staying and watching did not get a chance to compete with the idea of doing as his wife had asked. It was tempting to enjoy the opportunity of seeing two attractive women exchange an intimate greeting, but he thought it more important to be seen as a good husband and host. He entered the kitchen and found Mark placing the birthday cake on a circular silver board.

'Nice kitchen,' Mark mumbled distractedly.

His attention was fixed on centring the cake. Johnny didn't think he could have done a much better job if he had used digital callipers and a micrometer. 'Aside from the microwave and the kettle most of this kitchen is still in its original packaging,' Johnny assured him. He glanced at the cake and read the inscription HAPPY BIRTHDAY LISA. The royal icing was a brilliant white with lettering the same pink as Anne's current hair colour. He marvelled at his neighbour's ability to do so much with food. 'You're a genius,' he said, without realising he'd spoken aloud.

'Genius,' Mark echoed. 'I like that.' He glanced around the kitchen, finally satisfied the cake was set perfectly. The polished counters were empty and sterile. With the cupboard doors closed, it looked as barren and unused as a display kitchen in a showroom. A vase of roses sat by the side of the fridge-freezer and a bottle of red wine stood next to the microwave. Shaking his head Mark said, 'I can see you put a lot of preparation into tonight's birthday meal.'

Johnny shrugged. 'I got the number of Lisa's favourite Chinese restaurant. They've agreed to deliver a takeout. I'll send the order through later, once we've had a couple of drinks and settled down for the evening.'

Mark laughed and Johnny understood he was amused by their contrary attitudes towards the proper use of a kitchen. Considering the effort Mark invested in cooking and preparing meals, Johnny realised they were at opposite ends of that spectrum. Yet, for some reason he couldn't understand, the difference made them more compatible than if it had been a shared interest.

'How's Lisa's birthday gone so far?' Mark asked.

'She's spent most of the day at the Munster house with Anne.' He paused, snatched a bottle of wine from the fridge and found four glasses in an eye-level cupboard. In Mark's company Johnny was close to being embarrassed by his own lack of familiarity with the kitchen, but that knowledge didn't cause any consternation. Comfortable with his new friend, he simply went on exposing his ignorance as he searched through two drawers before finding a corkscrew. 'How did you get on with Debbie the other day?' he asked. 'She's been awfully quiet since the pair of you did lunch.'

'She hasn't said anything to you?' Mark raised an eyebrow. 'I thought she would have—'

'Are those drinks ready yet?' Lisa's voice trailed from the lounge.

'We're getting parched in here,' Anne added.

Mark glanced towards the plaintive sounds of the two women and shook his head. 'I'll tell you what happened later,' he promised Johnny. 'For now, it sounds like there are women in need of our attention.' Taking the glasses from his hand, he urged him to step through the kitchen door. The two men returned to the lounge.

Lisa and Anne were naked and kissing.

Their bare bodies slid together with a blend of passion and familiarity that was breathtaking to behold. Mark and Johnny stopped in the doorway and simply watched as the two women gave themselves over to the moment. Discarded clothes littered the floor and the back of the settee. The blinds had been drawn to make their liaison discreet and they lay naked in each other's arms. Their faces were pressed together, their tongues occasionally visible as they shifted and writhed. Lisa's fingers were pressed into the dark curls of Anne's pussy while Anne held Lisa's breasts in a loose, almost reverential embrace. Aside from murmurs of encouragement, Anne whispering, 'Yes', and Lisa cooing, 'Go on', they were bound by a spell of silence.

Johnny quietly marvelled that he and Lisa had clicked so well with the new neighbours. In the past, apart from swinging at parties, they had met up with the occasional single or couple. And, while those meetings had invariably led to fun evenings, they had seldom progressed to anything more. There had been one couple they had seen three times after their first encounter. The sex had been better each time but the pair never struck Johnny as being particularly close. He began to feel uncomfortable with them whenever their time together stretched away from the diversion of sex. Lisa, he remembered, had also been uneasy with the way the pair casually disparaged each other when out of earshot of their respective partners.

There had also been a single guy who was handsome, clean, presentable and devoted to pleasing Lisa. But, after a month of seeing him every weekend, Johnny and Lisa had grown tired of arguing that he must still use condoms before they did anything sexual. Eventually it had proved less complicated to simply stop seeing him than to go through the same irritating conversation every Friday evening.

There had been others, couples with whom they'd made a connection at parties, and singles who had stayed in touch for weeks after. But few of those relationships had led to anything more than extra names for the Christmas card list. With the possible exception of Debbie – who was more Johnny's sanctioned mistress than a legitimate swinging partner – all of them had eventually fallen into the realm of glossed-over memories. Throughout five years of swinging, Lisa and Johnny had found nothing that had the comfortable feel they were experiencing with Mark and Anne.

'Do you want these drinks now?' Mark asked.

'Or should we go back to the kitchen and wait until you two horny sluts have finished feasting on each other?' Johnny suggested.

Lisa and Anne separated. Neither appeared concerned about her nudity or the fact that they had been kissing. Each gestured to her partner to join them and Mark distributed glasses while Johnny poured the wine. The incongruity of their nakedness did not seem out of place as they all toasted Lisa's birthday. Nor did it appear odd when Lisa gushed excitedly about the CDs that Anne and Mark had given her as birthday gifts. She kissed Mark on the cheek, her bare breasts crushing against the thin cotton of his shirt, and she cheerfully hugged Anne as their unclothed bodies pressed close together. She didn't have any Elvis or Glenn Miller in her collection and Johnny knew she was genuinely delighted with the presents.

And still he marvelled at how easily the four of them had become a quartet.

'One of us will phone the order through to the Chinese in a while,' Lisa told Mark and Anne. Glancing at Johnny to include him in the conversation she added, 'Anne and I just thought we should start the evening with a little bit of fun.'

He rolled his eyes and feigned uninterest. 'Oh damn!' he moaned. 'Is that what we're going to have to do? I hope it doesn't take too long because I'm starving.'

The four of them sat together on the comfortable expanse of an overlarge settee. Johnny was next to Lisa who sat by Anne with Mark at her side. Anne reached across Johnny's wife and stroked her hand against the front of his shirt. 'Are you feeling left out because you're a hungry boy?' she teased.

Her fingers, the short nails painted the same colour as her hair, trailed down to the waistband of his jeans. She traced the bulging shape that lurked beneath the zip. He could feel a warmth emanating from her touch. When she pulled the zipper open and slipped her fingers inside the gaping mouth of his fly, his hardness returned with a fresh and furious force. Her fingers easily found his erection.

'You're neglecting your husband,' Lisa murmured.

Johnny glanced over at Mark who was stroking a lazy hand against Anne's bare backside. He couldn't see clearly from his position but he suspected Mark's fingers were trailing against the soft split of Anne's pussy lips. The thought made his excitement more intense. He could picture the woman's sex being lightly fingered and imagined the dewy wetness that would now glisten around her hole.

'Mark isn't being neglected,' Anne chided softly. Her fingers circled Johnny's erection. She eased the length from his jeans and wrapped her fist around him. Stroking casually up and down, pulling his foreskin back until the dome stood dark and purple, she told Lisa, 'I'm sure you can make Mark feel as though he's a part of your birthday celebrations.'

And Johnny saw that was all it took for the four of them to become interlocked. Lisa shifted position under Anne's naked body, pushing her buttocks towards him as she moved her face over Mark's lap. Johnny was able to stroke the shaved lips of his wife's pussy as she licked their neighbour's erection and Anne sucked on his shaft. Groans of satisfaction filled the room as the two men teased the women and the women licked and sucked with greater enthusiasm. No one spoke. No one needed to speak, he realised. They simply enjoyed the pleasure of sharing their bodies with each other. Johnny teased one finger and then two inside Lisa's pussy while Anne continued to run her tongue up and down his length. His wife's inner muscles gripped his hand with a fluid demand he hadn't expected. Surprised by her obvious excitement, he leaned awkwardly past Anne's head and slipped a kiss on Lisa's sex.

'You're doing that too well,' Mark warned Lisa.

'It's your fault for making it so tasty,' Lisa returned.

Anne giggled, spurts of her hot breath warming Johnny's cock.

And the shared intimacy was strong enough to hold them together for a glorious hour. Occasionally one member of the quartet would shift position to retrieve their wine glass and take a sip, or change to a posture that was more comfortable. But they stayed in the same loose line-up quietly revelling in the ambience. It was Johnny who eventually pulled away from the undulating melée – and that was only so he could slip out of his trousers.

His movement encouraged the others to shift position and the dynamic of the four bodies entwined was changed as they paired off. Anne came with him, constantly keeping her lips in contact with his stiff cock. Lisa straddled Mark and kissed his mouth as their loins pushed hungrily together. A part of Johnny wanted to think the pleasure was diluted now that they had become two pairs, but that word wasn't quite right. It was still exciting to see his wife grinding herself against Mark's erection. And there was no denying that Anne was performing a splendid job as her tongue lapped up and down his own rigid length. But the fact that they were once again two couples did not seem quite as fulfilling as when they had been a foursome. Nevertheless, as he buried his face into the downy hairs that concealed Anne's pussy, he felt confident that the quartet would soon be reunited.

'Harder!' Lisa gasped.

Glancing at his wife from between Anne's thighs, Johnny could see Mark was sucking her nipples as they writhed together. Knowing Lisa enjoyed rough handling of her breasts – light torment and an increasing severity of nibbles at the tips – he turned his attention back to Anne's pussy and listened as his wife gave instructions to another man.

'Harder. Don't just lick them. Bite them.'

Johnny's entire erection was inside Anne's mouth. She sucked at him, returning every probing kiss he delivered to her pussy with a long and luxurious lick along his length. The urge to climax was maddeningly strong but, because he was enjoying the stimulation so much, he refused to let his pleasure get the better of him.

Her labia were sticky and he had been hungrily drinking the wetness of her arousal. Her slender build was a contrast to Lisa's curvaceous figure and a constant reminder that he was enjoying himself with a different woman.

But this time it was Anne who broke the spell of the moment. 'This isn't right,' she declared. She tore her mouth from Johnny's shaft and pulled her pussy from his tongue. 'This isn't right at all,' she said decisively.

All three of them stopped. Johnny could see the tension in Mark and Lisa's posture and knew they shared his fears that Anne had suddenly rebelled against the idea of swinging.

'What isn't right?' Lisa asked.

'What is it, sweetheart?' Mark demanded.

'It's Lisa's birthday,' Anne explained. 'Lisa should be having all the fun.'

Lisa grinned. She had her fist wrapped around Mark's erection and a sliver of his pre-come trailed from her lower lip. 'Who on earth said I wasn't having fun?'

'You should have the boys,' Anne said. Her tone was decisive and she spoke as though her mind was already made up. She tapped Johnny's backside and pointed towards his wife and her husband. 'I'll sort out fresh drinks while you two make sure Lisa celebrates her birthday properly.'

'She can be a bossy little sprite when she sets her mind to it, can't she?' Johnny remarked.

Lisa said, 'You should have seen her negotiate the deal for the party house.'

'The Munster house?'

Lisa rolled her eyes as he eased next to her side. 'If that's what you insist on calling the bloody place.'

'You should try living with her,' Mark added. He winked at Anne as she refilled his glass and said, 'Live with her for a while and you'll find she goes beyond bossy and moves towards downright demanding.'

119

The comments were all delivered in a spirit of good-natured ribbing. Anne accepted them with a distant grin as she went from glass to glass. She showed no inhibitions about her nudity, or the way the other three were joining their bodies together as she served them. She simply encouraged her husband to remove his clothes and enter the developing spirit of the party.

'How do you propose I should celebrate my birthday properly?' Lisa asked.

Anne raised her glass and mumbled a brief toast to Lisa. Johnny and Mark echoed her as the four touched the rims of their glasses together. Drawing a deep breath, flushing only a little as she spoke, Anne said, 'If this were my birthday, and I had two handsome and capable guys available to me, I'd want to have them both.' Her blush deepened as she added, 'I'd want to have them both *at the same time.*'

'A DP?' Lisa grinned. She cast her gaze from Johnny to Mark. Turning her eyes back to Anne she said, 'You keep some feisty appetites hidden beneath that sexy little surface of yours, don't you?'

Anne's expression was pleasantly puzzled. 'What does DP mean?'

'Double penetration.'

She put a hand over her mouth. 'Jesus! You guys have got a phrase for everything. Cornholing, spitroasting, pearl necklaces and now DPs. Whatever next?'

'Whatever you fancy,' Johnny said quickly. 'Although any of those aforementioned plans work for me.'

Mark and Lisa were both laughing as Anne went to her discarded jeans. She rummaged through the pockets and produced a couple of condoms. Tossing one packet towards Mark she winked at him and said, 'Make Lisa's day, sweetheart.'

'And what will you be doing while we're all partying?' Lisa asked. She had taken the condom from Mark and was already unrolling it down the gleaming length of his thick shaft. 'Aren't you going to feel left out?'

'I want to watch the birthday girl having a good time,' Anne decided. She settled herself in a chair that faced the settee. Spreading her legs, revealing the wet split of her sex, she licked her index finger. Lowering it to her pussy, idly toying with herself as the three of them watched, she said, 'I'll just sit over here and watch you celebrate.'

Johnny embraced his wife, gave her a questioning look and was pleased to see her nod agreement. He waited as she straddled Mark's length with her pussy and then lowered herself on to him. Her labia were stretched by his thickness and her flesh dimpled inwards as his long shaft pushed inside.

She groaned.

He glanced at Anne. Her smile was broader than he had ever seen before. Her left hand held open the lips of her sex while her right idly teased the exposed flesh of her clitoris. It was difficult to tell if her concentration was fixed on the show that Lisa and Mark presented or the efforts of her own right hand. And, when Johnny was summoned to take his place behind Lisa, he realised he wasn't going to see how Anne's pleasure developed.

Lisa's hand encircled his shaft, guiding him towards her anus. She was fully lowered on to Mark, his thick shaft filling her pussy, and Johnny knew it was going to be a struggle trying to squeeze himself into the tight confines of her anus. Nevertheless, because his shaft was already dripping with Anne's saliva, and because he understood his wife was sufficiently aroused to accept him, he pushed against the taut muscle of her sphincter.

'Christ! Yes!' Lisa exclaimed.

Anne gasped.

Mark's strong hands went to Lisa's side and helped her to steady her balance.

Johnny continued to press his erection against his wife's rear, determined to push past her anus and adamant that he would help her to fully enjoy her birthday.

'Harder,' Lisa insisted.

She pushed her rear out to meet him as Johnny urged his hips forward. There was a moment when he didn't think her body could accept so much. And then his shaft slid through her sphincter and his cock filled her backside.

Lisa groaned.

Mark made an exclamation of pleasant surprise.

Anne squeaked behind them and Johnny knew she was getting as much pleasure from watching the DP as the participants were from their involvement. He pushed himself fully into Lisa's rear, savouring every glorious sensation as he filled her with his length. The flimsy walls of her bowel were pushed out of shape by the bulge of Mark's shaft in the neighbouring canal. Johnny could feel the steady pulse of the other man's length as it lay so close to his own. Lisa muttered directions for how she wanted them to use her.

'Mark, slide in,' she grunted. 'Johnny, pull out. Neither of you fall out of me because I'll never get you both back inside.'

They mumbled assent and began the slow learning process of discovering each other's rhythms. Lisa guided them, hissing for one to stop retreating while urging the other to push back inside. But, as her arousal increased, her commands dropped to inarticulate growls. Mark fondled her breasts, holding her nipples between his fingers and thumbs and lightly squeezing. Johnny pressed kisses against his wife's neck and throat, reminding her of his love each time he pushed deep into her bowel.

'Wow,' Anne gasped. 'Doesn't that hurt?'

'Oh! Yes!' Lisa giggled. 'It hurts so much I'm going to come my brains out.'

'I am so going to have to try that,' Anne said. Her tone had the breathy quality of a woman close to

122

climax. Johnny wanted to look back and see her enjoyment, but he couldn't bring himself to stop kissing his wife. Glancing at Mark, noticing the other man was smiling broadly over Lisa's shoulder as he watched Anne, Johnny realised the pleasure in the room was being distributed equally amongst them all. He continued to push in and out of his wife, measuring his pace against Mark's and listening for the telltale sounds that told him how close he was to experiencing Lisa's orgasm.

'It's like a live porn movie,' Anne breathed. 'You look so stretched, Lisa.'

'I am stretched,' Lisa admitted. 'Your husband is hung.'

'Johnny's not what you'd call small,' Anne said quickly.

The remark was pleasantly flattering. Johnny had to hold himself still for fear of climaxing beneath the praise. He pressed another series of kisses against Lisa's throat and waited until Mark had pulled his shaft to the lips of her pussy before plunging back inside.

Lisa moaned.

He could hear the undercurrent of excitement in her guttural cry and knew she was on the verge of coming. The idea that she was so close to orgasm made him want to hasten his own climax and allow the pulse of his ejaculation to push her to the same point of ecstasy. But, sure she would enjoy the experience better if he held off for as long as possible, he slowly slid back and allowed Mark's thick length to fill her pussy.

'I *so* have to try that,' Anne mumbled.

'I *so* want to watch you try it,' Lisa returned. She spat the words in breathless pauses, clearly caught up in a world of pleasure that wouldn't allow her anything more than mumbled groans of satisfaction. 'I *so* want to watch that.'

'Too much!' Mark grunted.

Johnny could feel the other man's eruption as his length spattered Lisa's pussy. Their shafts were pressed together, separated only by Mark's condom and the flimsiest sheath of flesh inside Lisa's body. He could feel each pulse that shivered through Mark's thick cock. He heard his wife groan, knew the orgasm was going to rip through her, and his own climax came with the same blistering force.

Anne shrieked as she came behind them.

Johnny could have echoed her cry as his own orgasm was torn through the length of his shaft. Mark continued to groan, his size barely dwindling as his cock continued to throb. Lisa bucked her hips hard against him and released a cry of the most anguished euphoria Johnny had ever heard.

The three of them pushed apart with a haste that bordered on being unseemly.

Lisa turned around, grabbed Johnny and smothered him with kisses. She stroked one hand against Mark's bare leg, smiling gratefully at him, and then turned her eyes towards Anne. Lisa's face was swathed in perspiration. Locks of hair clung dank to her scalp. Her cheeks were dusted with purple blushes that made her seem peculiarly feminine and desirable.

'Thank you. Thank you both. All three of you,' she muttered. Her voice teetered on the brink of hysteria. When Johnny embraced her again he could feel her heart racing. 'Thank you,' Lisa muttered again.

Anne trembled in her own chair, wearing an impish grin that suggested her personal pleasure had possibly been as rewarding as Lisa's. 'And that's just for starters,' she laughed. 'Once we've had the Chinese and a slice of birthday cake, perhaps we can try something even more daring?'

Lisa pulled herself away from Johnny and took a swig at her wine glass. She drained the contents in one long swallow. Gasping and wiping the back of her hand across her mouth, she laughed without humour and said, 'Now that's how a girl should celebrate her birthday.'

Mark removed the condom from his flailing length. His colour was high with the pleasure of satisfaction and Johnny could see the man was enjoying the learning experience of being with more than one person when he climaxed. More importantly, he could see Mark and Anne exchanging delighted smiles across the room and knew they had taken a lot from the impromptu beginning of the birthday celebration. 'I think –' Johnny began. He got no further. The chime of the front door bell rang musically through the house. Startled, he glanced at Lisa.

Anne snatched her T-shirt from the back of the settee and held it to her chest. 'I'll get it for you,' she said, rushing to the door. She was so quick no one had the chance to stop her. Johnny barely noted the peculiarity of her behaviour before she left the room. Lisa was using a Kleenex to wrap Mark's used condom and take it from his hands. Mark had slipped back into his clothes, not hurrying but not taking his time about the process either. Johnny caught his wife's puzzled expression and asked, 'Are you expecting anyone?'

'Of course not!' Her voice was defensive to the point of indignation. She was still naked, alone on the settee now as Mark stood up to tuck his shirt into his pants. Her legs were crossed and, in the weakest deference to modesty she could make, she had pulled a scatter cushion over her breasts. The stray hairs had been brushed from her forehead. Basking in the afterglow of her orgasm, Johnny thought she looked satisfied and magnificent. 'Who the hell can it be?' Lisa demanded. 'It's not your parents, is it?'

Uneasily, he shrugged and then stepped into his jeans. 'They usually phone before they come round here. They know better than to surprise us on your birthday.' Lisa nodded, mentally revisiting those awkward occasions that had arisen with the unexpected arrival of Johnny's parents or Lisa's mother. They were still pondering the question of who could be calling when Anne returned to the room, a blonde by her side. Johnny could only gape.

Mark passed Anne her magenta jeans and quietly took charge of the situation. 'Introductions aren't really necessary,' he said, directing his words between the blonde, Johnny and Lisa. He cupped the newcomer's shoulder and gave her a gentle peck on the cheek. 'Johnny and Lisa you already know. Anne, the lady who welcomed you in here, is my wife. But she and I are leaving now, so you'll be alone with these two.' He turned to smile at Johnny and Lisa. 'Happy birthday, Lisa,' he said, beaming. 'I hope you enjoy playing with Debbie.'

10

Lisa's Present

'Would you like a glass of wine, Debbie?'

'God! Yes!' She took the glass in hands that trembled as though she were in the grip of a seizure. When the wine had been poured she drained the contents in one vicious swallow.

Lisa considered apologising for her nudity and then decided that would only draw attention to the condition. Debbie appeared so nervous and distracted it seemed likely she hadn't noticed. Puzzling over the woman's arrival, and anxious about her obvious distress, Lisa asked, 'Is there something wrong? You seem very nervous.'

'I've never . . .' Debbie began. She glanced around the room with a hunted expression. When Johnny returned from seeing Mark and Anne to the door – and Lisa thought that chore had taken him longer than she would have expected – Debbie's features briefly dissolved into something like relief. Returning her gaze to Lisa, clearly remembering she had been in the middle of a sentence, her apprehension returned and she hissed, 'I've never done this before.'

Lisa frowned. 'You've never wished someone happy birthday before? Are you a Jehovah's Witness?'

Johnny laughed and placed a fraternal arm around Debbie's shoulder. Smiling too broadly he shook his head and ushered Lisa back to her place on the settee. 'Sit down, birthday girl,' he commanded. Hugging Debbie affectionately he said, 'If you don't want to do this, no one is forcing you.' His tone sounded earnest and Lisa recognised it as his most rational and sympathetic voice. When Johnny spoke in this way the simplicity of his values and the good nature of the man she loved were at their most apparent. Her adoration for him soared. 'I don't care what Mark said that's brought you here tonight,' he continued.

Lisa saw Debbie flinch when Johnny mentioned Mark's name. She wondered what Mark had to do with the unexpected arrival of Johnny's secretary. But there was no time to ask the question because Johnny was continuing to placate their visitor.

'No one does anything in my home unless they want to do it,' Johnny went on. 'If you just want to sit down and have another glass of wine to celebrate Lisa's birthday, no one will hold it against you or think any the less of you.'

'I'd think less of me,' Debbie spat. 'And I want to do this.' She regarded him with eyes that were large and pained with the enormity of some personal decision. 'I *need* to do it,' she added, as though stressing the word clarified the explanation. 'I'm just anxious because I've never done this before.'

Johnny nodded.

Lisa glanced from one to the other. 'What the fuck are you two talking about?' She stared at Debbie and asked, 'What is it that's making you so anxious? What is it that you want to do?'

Debbie paused before answering. She shook her shoulders and it was almost as though she was shaking off the last of her doubts. The hunted expression in her eyes vanished and she regained her usual austere composure. Shrugging herself free from Johnny's loose embrace she stepped into the centre of the room. She wore a dark business suit. The short skirt and crimson blouse added a stylish femininity to the otherwise masculine cut of the clothes. If she had been the model of indecision and self-doubt before, she was now an icon of self-control and poise. Standing with her legs shoulder distance apart, placing one hand on her hip and pointing the other at Lisa, she sang, 'Happy birthday to you . . .' Her voice had the breathy quality of a Marilyn Monroe impersonator singing the same song to an imaginary JFK. 'Happy birthday to you . . .'

Lisa glanced from Debbie to Johnny, her eyes growing wide with surprise and delight. The shock of Debbie's arrival and the worry about her signs of upset and apprehension were immediately forgotten. Realising that Debbie was there as a birthday present was enough to make everything else seem unimportant. 'You planned this?' she gasped. 'You knew about this? You set this up?' Johnny didn't get the chance to reply before Debbie continued with the next line of her song.

'Happy birthday, Lisa We-est!' She reached for the lapels of her jacket, tore them apart, and then tossed the garment to one side. 'Happy birthday to you!'

Lisa shrieked with laughter. She patted her seat, encouraging Johnny to join her as they watched Debbie perform a second verse of the song. The woman no longer seemed as anxious as the timid creature who had first appeared by Anne's side in the doorway of the lounge. She now held herself with the grace and confidence that Lisa was used to seeing.

On those few occasions Lisa had reason to visit Johnny's office, she had always been won over by Debbie's air of cool and efficient composure. As Debbie began the second verse of her song, Lisa could see every inch of the desirable ice goddess she had lusted after. She crushed her thighs together as the rush of arousal flooded through her loins. A wave of glorious flowing warmth swept over her and she was briefly dizzied by the thrill of excitement.

'Happy birthday to you . . .' Debbie gave more of herself to the performance this time. The short skirt of her business suit was unfastened as she sang the words. It fell to her ankles and pooled around her stiletto heels, revealing the lacy tops of her black stockings. She stepped out of the skirt and became a striking figure of desirability, dressed only in her lingerie with a crimson blouse covering most of her modesty. Briskly, she released the three buttons on the blouse while singing the next line. 'Happy birthday to you . . .'

Lisa clutched Johnny. If she had glanced at him in that moment she would have seen the amazement etched into his face. And, if she had seen he shared her disbelief, she might have wondered what had inspired Debbie to come singing and offering herself on her birthday. But because Debbie was presenting such a captivating show, Lisa couldn't snatch her gaze away from the woman.

'Happy birthday, Lisa We-est!' Debbie shrugged the blouse from her shoulders. It fluttered to the floor as she revealed herself in a black bra that was cut from the same satin as her thong, panties and suspender belt. She held her arms by her sides in a twenty-to-four position and sang the final line in a passable crescendo. 'Happy birthday to you!' To conclude the song she fell down on one knee in front of Lisa. Staring directly into Lisa's eyes, a gentle smile lighting on her perfectly glossed lips, she dropped her voice to a husky whisper. 'I believe I have something you wanted for your birthday.'

'God! Yes!' Lisa shrieked. She glanced at Johnny in awe.

He had regained sufficient composure to appear nonchalant. Diplomatically, he nodded at Debbie, and Lisa turned her gaze back to their guest.

'Do I get a kiss from the birthday girl before we begin?' Debbie asked.

Lisa could feel her heartbeat fluttering. Eddies of the pleasure she had enjoyed with Mark and Johnny still trembled in her body. But they weren't as thrilling as the idea of kissing Debbie. She moved forward, conscious of her own nudity and ruefully aware that she was nowhere near as imposing as the blonde beauty in her arms. Those considerations were easily brushed aside before her lips touched Debbie's mouth. She was used to getting close to a variety of women at swingers' parties and seldom considered good looks to be anything more than a pleasant bonus. More important, to Lisa's thinking, was an attitude of open-minded adventure.

Her fingers found the curve of the blonde's perfectly sculpted waist. The two women pressed together with a feral hunger. Lisa's breasts were crushed against the stiff satin of Debbie's bra and, as gravity forced them to roll on the floor, she felt her legs being caressed by the sheer fabric of the blonde's black stockings. A furious longing broiled inside her sex.

'My God!' Debbie marvelled. She pulled her lips away for the briefest moment. Her eyes shone with genuine incredulity. 'I'm really kissing a woman!' she gasped.

Lisa grinned at her surprise. She didn't know what had brought Debbie to their home this evening. And she wasn't sure how or why Mark was involved. But she could see that events were going to progress towards a memorable birthday. 'Yes,' she agreed. 'You're really kissing a woman. Want to do a little more?'

Debbie chuckled as her fingers moved to the back of Lisa's bare waist. Her hand smoothed over Lisa's buttocks and reached under the tops of her thighs. Her actions were slow, cautious but deliberate, and Lisa understood exactly what the blonde was trying to do. Anxious to make her guest feel as comfortable as possible, Lisa parted her thighs so it was easier for Debbie to reach her sex.

When the first finger stroked her pussy lips, both women shivered. Debbie snatched her hand away as

131

though it had been burnt. She regarded the tip of her finger and admired the wetness that coated her flesh. Her smile grew lascivious.

'You really are game for this, aren't you?' Lisa muttered.

'I hadn't realised quite how game,' Debbie replied. Instead of adding further words she pushed her face forward and enveloped Lisa's mouth with another kiss. Once again they writhed together on the carpet as their hands caressed bare skin and their bodies pressed together.

Johnny remained on the settee behind them. Lisa felt confident ignoring him, knowing he wouldn't think he was being left out. They were both familiar with the unwritten protocols of swinging. If Debbie wanted him to join their coupling she would say as much and they could become a triple. If Lisa felt a desperate need to have her husband participate, she would ask Debbie before issuing an invitation to Johnny. A part of her reflected that the gentility of dancing so carefully around each other's sensibilities was a harsh contrast to the animal passions that marked the most memorable swinging encounters. But she had also learnt that consideration for other people's sensibilities was the one thing guaranteed to make any swinging event work to everyone's satisfaction.

Debbie pushed Lisa to the floor and leered over her. She still looked resplendent in her gleaming black lingerie. Lisa's inner muscles squirmed with torrid anticipation. She saw Debbie's ice-blue gaze trail over her body and was elated by the smile of anticipation that twisted the woman's lips. Her arousal had been strong before. Now it smouldered with a fresh intensity that swathed her in perspiration.

'I'm new to this,' Debbie murmured. 'You'll have to tell me what I'm expected to do next.'

'Would it be easier if I showed you?' Lisa suggested. She didn't wait for Debbie's reply. Instead, she grabbed the woman's arms and shifted positions so Debbie was lying down and Lisa was hovering over her. She eased Debbie's bra strap aside, teased one perfectly round breast from its confines and suckled the stiff nipple. The puckered flesh grew taut inside her mouth. The tip swelled like a miniature erection. Lisa pursed her lips around it as though she was trying to encourage an ejaculation. She didn't move her mouth away until she heard Johnny's secretary groan with satisfaction. Hesitating briefly, wondering if she should treat the woman's other breast to the same ordeal or continue her exploration with bolder moves, Lisa eventually stroked her tongue down over the sculpted four-pack of Debbie's bare stomach. When her mouth met the fabric of Debbie's suspender belt, Lisa lowered her head so her fringe tickled the woman's bare torso.

'That is so exciting,' Debbie panted.

'It gets better,' Lisa promised. True to her word, she moved her mouth lower, across the front panel of Debbie's thong. She could taste the sweet scent of the woman's arousal, a heady fragrance that fuelled fresh heat between her own legs, and she allowed the perfume to make her a little giddy before she continued. Glancing up at the blonde, seeing the sultry smile of encouragement that parted the woman's lips, Lisa daringly planted a kiss upon her crotch.

'Sweet Jesus,' Debbie whispered. She spread her thighs a little further apart, as though she was trying to make herself more accessible.

Lisa used the tip of one finger to ease the black thong aside. Delighting in the moment, not sure how she had come to have the beautiful Debbie lying on the floor before her, but revelling in the pleasure that it had happened, Lisa pushed her tongue against the shaved flesh of the woman's hole.

Debbie groaned.

It wasn't the first time Lisa had gone down on another woman. In truth, it probably wasn't the hundred and first time. But this was different: this was Debbie. When Lisa had discovered that her husband had cajoled his way between his secretary's thighs, she had been delighted for him but mildly jealous that Johnny was getting to experience the woman. Debbie presented a cool façade that would have been exciting in and of itself. With her striking height, stunning good looks and impeccable fashion sense, she was, for Lisa, a symbol of her most lurid desires. She didn't know whether she wanted to *have* Debbie or if a part of her wanted to *be* Debbie. She only knew that now the opportunity was available to her she was going to enjoy every wonderful moment of discovering the woman's body.

Lisa licked Debbie to a fast and crushing climax.

Whatever composure the woman had shown was devastated as the orgasm shook her body. She cursed till Lisa gasped with astonishment and then rolled and thrashed her way through a gamut of satisfied responses. She shivered and trembled, her eyes wide with astonishment. Shaking her head, regarding Lisa as though the woman had just revealed the meaning of life, Debbie pushed her to the floor and began to lick and tease and excite.

It was not as satisfying as her earlier experience with Mark and Anne. Because she couldn't feel herself connecting to Debbie with the same understanding that she had for Anne, Lisa didn't even think it was as intense as the pleasure she had enjoyed earlier in the week during the second meal she and Johnny had shared with Mark and Anne. But, although the pleasure wasn't as satisfying or intense, she still marvelled that she was having Johnny's ultra-sexy secretary.

They rolled apart, spent but panting for more. As though neither could bear the thought of the moment ending, their hands remained gripped together. Lisa held Debbie's shoulder. Debbie stroked Lisa's breast.

134

Both were exhausted yet neither seemed able to pause for breath, thought or sustenance. 'I suppose I should go,' Debbie said with a frown. 'You two probably have other things you'd like to do this evening and I must have taken up—'

'Stay with us for our meal,' Lisa broke in.

Debbie glanced at her and seemed to cower away from the invitation.

'Johnny's just going to phone the order through now,' Lisa said quickly. 'We'd love to have you as our guest if you'd like to stay with us.'

Debbie regarded her doubtfully. 'Are you sure it's not inconvenient?'

Her humility was enough to make Lisa grin. Women at swinging parties often quoted the line: *once you've had sex with a woman it's difficult to be a bitch to her.* Lisa had thought there was an element of truth in the remark but she had never seen it so perfectly illustrated as in Debbie's transformation from frosty ice maiden to humble houseguest. 'You must stay,' Lisa insisted. She glanced at Johnny and said, 'You've taken Debbie for enough meals. I'm sure you know what she likes. Order for all three of us and then hurry back here.'

Johnny disappeared to call the order through from the kitchen.

Alone, Lisa relaxed against Debbie's firm, toned body and they chatted easily together. At first Debbie laughed at the easy way Lisa ordered her husband around, reflecting that it made a stark contrast to the way he gave the orders to everyone in their office. As the barriers between them melted, Lisa quizzed Debbie about her family background and the genetics that had led to her blonde good looks. They were still talking when Johnny returned from the kitchen and told them he was going to drive out and collect the meal rather than imposing on the restaurant.

Both women pecked him on the cheek and told him to hurry safely back.

They returned to the comfort of the settee as soon as he had gone.

'It was your booking at the Red Mill that got cancelled, wasn't it?'

Lisa nodded. She wished Debbie hadn't brought up the cancellation because she'd been trying not to brood on that particular irritation. Admittedly the upset had benefited her to some degree: without the cancellation Anne would never have had the need to find an alternative location. But it was making the organisation of the party seem like harder work than she had wanted to invest.

'I took the message of the cancellation,' Debbie explained. 'I phoned them back to find out what had happened but everyone was pretty cagey about the reason. Someone said it had been a double booking and it dated back months ago, but I had to go through three people before I was fobbed off with that lie.'

'Lie?' The hairs on the nape of Lisa's neck prickled. 'What makes you think it was a lie?'

Debbie rolled her eyes. 'If it was a double booking I'd have been told that by the first person I talked with. Not the third. It was a lie.'

'Then why do you think they really cancelled?'

Debbie paused for a moment. Sitting still, finally relaxed, Lisa could see that the woman no longer seemed as distant and unapproachable as she had been before. She didn't know if the change had come about because Debbie's appearance was now untidy and dishevelled or if the woman's aura of distance had finally been breached by the things they had done together. For whatever reason, Debbie looked far more friendly and accessible.

'I've asked a couple of colleagues at the Red Mill to get back to me on that one. But, until I hear their responses, there's no way of telling for certain why they cancelled your booking. If you want my personal opinion, I think someone deliberately set out to screw things over for you.'

'I don't understand. What are you saying to me?'

'I'm saying that someone told the Red Mill to cancel your booking because they don't want your party to happen.'

11

The Slut

It was unusual for Anne to be in control of the Kents'
kitchen. She handled the experience with the same
embarrassing lack of familiarity that Johnny had displayed in the Wests'. She explored two cupboards
before she found cups, but then got lucky and found
instant coffee and teaspoons on her first attempt. She
boiled the kettle, filled two mugs and handed one to her
husband.

'Am I a slut?'

Mark frowned. 'Who the hell has called you a slut?'
The hand that wasn't holding a mug had turned into a
fist. 'Tell me who said it and I'll pop them so fucking
hard they—'

'No one called me a slut,' she broke in. She placed a
hand on his bulging bicep. The muscle was large and
taut with tension. 'I'm just worried that I'm depraved or
something. I'm worried that I might have become a slut.
And I'm not sure that's what I want.'

His fist loosened but his smile didn't return. He stared
at her with uncertainty and disbelief. 'Why on earth
would you think that?'

'Shit! Mark! That's a dumb question, isn't it? You've
just fucked our neighbour while she was getting a
cornhole with her husband. I sat watching as I flicked
my bean off.' She paused and realised she had probably

not grasped the full intricacies of the swinging vocabulary. More importantly, her tone was rising and filled with an anger that she didn't understand and couldn't control. 'Doesn't that sound depraved to you?' she demanded hotly. 'Doesn't that sound like the behaviour of a slut?'

He took a sip at his coffee and flinched, surprised by its heat. 'We don't have to carry on seeing Johnny and Lisa if you don't want to,' he said calmly. 'We agreed as much before we got physically involved with them. And that still stands. If this . . .' He waved his hand in the air as he tried to find a word for the relationship they shared. Coming up blank, he simply continued, 'If this is getting too much for you, we don't have to take things any further. We don't have to do another thing with them. Johnny and Lisa will understand. And, if they don't, their feelings are the least of our concerns.'

'I know what we agreed,' she snapped. She raked splayed fingers through her spiked crop. 'I know all of that.' Storming out of the kitchen, striding purposefully to the dining room and coming back a moment later with a cigar in her hand, she went to the back door and sat down on the step. She lit the cigar and took comfort from the acrid taste. 'I know what we agreed,' she continued softly. 'I know we can stop seeing them whenever we want.' She drew on the cigar, paused for a moment and then said, 'But I don't want to stop seeing them. And I don't want to be a slut either.'

Mark shook his head. Putting his coffee aside and joining Anne on the step, he placed an arm around her shoulders and she squeezed into the comfort of his embrace. 'We talked about this a lot before we made the decision to try swinging, didn't we?'

'We talked it to death,' Anne grunted. 'I'm surprised, by the time we got round to doing it, we weren't bored with the whole idea.'

He laughed dryly. 'We discussed all the various issues of jealousy that we might come up against . . .'

'I'm not jealous,' Anne assured him.

'. . . and we talked about the danger that one, or both, of us might get insecure with the arrangement.'

'I'm not insecure either.'

He was nodding. 'I know you're not jealous. And I know you're not insecure. And I'm wondering if that might be the problem.' —

She sat for a moment, savouring the cigar – a gift from Johnny, she remembered – and enjoying the cool night air against her face. She was being embraced by the man she loved and admiring the moonlit landscape of the garden in their new home. Her stomach was warmed by the weight of a recent climax and her body felt rested and relaxed. If not for the nagging feeling that she was guilty of a great and undiscovered wrong, Anne thought the moment would have been close to perfect.

'How did you persuade Debbie to visit Johnny and Lisa this evening?'

He chortled. 'I had no idea that would be so easy,' he admitted. 'We knew each other before when she worked for Cox's. Did I mention that?'

Anne nodded, not so much listening to his words as enjoying the sound of his voice. She wanted to discuss her feelings, and talk with him to help him understand what she was going through. But she realised her inexplicable anger was still simmering and she didn't want to risk hurting him with an unexpected outburst. Consequently, she thought it would be best to distract herself by asking Mark about Debbie. Her husband had a way of speaking that made her feel as though she was the most special woman in the world. As a salesman he could talk anyone into anything and she knew that a lot of that skill had to be credited to his smooth, easy-to-listen-to voice. And, as she listened to him, she believed she could understand how he was able to persuade so many people to trust his judgement and advice.

'I'd heard she had a crush on me back then,' Mark explained. 'But, because I was involved with someone at the time, I'd never pursued her interest.'

'Who were you involved with?'

'The same lady with whom I'm still involved,' he said, squeezing her against his side.

Anne forced a thin smile.

'Anyway, I arranged to meet Debbie for a meal and, because she'd always had a thing for me, it was easy to guide the conversation to the subject of sex. I asked her what she looked for in a sexual partner and she described me. She asked me what I looked for—'

'And you described her?' Anne guessed.

'No,' Mark said simply. 'I told her I liked women who were shamelessly uninhibited. Johnny had told me Debbie liked anal, so I made a point of mentioning that. But he'd also mentioned that she treated the act as something unwholesome and forbidden. It made me think that she liked doing things that she thought were considered taboo. I have to admit, if that card hadn't worked, I don't know how I would have persuaded her to turn up at their house this evening.'

'You simply told her that you like women who present themselves to other women as birthday presents?'

His grin stretched. 'I was a little more subtle than that,' he said carefully. 'But if you're going to trim down my dialogue to one of your snappy little synopses, then I guess that pretty much sums it up.'

She squeezed against him for a moment and then pulled away so she could draw on the cigar again. Feeling as though she had regained control over her anger, and still wanting to discuss the subject that had been weighing on her thoughts, she told him, 'I'm not jealous about you and Debbie. And I'm not jealous about what you were doing with Lisa this evening. Why should I still feel as though there's a problem if I'm not jealous?'

'We're not brought up to believe promiscuity is acceptable,' he began. 'But you and I have both been open-minded to the idea of sharing, swinging and swapping. Like you say, we'd talked the idea to death before we made any move towards acting on our fantasies. I think, now that we've broken the taboo and actually acted on our fantasies, we're both a little shocked that we don't feel jealous or wronged or daunted in any way.'

She considered the words, turning them over as she rolled the cigar between her fingertips. The explanation sounded right but did not go any distance towards lessening her inexplicable anger. 'I'm feeling bad because I'm not feeling bad?'

Mark was silent for a moment. 'I think my way of phrasing it was more eloquent. Your way makes it sound like a drunk's riddle.'

'I watched you fucking Lisa this evening,' she breathed. As she said the words the image of Mark's sheathed shaft plunging into Lisa's shaved pussy filled her mind. She was no longer looking at the dusky grey shadows that enveloped the moonlit garden. She could only see the glistening pink flesh of her husband pushing into her naked friend. His mouth was around her nipple. Lisa was gasping and lost in the throes of an approaching climax. Their bodies were melded into an intimate embrace that he had only previously shared with her. The memories made the inner muscles of her sex convulse with a hungry shiver. 'I watched you fucking Lisa,' she breathed. 'And, instead of being angry, jealous, sickened or outraged, it just made me horny.'

He tightened his hold around her. 'I could see you were horny. You looked like you were enjoying yourself.'

Anne pulled away from him. 'Then that makes me a slut, doesn't it? I was horny then. I'm horny now. And surely it's not right for a woman to be getting off on something as depraved as kissing the woman next door? Or watching her husband fuck one of the neighbours?'

'You're horny now?' He waggled his eyebrows.

She punched his arm. 'Don't make fun of me.'

'I wasn't making fun. I just figured, if I can't resolve the problem that's making you believe you're a slut, I should take advantage of the symptoms rather than trying to cure the disease.'

She paused for a moment, wondering if she should be angry at his lack of consideration or if she should join him by laughing at the ridiculousness of the situation. Remembering all the times they had shared together before they risked so much, sure they still loved and wanted each other and knowing Mark was probably feeling just as confused, she tossed the cigar into the darkness and reached for him.

'Do you think you can satisfy me?' she asked, pushing him to the floor of the kitchen. It felt good to be straddling him. His embrace was a comfort. Between her legs, pressing at the crotch of her jeans, she could feel the weight of his erection. Remembering where he had been, and how much pleasure Lisa had gleaned from being with him, made her excitement soar. Anne caught her breath and pressed a kiss against his throat. 'Well?' she pressed. 'Do you think you can satisfy me?'

'I can make a damned good attempt.' He gained the upper hand without any effort. He lifted her from the step, kicked the door closed and carried her into the kitchen. Placing Anne in front of the sink, Mark bent her over and pulled her jeans away from her waist. He didn't bother removing the denim from her legs but left her knees bound by the unyielding fabric.

Anne didn't know if she was experiencing an impromptu form of DIY bondage or her husband was simply too impatient to remove her clothes. She did know that her pussy was on display for him. Hearing the sound of his zip being pulled down, then catching

143

the gamey scent of his erection, she knew he was going to slide into her before she had a chance to think if it was what she really wanted. Considering the heat that now smouldered in her loins, and the urgent throb that pounded inside her swollen sex, she guessed there wasn't a decision to be made. But she still couldn't understand why her body was responding so positively to stimulation that should have killed her arousal.

'I might not be thinking of you while we fuck,' she told him.

He pressed the tip of his cock against the gaping lips of her sex. It rolled up and down her labia, filling her with an excitement she hadn't anticipated. The urge to push back and have him fill her hole was almost unbearable. But because the waistband of her jeans loosely bound her knees, and her position over the sink didn't allow for much movement, the best she could manage was to squirm against him. 'I might be thinking of something other than you fucking me. I might be imagining you are someone else.'

'Is that supposed to upset me? Or turn me on more?'

'I might be thinking of the way your cock was inside Lisa,' she gasped. 'Or the way Johnny rode Lisa's backside.' She knew she shouldn't have said the words. Aside from taunting Mark with comments that might cause him distress, she was also painting mental pictures that increased the temperature inside her sex. She couldn't recall her arousal being stronger, and she knew, when her husband did push against her, he would slide easily inside.

As though he had read her mind and was trying to prove her right, Mark thrust into her hole. The muscle separated as though he was slipping into melted butter.

They both groaned.

Anne realised the entire evening had been a slow build to this moment. Kissing with Lisa, watching her husband and another woman, masturbating while the other three fucked together, all of that had been getting her wet for this instant. Mark's length slid effortlessly through the lips of her sex until his thickness filled her hole. The sensation of being close to bursting made her moan and she knew he still had more to deliver. Anne clutched at the cool metal of the sink, gasping for breath and shivering as the pleasure gripped her.

He forced himself forward, pushing every millimetre of his length as deep as it would go. Anne quietly cursed the jeans that bound her knees because she knew, if not for them, she could have opened herself more fully and easily to the penetration.

Mark grunted as he finally urged the last inch of his shaft into her sex.

'I might be thinking of the taste of Johnny's cock,' she taunted. 'Or the flavour of Lisa's pussy.' She snatched the words between gasps for air. 'You know that I've sampled both. I could be thinking of either of those things.'

He began to draw out of her, but the movement was not made with indignation as she'd expected: Mark was only pulling back so he could push into her with more force. Carefully, he began to build to a slow and maddening rhythm.

'If it makes your satisfaction better,' he panted, 'why should I be upset by your thinking of any of those things?' He continued to plough back and forth. His pace was relentless and her pussy slurped around him when he hastened his speed.

Her thighs were crushed against the front of the sink but that minor discomfort was overshadowed by the pleasure he forced through the muscles of her sex. She started to speak, and then the air was pushed out of her as he thrust back inside. An orgasm was welling in the pit of her stomach. But Anne wouldn't allow the satisfaction to take hold. Still fretting about her response to all that had happened in the last few days, needing to understand what had driven her reactions this evening, she allowed a surge of sensations to trickle through her sex and then steeled herself against further enjoyment.

'Doesn't it make me a slut?' she demanded. 'Doesn't it make me a slut that I'm getting off on these things instead of feeling jealous or angry?'

Mark pulled himself from her sex and turned her around.

A moment later he had pushed himself back between her legs. She didn't know how his length managed to find her hole while the jeans remained round her knees but he slid inside her as though her pussy was where his erection belonged. Finally he kicked the jeans away from her, grabbed her backside and encouraged her to wrap her legs around his waist. He carried her upstairs to their bedroom, his erection filling her as they went. Each step caused the pleasure to bounce through her sex. The end of his thick shaft repeatedly nudged the neck of her womb. Anne had been struggling to resist the rush of excitement before. Now, as he carried her towards the bedroom, she felt close to climaxing each time she exhaled. She shivered as he laid her down on the bed and the excess of pleasure took her close to forgetting the cause of her confusion and anxiety.

Mark knelt between her thighs, his shaft still plugging her sex and one hand tenderly stroking her cheek. The lights were off and it reminded her vaguely of the first times they had made love together when they were a young courting couple. It had been so long since they had sex without a light on, the experience was almost as kinky as what they had enjoyed with Johnny and Lisa.

'You asked me if I thought you were a slut,' he began.

Despite the effort of carrying her upstairs his voice sounded remarkably controlled and he was breathing freely. She supposed that was one of the advantages of not smoking and absently wondered if she should follow his lead in kicking the habit.

'If a slut is someone who enjoys sex,' he continued. 'Then you're a slut.'

She cried out, shocked by the words. Tears welled in her eyes and she was thankful he wasn't able to see them. The worry that she had become a slut, that she *was* a slut and living a slutty life, had been tormenting her since they left Lisa and Johnny's. She had thought, in confessing her fears to Mark, he might say her worries were groundless or that she was fretting for no reason. To hear him call her a slut was like a slap across the face. She didn't think he could have found a way to inflict a greater hurt.

She tried to pull away from him, anxious to end the sex and forget about the low-grade fever of arousal that still broiled within her loins. It was proving to be an evening of firsts, she thought miserably. It was the first time she had watched her husband with another woman, the first time she had masturbated in front of other people, and now this was the first time they had argued while having sex. The tears she had been trying to contain grew impossible to hold back, and poured down her cheeks. Again, she struggled to pull away from him.

Mark held her in place and continued sliding between her thighs. 'If that's your definition of a slut, then that's what you are,' he grunted. 'But if you think a slut is an insult for someone who is mindlessly promiscuous . . .'

He had started panting and she didn't know whether the effort in his voice came from the physical exertion or the psychological challenge of trying to make his point.

'. . . if you think a slut is an insult for someone who is mindlessly promiscuous, if you think a slut is someone who conducts herself without any thought for her partner's feelings, then you're not a slut. If that's your definition, then you couldn't be further from being a slut.' He pushed into her with a final thrust, as though his ejaculation was the fullstop to his sentence.

Anne's responding orgasm – more muted than she had expected but still powerful enough to make her scream – helped clear her thoughts. Her stomach was cramped with a spasm of pleasurable pain. She exulted at the sensation of his shaft throbbing inside her sex. The hot douche of his semen spattered against the neck of her womb. And the wave of euphoria allowed her to understand what he had been saying.

She wiped a hand against her eyes, frantically drying her face and thankful he couldn't see the senseless tears she had shed. Trembling in his embrace, hoping he would believe the shivers were a natural part of her subsiding pleasure, she kissed him gratefully and encouraged him to lie next to her. It didn't matter that neither of them was fully undressed. All that mattered was that they shared an embrace and reminded each other they were still in love.

'That was pretty impressive,' Anne muttered. She was relieved that her voice was normal and unstrained, with no sign of her recent torment. Her hammering heartbeat sounded like the pounding she heard after her most powerful orgasms.

'Which part was impressive?' She could sense his smile. 'My carrying you upstairs? Or my supplying dictionary definitions while treating you to fantastic sex?'

She giggled – and caught the sound for fear it would turn into hysterical laughter. 'Both were pretty impressive,' she decided. 'You getting my jeans off with just one foot was quite a clever trick. You'll have to show me how to do that one day.'

'I don't mind giving lessons on that,' he replied lazily. In a more serious voice he asked, 'Are you still feeling bad?'

She drew a deep breath. 'Am I feeling bad about not feeling bad?'

'Yes.'

She shook her head and then realised he wouldn't be able to see that in the dark. 'I'm not going to let myself,' she told him. 'You're comfortable with the situation. I'm comfortable with it. We're enjoying ourselves and we're not doing anything wrong. I just need to get used to the idea that I can have fun doing things that aren't usually accepted by society's norms. I shouldn't feel guilty any more.'

He was silent for a moment. 'Fine words,' he pronounced. 'Although you're a writer so I guess that's your forte.'

She cuddled into him and was rewarded when he placed a protective arm around her shoulders. The intimacy of an embrace was the exact comfort she needed. 'Writing's my forte,' she agreed. 'Just like it was your forte to talk Debbie into going round to the Wests' this evening.'

His chest shifted up and down, as though he was trying to suppress laughter. 'That was an impressive piece of sales patter, even by my standards.' Another moment's silence, and then he asked seriously, 'Do you think you'll be able to live by those fine words of yours?'

She shrugged and cuddled tighter against him. 'I'm not really sure. I hope so because I like Johnny and Lisa. And I love the things the four of us have done together so far. I guess the real test will be tomorrow night at the party.'

12

Becky

Even though it wasn't yet nine o'clock in the morning Becky knew she looked magnificent. She posed in front of a full-length mirror, admiring the rubber-clad dominatrix staring back at her. Her long, shapely legs were encased in black rubber stockings. They ended at the tops of her thighs, revealing a tantalising glimpse of milky flesh before cutting off to the harness of her strap-on. It wasn't the formidable weapon she had boasted about while speaking to Tara. This was a mere ten inches of erection with a relatively slender girth. It sprouted from her loins, thrusting jauntily upwards and providing a delicious contrast to the femininity of her curvaceous figure. The rubber basque, impossibly narrow at the waist and so low-cut her breasts almost spilled free each time she exhaled, clung to her skin like shrinkwrap. With the accoutrements of elbow-length gloves and a coiled leather whip, and her hair tied back in an austere scrunch, Becky didn't think any other woman on the planet could have looked as formidable or as sexy.

'Tell me again,' she insisted. 'Who is the greatest hostess of all time?'

Behind her Tara and Alec exchanged a glance. They were both naked, kneeling on the floor, and clutching mobile phones. Before them they each had an open copy of the Yellow Pages.

'You're the greatest hostess, Becky,' Alec mumbled.

Tara glanced up at her with genuine adoration. 'He's right, Mistress Becky. You really are the greatest.'

Becky grinned and drew herself up to her full height. Strutting confidently around the room, glancing down at the pair occasionally so she could enjoy the sight of them cowering at her feet, she savoured the satisfaction of control before looking at the clock. The second hand was making its final journey to mark the end of the hour. 'Just so we're all clear,' she began, 'I'll go over the rules for a final time.'

Alec groaned.

Becky pretended not to hear the sound.

'Tara: you will start phoning from the bottom of the catering section. Alec: you will start from the top. You know your scripts. You know our ultimate goal. Each time you talk with someone not involved with Lisa West's pathetic party, I shall lash you across the backside.' She flicked her whip through the air, snapping the end so it made a sound like a twig breaking.

Alec winced.

Tara bit her lower lip to suppress a hungry smile. She trembled against the bedroom carpet.

'The first one of you to successfully cancel the caterers will receive a special reward,' Becky announced. To illustrate what she was suggesting, she stroked one hand along the ten-inch length of her strap-on. She glanced at the clock again and saw the second hand sweep past nine o'clock. 'Make your phone calls,' she instructed. 'It's time to begin.' She snapped her whip again and this time it sounded like a gunshot.

Dutifully, Tara and Alec did as they were told.

Becky listened as the pair hastily dialled numbers. She was touched by a thrill of power as she realised they were obeying her orders and scared of her wrath. She was also excited that they were going to ruin Lisa's party before it had a chance to properly begin. Another glance in the full-length mirror reminded her she looked like a dominatrix and she settled into the role with a sigh of contentment. Her pussy muscles quivered with mounting excitement and she began to casually strut around her subordinates as they stammered into their telephones. The joy of dominating was stronger than the rush she usually enjoyed while strutting around her swingers' parties. There she was used to everyone fawning on her, congratulating her on organising a splendid party and praising her for balancing incredible skills as a hostess with an ability to appear beautiful and desirable. But here, although there were only her husband and Tara to make her feel like a goddess, Becky knew the subordinates were genuinely scared of her. Mischievously, she contemplated scoring a mark against Alec's rear just to remind him that she was in charge. She dimissed the idea when he began speaking, not wanting to distract him if he was in the process of cancelling Lisa's caterers.

'I'm not sure if this is the right number . . .' Alec began.

Tara said, 'I'm calling on behalf of my friend Lisa West.'

'She had caterers booked for a party this evening.'

'But the party isn't going to happen tonight.'

Alec's backside, taut and muscular, stuck high in the air. She trailed the tip of her whip against his bare cheeks and grinned as he shied away from her. He was an attractive man, a desirable asset when she hosted her parties, and the pleasure Becky got from tormenting him never failed to kindle her excitement. She paused and reached down to stroke the bald flesh of his scrotum. Because they so regularly attended parties she insisted he kept his body free from pubic hair. Her gloved hands flowed smoothly over the taut skin of his sac and she could feel his erection growing harder as she touched him.

Glancing up, she saw Tara's magnified eyes regarding her through her bottle-bottom spectacles. A wide-lipped smile revealed the woman's buck teeth. Her myopic gaze was fixed on Becky's hands as she fondled Alec's balls. Into her mobile phone Tara said, 'Her auntie died. It was very sudden. And upsetting.'

'Her husband's left her,' Alec said into his phone. He paused a moment and then added, 'Yes. A terrible shame.'

After giving him a gentle squeeze – just enough to have him stiffen and catch a breath – Becky retrieved her hand from Alec's scrotum and marched to Tara's rear. The kneeling woman was blessed with the perfect body, a gift that Becky supposed might compensate for her plain and unattractive face. She traced a finger between the cheeks of Tara's buttocks, exciting a shiver that almost distracted her from her phone call. The button of her anus was a puckered invitation to tease. The lips of her pussy remained sealed, although Becky could see a sliver of wetness glistening on the outer labia.

'Oh! You weren't catering for her party?'

Becky moved her hand away from Tara's rear. Standing erect, aiming the whip, she fired a brisk stripe across her milky buttocks. Tara stifled a howl and used both hands to grip the telephone.

'OK,' she grunted. 'Thanks for your time.'

'Not one of yours?' Alec spoke as though he was repeating someone else's words. 'Thank you anyway,' he murmured.

Becky slashed her whip across his back. Ordinarily she would have classed the shot as ineffectual. The brunt of the impact landed loosely between his shoulder blades and didn't look as if it had inflicted any sexual injury. But she saw the tip disappear between the cheeks of his backside and watched him stiffen as it nipped at his balls.

'Shit! Becky!' he snapped. 'That really fucking hurt.' He had dropped the phone and cupped himself tenderly.

'It was *really fucking* meant to,' she returned with equal hostility. 'Now stop clutching your nuts, pick up your phone and dial the next fucking number. I want the caterers cancelled in the next hour. We've still got a lot to do this morning. And I've got an appointment booked at the salon for noon.'

Tara was already making her second call. She wore a broad smile, as though she was enjoying the thrill of obeying Becky's commands and suffering her subsequent wrath. Alec seemed less pleased but, with unnecessary bad grace, he picked up his telephone and began to dial the next number on his list. He paused before keying in the number and asked, 'Why have you got a salon appointment booked for noon?'

She rolled her eyes. 'Duh!' she snorted contemptuously. 'I want to look good for tonight's party, don't I?'

He shook his head. 'Why the hell do you want to look good for a party you're trying to cancel? That doesn't make any sense.'

Becky slashed the whip across his backside. The snap was harsh and left a long horizontal line cutting across both cheeks of his rear. 'I want to make sure that I look fantastic, so everyone can compare my perfectly composed beauty with the spectacle of Lisa's ruined and tear-stained appearance.' She snapped the whip again, grinning as he howled. 'That's why I've got a salon appointment for twelve. Now, stop asking questions and start dialling caterers.'

Tara was on the phone to the second number on her list. 'I'm not sure if this is the right number . . .'

'I'm calling on behalf of my friend Lisa West,' Alec said into his phone. He glared at his wife with open hostility as he talked to the voice on the other end of the line.

Becky listened, and then striped them both for a second time when they each proved unsuccessful. She

154

enjoyed playing the part of a dominatrix and, although it was satisfying to receive Tara's goofy smile each time she striped the woman's bottom, she got more of a thrill from landing the whip on her husband's rear. Alec had a cutting tongue when he chose to stand up to her and each time she got a chance to land a punishing blow upon his rear, she saw it as payback for one of his more scathing remarks. After four calls his buttocks were striped with a pleasant crisscross of red lines. And, although he glared at her as though the sensation wasn't pleasant, she noticed his erection didn't dwindle.

'This is fucking hurting,' he spat.

'Then hurry up and call the right one,' Becky returned.

'What's my reward going to be if I get the right one?' he asked. He glanced at Tara, the focus of his gaze narrowing as he admired her bare curves, and Becky understood what he wanted. She was stung for a moment by the realisation of his treachery. She had dressed for him and Tara in her dominatrix outfit and gone to the trouble of fastening herself into the complicated harnesses of the ten-inch strap-on. Quite why he would want to be rewarded by sliding into Tara's tight pussy, rather than have his beautiful wife ride his arse with her ten-inch dildo, was a mystery she couldn't comprehend. Snorting with disdain, brandishing the whip at him, she said, 'Call the right number and I'll let you watch me fuck Tara.'

Grudgingly, he dialled the next number on his list.

Becky heard Tara thanking the person on the other end of her telephone call and she passed her a questioning glance.

'It wasn't that one either,' Tara said sadly.

Becky slapped the whip hard across her backside.

The calls continued, punctuated by the hissing sound of the whip slicing through the air and the occasional retort of flesh being bitten by leather. The mood of black arousal grew thicker as the minutes ticked past. Alec dialled with frantic haste, trying to call the right number and clearly anxious to avoid further punishment. When Tara finally succeeded in finding the caterers whom Lisa had employed, both subordinates were sporting backsides that were crimson with red lines.

'I didn't want you going to unnecessary inconvenience ...' Tara purred. She smiled triumphantly at Becky and gestured with a thumbs-up signal.

Alec glared at her.

'I understand that,' Tara continued. Her voice faltered as Becky knelt behind her and rolled the end of the strap-on against the wetness of her sex. 'I just thought I'd call and let you know, so you weren't sending your people out to a party that wasn't happening.'

Becky pushed forward before Tara had ended the call. She took a tight hold of her hips and pulled the woman towards her as the dildo plunged inside. They both stiffened with pleasure. Becky didn't know why she found it so satisfying to use the dildo. The base only pressed against her pelvis and the friction was not particularly exciting. Yet the action of having a woman beneath her, groaning as she was ridden and filled, always thrilled Becky with a sensation of power and control.

'Thank you,' Tara said softly. She was speaking into the phone, clearly anxious to end the conversation so she could enjoy the devastating ride that Becky was trying to administer. She pressed the red button on her mobile, concluding the call, and then groaned. 'That feels perfect, Mistress Becky.'

Becky chuckled. She glanced at Alec and saw he had put his phone aside and was now stroking the thick length of his cock. His smile was a gratuitous leer and, as she watched, his fist began to work faster. She released her hold on Tara's hips and slapped the end of his erection.

Alec gasped and then howled. 'What did you do that for?'

'You didn't cancel the caterers,' Becky reminded him. 'Therefore you don't get the reward of watching me fuck Tara.'

'But I . . .'

'Turn around,' she insisted. Her tone was strident. 'Don't keep looking at us. Face the corner.'

'But I . . .'

'There are other jobs for you two to do this morning.' Becky sniffed pompously. 'Turn around. Face the corner and wait until I give you an instruction to move. If you succeed with the other job I have for you, you'll have earned your reward and you'll enjoy it more.'

He glared at her for a full minute. She could sense he was longing to disobey. Becky narrowed her eyes, savouring his scowl and rolling her hips as she waited for him to do as she had instructed. The ten-inch dildo slurped deeper into Tara's sex and then pulled out until it was almost spilling from the tight slit.

'Turn around,' she said again.

Groaning angrily, Alec finally turned to face the corner of the room.

Becky plunged the dildo deep into Tara and made the woman howl. She rode her pelvis with a brisk pace, delighting in every sensation she injected into Tara's receptive body. The woman trembled, shivered, moaned and pushed herself back as she demanded more. Savouring the sensations, Becky quickened her tempo and ploughed in and out with greater haste.

'That feels good,' Tara muttered.

'That feels good, *Mistress Becky*,' Becky prompted.

'Mistress Becky,' Tara agreed. 'Mistress Becky. Mistress Becky. I'm sorry.'

Becky thought of spanking the woman's backside for the oversight, and then decided it was too much trouble.

She gave her hips a final thrust forward and was rewarded by Tara's cataclysmic cries of release.

The bespectacled woman shrieked, pushed herself back onto the full force of Becky's thrust, and then collapsed on the floor in a writhing pantomime of orgasm. Her hands flailed at the carpet. She shifted positions from a foetal curl to an arched exclamation. And then she was gasping and laughing as though the pleasure was a completely unexpected by-product of what they had been doing.

'Here, Alec,' Becky snapped. She stepped over to her husband and pushed the glistening length of her dildo close to his face. 'You can lick this clean now.'

He glared at her. 'You take things too far, Becky.'

She daubed the rounded end of the dildo against his cheek. It left a silver smear of wetness. The moisture was a viscous reminder that the length had just been buried in Tara's pussy. 'Don't answer me back, boy,' she snapped. 'Just lick it clean before Mistress Becky loses patience with you.'

There was a brief instant when she thought he might rebel. He stared up at her with a loathing she had seldom seen before. Then she saw his gaze flash in Tara's direction, watched her husband admire the other woman's model-perfect figure and was relieved to see him place his mouth around her erection. He licked her clean without any discernible show of enthusiasm. But, because he was a subordinate and she was playing the role of the Mistress, Becky didn't think he needed to lap at her erection with any great display of appreciation.

'Doesn't he look good sucking my cock?' Becky asked Tara. She placed her hand on the back of Alec's head before asking the question, holding him in place with the erection in his mouth as Tara stared at them both and then smiled. Alec's cheeks turned red as he blushed and Becky quietly congratulated herself on knowing exactly how to compound his shame and humiliation.

Familiar with her husband's mood swings, Becky figured the embarrassment would keep him aroused and ensure that he did everything she demanded in her final attempts to destroy Lisa's party. 'Doesn't he look absolutely fantastic with his mouth around my ten inches?'

'He looks delightful,' Tara agreed.

Becky noticed the way she admired Alec and realised there was a danger her subordinates were growing too interested in each other. Deciding the best way to rule them was to divide and conquer, she pushed Alec from her length and clapped her hands so they were both staring at her. 'OK!' she gasped. 'It's time we got back to business.'

Tara turned her attention back to Becky.

After allowing his gaze to linger over Tara's body for a moment longer, Alec raised his eyes and looked at Becky. 'What do you want us to do now?'

She contemplated reminding him that he should call her Mistress Becky, and then decided it wasn't worth the effort. There were still a lot of calls to be made and not enough time to waste on meaningless power struggles. 'The entertainment is cancelled,' she declared. 'The caterers are now out of the picture. And the venue she's using isn't her first choice. Shall we pick off the guests now?'

Alec groaned.

Tara shivered.

Becky went to her handbag and produced two identical packets of folded pages. There were three sheets in each bundle with approximately a hundred names on each page. 'You start from the bottom of page three,' she told Tara. Glancing at Alec she said, 'You start from the top of page one.'

'And what are we telling the guests?' Alec asked.

'You're telling them there's been a rumour that Lisa is asking more than double the usual door charge to enter her party.'

'No one will stand for that,' Alec told her.

Becky shrugged. 'Isn't that the point?'

'But what if someone phones her and asks her if it's true?'

Again, Becky shrugged. 'I can see one per cent of them doing that,' she said in her most official voice. 'And I can see one per cent of them not caring, and paying twice the amount it would cost to attend one of my parties.' Her grin turned sinister as she said, 'The other ninety-eight per cent will simply believe what they've been told and won't bother turning up for the shambles that was Lisa's party.'

Alec shook his head. 'Haven't you done enough to fuck over this party?'

'No!' Becky insisted. She snapped the whip and both he and Tara flinched from its crisp retort. 'It's not nearly enough,' she screamed. 'I cancelled the Red Mill, and that didn't stop her. I've cancelled her entertainment and her catering. And we're not going to stop today until we've told each of her guests that the door charge has doubled. If Lisa West doesn't yet know that no one wants her stupid party, then I'm going to make sure she learns that lesson. And tonight, once everyone sees what a fuck-up she's made of the whole affair, I'll be feted as the queen of swinging parties.' A triumphant grin turned her features pretty. In her mind's eye, she was already watching the other woman's tears as Lisa knelt sobbing before her and admitted she simply wasn't as good as Becky.

From a distance, she heard Alec and Tara dialling the first of the calls. As satisfaction swelled in her chest, she felt convinced that Lisa's party was going to be a huge disappointment.

13

Surfing

'Tonight's party is going to be a huge disappointment,' Lisa reflected.

Johnny nodded. He sat in his bathrobe, a coffee mug in one hand and a copy of the Saturday morning paper in the other. His hair was dishevelled, his face had the spongy texture she noticed when he got too little sleep, and the whites of his eyes were pink from alcohol and exertion.

And she still believed he was the most attractive man in the world.

'It's going to be a flop,' he declared. 'No one will turn up. Everyone will hate it. And, I've heard, there's a danger your fanny will heal up.'

Lisa turned in her seat and glared at him.

They were sitting in the spare bedroom that was known as 'Johnny's Computer Room'. The walls were a sterile white and the dark carpeting was matched by the blinds at the window. Halogen lamps made the light unbearably bright for so early in the day. She thought they bleached her tan and made her skin look anaemic. Aside from the two swivel chairs, both black, high-backed and allegedly leather, the only furniture was a large desk and Johnny's computer.

'I wasn't fishing for compliments or reassurance,' she growled.

Lisa didn't understand Johnny's computer and had never made any attempt to further her knowledge. But there were some chatrooms she and Johnny often visited (with Johnny typing at her dictation) and Lisa had thought it might be a good way to make a last-minute announcement about the party they were throwing. Johnny had signed them into a swingers' room under the identity *Party Couple* and Lisa sat topless in front of a webcam as a barrage of questions and comments flashed up on the screen. As she turned away from the camera and glared at her husband the barrage of questions became a string of protests begging her to turn her breasts back to the lens of the webcam.

'I was just pointing out,' she continued, 'after all that happened last night, the party is going to be a letdown.'

He folded his newspaper, put it aside and grinned. Observing what was happening on the screen he signalled to her to turn back. 'You enjoyed your birthday?'

'I don't know which part was best,' she marvelled. 'I mean, I got to screw Debbie!'

'She's a very sexy lady, isn't she?'

Lisa shook her head. 'But not only did I get to screw Debbie,' she enthused. 'The stuff we did before with Mark and Anne . . .' Her voice trailed off and she shook her head. The smile on her face was tight with disbelief. 'That was truly amazing.'

'It was pretty powerful,' Johnny agreed. He joined her in the chair, encouraging her to stand for a moment before taking the seat and then allowing her to sit on his lap, and began to fondle her breasts. She knew that he was doing it partly to improve the show being presented to those in the chatroom but, as was always the way with Johnny, she realised he was also doing it for her pleasure. His fingers found her nipples and he held them with excessive gentleness. Rolling the flesh lightly between his fingers and thumbs, pulling ever so gently, he made the tips turn hard with arousal. And, although her body ached from an excess of pleasure the night before, she could feel her pussy responding to his caresses with a rush of fluid warmth. Her inner muscles trembled and she realised she already wanted him again.

Glancing at the computer screen, watching her own image transmitted to a chatroom inhabited by a hundred or so swingers and voyeurs, she was comfortable that only her breasts were being shown. The webcam was set at an angle that wouldn't catch her face and none of their audience could hear what she was saying to her husband. The picture on screen, although relatively small, showed two pert orbs being deftly fondled by a pair of large hands. Johnny's wedding ring glinted brightly beneath the halogen lighting and her chest began to heave as the arousal surged through her. Memories of the previous evening were already making her pussy damp and she wondered how much of a show they might end up providing for the chatroom audience.

In the past she and Johnny had watched couples wanking, sucking and fucking before their webcams. There was one regular woman who would frig herself to climax with a variety of dildos, bananas or cucumbers. Another frequently showed herself squirting through a self-inflicted orgasm. A lot of single men masturbated in front of their cameras. And then there were couples, like Johnny and herself, who occasionally played together for their own pleasure and the benefit of an unseen audience.

There were times when Lisa considered the chatroom exhibitionism to be tawdry and beneath her. The sight of too many men masturbating could kill her arousal, and some of the more vulgar comments came across as threatening or unkind. But, whenever she was caught in a particular mood of excitement, Lisa couldn't resist pushing her own boundaries that little bit further and did as much as she could to excite the ever-present roomful of voyeurs.

Someone on screen asked them why they were called the party couple.

Johnny moved his hands from Lisa's breasts so he could type his response on the keyboard. He explained they were hosting a swingers' party that evening. He added that there was a door charge but the invitation was extended to every couple in the chatroom if they wished to attend. He concluded his message by typing out one of his many email addresses and saying he would send further details to anyone who contacted him privately. As soon as he had pressed the SEND button, he moved his fingers back to Lisa's breasts and fondled her again.

She sighed. Her breasts tingled from the throb of excitement. She didn't usually consider herself an exhibitionist but there was something darkly thrilling about showing herself in the safe environment of a swingers' chatroom. A part of her understood that those who were watching would not think there was anything remarkable in what she was doing. But that didn't stop her from responding to the familiar excitement of being more daring than the vast majority of her contemporaries. She grinned as she read a string of messages, each one offering a compliment, begging to have a private conversation with her, or suggesting her partner touched her more intimately.

A series of beeps from the computer caused Johnny to release his hold on her breasts. He typed without shifting from underneath her. To make sure the audience weren't only staring at her bare breasts, Lisa stroked the tips of her fingers against her nipples. The contact was not as thrilling as Johnny's caresses had been. But the image on screen, with her own painted nails scratching at the circles of her areolae, inspired a rush of fresh messages.

'Tonight's party won't be a disappointment,' Johnny mumbled. 'Aside from the fifty confirmations we've already had, there's another dozen here showing interest.'

She giggled and squirmed on his lap. 'Why not point the camera down and see if we can garner a little more interest?'

Obligingly, Johnny shifted the small webcam so it pointed at Lisa's groin. He pushed their chair back a little, so the lower half of her body was exposed to its leering eye. Because she was naked her bare pussy lips were immediately shown on screen. The thickening length of Johnny's semi-soft penis sat against the wet flesh of her labia. Neither of them had planned to make their web-show so graphic but, with arousal governing her actions, Lisa didn't want to miss the opportunity. She watched the computer screen and was delighted to see a string of messages pleading for her to take the cock between her legs. Johnny read a couple of them out loud, mumbling something disparaging about the grammar and spelling. But that didn't stop him from sliding a finger against the split of her wetness and opening her sex to the lens of the camera.

The light beneath the edge of the table lacked the ferocity that had blazed against her breasts. And, while her upper half had seemed unhealthily pale (save for the magenta flush of her nipples and areolae), her thighs and pussy looked orange as the computer's software struggled to show her with the limited light available. Nevertheless, even though her skin looked as if she had been dipped in one of the nastier salon tanning liquids, she couldn't fault the exciting sight of her pussy lips as they appeared on screen. She groaned as the tingle of pleasure shivered through her loins and couldn't decide if the arousal had been caused by Johnny's caresses or her own thrill at showing off.

'Do you think Mark and Anne have ever tried anything like this?'

'It wouldn't surprise me,' Johnny said calmly. 'They've never swung before. I believe them when they say that. But I don't think that pair have ever been Norman and Norma Normal.'

Lisa laughed, quietly agreeing that Mark and Anne were far from being the dull couple they had expected to meet when they first went to dinner with them. Johnny's fingers continued to tease the split of her sex as he added, 'You don't think we're getting too attached to them, do you?'

'Mark and Anne?'

'Yes. We've barely known them a week. Yet they celebrated your birthday with us last night. You've seen Anne nearly every day since that first party at their house. We'll be seeing them at the party tonight. Aren't you worried we're overcrowding them a little? That, maybe, we're overcrowding each other?'

She stared at the image on screen. Her sex was open and wet. The pink flesh of her pussy, sporting a tangerine hue, was visible to a list of unknown voyeurs. She was torn between concentrating on the conversation and enjoying the exhibitionism. Squirming under Johnny's skilful touch, loving the way he traced his fingers against her pussy lips and casually inspired her need, she reached down between her legs and began to stroke him hard. The screen image was a blur of his hands touching her labia and her fingers encircling his cock. A list of messages alongside the image begged her to accept his length while others insisted she should stroke him harder. The eagerness of the audience was almost as powerful an aphrodisiac as the sensuous silk of her husband's caress.

Surprised by the intensity of her responses, Lisa wondered if Anne would enjoy experiencing internet exhibitionism. And it was only when she realised her thoughts had come back to Anne that she remembered she hadn't answered Johnny's questions. 'Are you uncomfortable being with Mark and Anne?' she asked slowly.

'Christ! No!' he exclaimed. 'I like Mark. I consider him a genuine friend. And I think Anne's adorable. And incredibly sexy.'

Lisa frowned. 'Then why pick problems where there aren't any?'

Because she was sitting on his lap, she felt him shrug his response. 'I was just saying,' he mumbled defensively. 'You know I like to think things through and get every detail worked out before I progress with anything.'

She had him hard. Her husband's erection now filled the tiny webcam image they were broadcasting to the chatroom. Because his cock was thrusting upward it all but concealed the view of her splayed pussy lips. Lisa eased forward, lifting herself slightly so she could place his length against her sex. The picture made for a lurid image that exacerbated her arousal. If she hadn't been wet before, when a hundred or so voyeurs were watching, Lisa knew her pussy would soon be gushing as she admired the sight of him, so close to penetration. The visuals reminded her of images she had seen in countless porn films. There was nothing romantic or edifying about their content and the same could be said for the webcam picture on Johnny's computer screen. But because this showed her wet pussy on the brink of being pierced by her husband's hard cock, and because it was being viewed by a chatroom filled with appreciative strangers, Lisa didn't think it would be possible to see anything more exciting.

Slowly, partly to draw out her own pleasure and partly to tantalise her audience, Lisa lowered herself onto Johnny's erection. His length slipped casually inside her. On screen her sex devoured him as though it had its own unhurried purpose. The outer lips of her sex clung tight to his thick length. The webcam remained constantly trained on the union of his hard cock and her wet pussy.

The list of screen messages flashed past in a blur. Lisa saw the majority were enthusiastic encouragements. Some coaxed her to do more: show her ass, finger her clit or suck his erection. Others demanded she type a message and describe every sensation the penetration inspired. She felt breathless as she read each line. Thrilled to be the centre of attention, Lisa even considered pecking out a response on the keyboard.

Johnny reached past her before she could formulate a reply in her head. She dimly realised he was sending out another batch of emails concerning that evening's party. She grinned and was surprised to find she could still look forward to the pleasure of the party even while she was enjoying the depravity of fucking and flaunting herself to a vast and unseen audience.

'I was just worried that we might be getting too close to Mark and Anne,' Johnny explained. He had the enviable ability to talk and type without making a spelling mistake or losing his erection. Lisa quietly marvelled that he could multitask so efficiently and then decided that was probably one of the reasons why she loved him so dearly. Keeping her adoration quiet, not wanting to offer praise and potentially make him conceited, she raised and then lowered herself on his length. The on-screen image showed him sliding easily in and out of her wet hole.

'That was the only reason I voiced my doubts,' Johnny added as he pressed the SEND button. 'I'm quite comfortable with the relationship. But I don't want any of us getting hurt. I'm particularly anxious that neither you nor I get hurt.'

'If they grow bored with us—' She stopped abruptly and decided to begin again. 'If we grow bored with them—' Again, the words sounded callous, as though she didn't care about the feelings of their neighbours. She shook her head and tried to focus on the conversation rather than the glorious sensations being driven through her sex. 'If we grow bored with each other,' she managed, 'if the whole relationship becomes too involved, too complicated or too messy, we can always call it off. But until that happens, I think we should enjoy the friendship and the fun.'

'You like Anne, don't you?'

She tightened her smile, exasperated by the way he could pick on a single detail that made her feel guilty. The truth was that she did like Anne and she had never before had a genuine female friend who also knew about her involvement with swinging. The gregariousness of the parties Lisa attended, the recreational sex and casual liaisons with virtual strangers, all that was balanced by a regular life that was kept separate and secret. No one in their families knew that Lisa and Johnny enjoyed an open relationship. Aside from Debbie, none of Johnny's work colleagues had any idea how he spent his time away from the office. And in her own small social circle of old school chums, family friends and occasional acquaintances, Lisa knew she was thought of as quiet, prudish and normal to the point of banality. The easy bond she had formed with Anne was a relationship she had never enjoyed before, and she was reluctant to let Johnny caution against the wisdom of developing such an attachment. Anne offered Lisa a chance to talk openly about an important part of her life that she had only ever discussed at length with Johnny. Admittedly there had been occasional conversations during the lulls at some of the less dynamic parties, but never anything like the powerful connection she had made with Anne.

'I do like Anne,' she said. 'I like Mark. More importantly, they like us. Also they're the first couple we've met that don't think you're an anally retentive cretin.'

Johnny had placed his hands on her sex. On screen her thighs were splayed to show his cock penetrating the gaping lips of her sex. The image was clear and glossy. The dark pink of her pussy glistened wetly for the camera. As he thrust in and out, a huge list of encouraging messages washed across the screen.

'I'm not anally retentive,' he muttered.

She absently patted his hand, then moved her fingers up so she could stroke the pulsing nub of her clitoris. The picture on screen was pitifully small but her arousal was strong enough to have engorged the bead of flesh. She could see it throbbing for the audience's viewing pleasure. Her excitement reached a fresh level of arousal and she told herself it was not wise to continue a conversation that could result in an argument. Together they were increasing the guest list for the evening's party. More importantly, they were enjoying their roles as the centre of attention in the chatroom's lurid show. To spoil that mood by raising a senseless argument would have been an act of madness.

'Of course you're not anally retentive,' she agreed. 'And the cretin tag is probably unjustified . . .'

'Probably?'

She brushed the question aside. Her finger rolled against the bead of her clitoris. Her arousal was strong enough to tingle in an electric surge that erupted up from her groin. She was deftly playing with herself, her husband's cock was sliding between her legs, and she was being admired for being sexy, exciting and daring. She remembered being surprised that Johnny could multitask so effectively and realised that, if she could continue her half of this conversation with tact and diplomacy, she was close to displaying the same spectacular achievement. 'But you know what I'm trying to say, don't you?' she pressed. 'Couples like Mark and Anne don't come along every day. If they are the perfect match for us, I don't want to fuck things up and stop things before they've properly started. I especially don't want to end our relationship with them just on the off-chance that things won't work out. To my mind that would be a really stupid thing to do.'

He stayed silent for a moment, teasing her sex wide open and coaxing her closer to a climax. Another batch of messages had dropped into his inbox, and Lisa supposed he would get round to responding to them shortly. But, for the moment, it looked as if his concentration was divided between pleasing her and responding to what she had just said.

Not hurrying him, knowing there was all the time in the world to wait for her beloved husband's reply, Lisa simply slid up and down his length and stroked more urgently against her clitoris. The orgasm swelled between her legs and she didn't know if it came from her own skilled touch, the presence of Johnny's cock or the attention of the internet voyeurs. She did know the orgasm was going to be strong when it came and, again, she was struck by the knowledge that she had to share the source of this excitement with Anne.

If Johnny genuinely thought things were moving too quickly with Mark and Anne, or if he seriously believed they were heading towards dangerous territory that could upset the balance of their own relationship, Lisa knew she would heed his warning and make a conscious effort to slow things down. But, unless he gave her an explicit instruction not to, Lisa was adamant that she would introduce Anne to the joys of online exhibitionism.

She giggled as she thought how they could put on a show of cunnilingus for the ever-present voyeurs who lurked in the chatrooms. The thought of all the interest that particular show would cultivate heightened the temperature inside her sex. Panting easily, she slid more quickly up and down Johnny's length.

'It would be nice to think we'd found a couple who shared our appetites and standards,' he said eventually.

Even though she was teetering on the brink of orgasm, Lisa forced herself to concentrate on what he was saying. The prospect of her impending climax was important but she knew it was more important to complete this discussion and fully understand each other. She glanced at the screen, pleased by the prettiness of her own pussy and the enviable thickness of her husband's cock. The sight made her inner muscles wetter but she kept her pace at the same steady rhythm. 'Go on,' she encouraged. 'I'm listening.'

'It would be good to have swinging friends who we could play with,' he told her. 'And it would be great to give up the facile searching and messing about that sums up the majority of downsides we've discovered with swinging.'

Lisa nodded ruefully. In the blink of an eye she could recall the countless singles and couples they had attempted to meet over the past five years. Each time had been a torment of nervousness, fear and breathtaking anticipation.

A lot of the dates had been set up through classified adverts in magazines until Johnny had discovered the internet. And the routine was predictable enough to verge on being boring.

Johnny placed an ad and two dozen people responded.

Johnny replied to those responses, asking for photographs and a brief outline of what they expected from an encounter with a swinging couple. Half of those two dozen would reply. Johnny sent undraped pictures of himself and Lisa to six of those twelve – the other six having proved themselves unsuitable, unsettling or incompatible in some other way. They would then expect three of those six to respond with telephone numbers or the time and location for a suggested meeting. And from those final three, if they managed to get a successful night with one of the respondents, Lisa considered that they had done well.

She glanced at the screen and watched her sex slide up and down her husband's length. Comments were still blurring the screen, praising her and blessing Johnny's good fortune. But it was on the image of her sex engulfing Johnny's shaft that she concentrated her attention. He looked so perfect inside her hole, his shaft fitting exactly as she needed and touching all the right places deep inside her sex. She worked herself more quickly, and tried not to think of the annoying experiences and frustrating disappointments that had chequered their swinging career.

She had sat through too many stilted conversations in unknown pubs. She had endured enough liars and truth-benders to no longer feel the thrill of anticipation that she used to enjoy. There had been single men pretending to be married couples and single women pretending to be twenty years younger than they genuinely were. They had received undraped photographs from men who had used CorelDraw to alter the size of their penises, as well as photographs from women who glibly announced that this wasn't a picture of them, but it's how they would look if they were naked.

The adventure of swinging had been a great deal of fun and a lot of the time, Lisa thought, it had been exceptionally rewarding. But the deceit and nuisance of people backing out of dates or simply proving themselves to be liars was something she had never enjoyed. The frustration of trying to communicate with people who were operating on a different wavelength was more maddening than she could begin to explain. And the idea that Mark and Anne might be the special couple she and Johnny had always wanted to find ignited a spark of hope that she hadn't dared consider for a long time. Privately, Lisa believed that they might finally be able to enjoy all the benefits of swinging without having to suffer any of the downsides. That thought alone was almost enough to make the climax hurtle from her loins.

'Which couple said I was anally retentive?'

She laughed. 'What makes you think it was just one couple?'

'Do I really come across as being like that?'

'Not until you open your mouth.'

'Damn it, Lisa. That's not funny.'

She grinned at him. 'It made me laugh.'

He pushed his erection up, the sudden lunge inside her muscles severing her mirth and slapping her thoughts back to the sex they were enjoying. The computer screen was a rush of messages, their tone more vulgar now, as though the voyeurs had sensed she was close to release. Johnny reached past her, typing another message to advertise the party and reveal his private email address if anyone wanted contact information. His hands moved back to her breasts and, as he squeezed her nipples and coaxed her closer to orgasm, Lisa knew this was being done for her pleasure and not to thrill the voyeurs. She rode him with a quickening pace, her sex hungrily devouring him. The barrage of sensations flickered through her pussy muscles and, as the first wave of climax struck, she pushed herself hard against him.

His ejaculation struck her as being a reflex response. Her inner muscles clenched hard around him and Johnny was left with no option but to release his pent-up climax. She watched on screen as the base of his shaft thickened and pulsed, and she revelled in the pleasure of having his seed flood her hole. Writhing against him, she tried to milk every last drop of pleasure from the union. Eventually she sat back and mumbled a brief but sincere thank you.

He kissed her cheek and they exchanged gasping platitudes of love. And, even though they repeated the words a dozen or more times each day, Lisa knew they were spoken from both sides with absolute sincerity. Johnny reached past her, pressed a button to end the images being shown by the webcam and then went through the process of responding to the substantial list of enquiries they had received. She saw he was transmitting the same message to every respondent, copying and pasting a huge block of text that included the type of party, vague details about the location and a contact number for anyone wishing to attend. Lisa eased herself from his lap and went to make them both a coffee, finding a bathrobe en route. When she returned she discovered Johnny was still typing and she settled herself lazily in the other chair. Picking up his newspaper, flicking idly through the pages, she allowed the last eddies of pleasure to subside as she prepared herself for the day ahead.

'Answer me seriously,' Johnny began. 'Do you think we should be easing away from Mark and Anne? Do you think we should be putting a bit of distance there, just in case either they're not ready for us or we're not ready for them?' He glanced over his shoulder and she could see from his expression that he was genuinely asking for her opinion.

She felt her cheeks grow red with a moment's embarrassment. 'That's going to be kind of difficult,' Lisa said carefully. 'Anne and I are spending the day making the last adjustments to the house before the party. Also, I've arranged for her to interview someone else from the swinging scene at the party house this afternoon, so she's got a more rounded picture of what goes on. Tonight, as you know, Anne's going to be co-hosting the event with me. And tomorrow, after the clean-up at the house, I'll be helping her with writing her article on swinging.' She flexed her apologetic smile wider and added, 'We've made plans together for most of next week. For the immediate future, it's going to be kind of difficult to ease ourselves away from them.'

'Christ!' he grumbled. 'Chang and Eng spent more time apart than you two.'

Lisa bit her lip. She knew Chang and Eng were the first recorded Siamese twins and she resisted the temptation to laugh or take umbrage. Johnny's flair for sarcasm was a nuisance that she disliked even when it made her want to roar with laughter. She paused for a moment and then said, 'Perhaps it would be easier if you kept your distance, though? You've got no need to see Mark after tonight's party, have you?'

His grin was bashful, almost as though he was ashamed of himself. 'I promised Mark I'd help him lay an ornamental fountain in the rockery at the back of their garden. I think we're scheduled to do that some time on Sunday afternoon.'

She raised an eyebrow.

'And I did tell him to call in at the office next week.' He turned his attention back to the computer, finishing off the last of his email responses. 'I have a few contacts who might be interested in the bespoke solutions his company provides,' Johnny explained. 'Mark and I are going to meet up on Wednesday lunchtime and maybe make an afternoon of it.'

'I see,' Lisa said shortly. 'And which one of you two is playing the role of Chang and which one is Eng?'

'Touché,' he mumbled dryly.

She tossed the paper aside, eased out of her seat and kissed him lightly on the cheek. The scrub of his beard grazed her lips and she thought of reminding him he would need to shave before the party that evening. 'You could be right. Things might be moving too fast and the four of us could all end up getting hurt. But it feels right to me. Does it feel right to you?'

He nodded.

'Then let's just play the game as it happens,' Lisa suggested. 'If things work out, then it's great for all of us. If things don't work out, then at least no one can say we didn't give it a shot.'

'And how will we know if things are working out?' he asked softly.

She shrugged. 'I guess we'll have a pretty good idea after tonight,' she reflected. 'This will be their first party. If we still want them and they still want us after we've

176

all attended the same party, it will give us a pretty strong idea of whether or not we've got a future as a foursome.'

He nodded. 'If that's the case, then I hope you were wrong when you predicted tonight's party would be a disappointment. For your sake, my sake, and for the sake of Mark and Anne, I hope it's a resounding success.'

She laughed, kissed him and shook her head. 'I can't see it really being a disappointment,' she admitted. 'And, although last night was good, I don't think this evening will be an anti-climax either.' Her smile was confident and self-assured as she said, 'In truth, I can't see anything going wrong with tonight's party.'

14

Tara

In Anne's experience there were two types of interview subject: those who couldn't stop talking and those who wouldn't start. She had encountered both sorts during her career as a freelance writer. She had grown weary with the chatterboxes who spilled information like clumsy drunks carrying a tray of drinks. And she had become vexed with the mutes who grunted their non-committal monosyllabic positives and negatives. But she couldn't ever recall meeting anyone who stretched across both extremes like Tara.

'Are you attending Lisa's party this evening?'

Tara looked away. 'I guess.'

'What do you expect to get out of this evening's party?'

'I dunno. Whatever.'

'What do you think you'll do at the party?' Anne pressed. 'Do you attend with a specific goal in mind? Or do you go and just take events as they come?'

A shrug. 'Whatever.'

Anne pursed her lips, annoyed that control of the interview had slipped from her grasp. Lisa had introduced Tara half an hour earlier. The preparations for the party were complete, with space laid out for the entertainers to simply turn up and perform. Because they were bringing their own PA system, and Anne couldn't tolerate the thought of an afternoon without music, she had brought a CD player and a collection of Elvis and Glenn Miller discs to help the day pass more pleasantly. The King was currently going through a medley of ballads that echoed impressively around the near-empty hall. His syrupy voice – the most potent aphrodisiac Anne knew – rang from the wood-panelled walls that would surround the night's decadence. It created, she thought, the perfect ambience to put anyone in an erotic frame of mind.

The massive table that dominated the dining room was covered with a pristine white cloth in readiness for the caterers. Mark and Johnny had dutifully gone through the process of collecting three cases of wine, two crates of beer, a box of assorted spirits and mixers as well as the rented glasses Lisa had ordered for the party. The pair had settled themselves behind the bar, exchanging a macho banter of coarse jokes and gruff camaraderie. And, although they presented an image of testosterone-charged masculinity, Anne had noted that neither of them touched the alcohol and both refrained from using vulgarities. She also thought they seemed surprisingly comfortable with each other and the realisation made her grin, happy that her husband had found such a good friend in their neighbour. Maddeningly, she thought, it seemed as if the only thing not going well was her interview with Tara.

'I love your hair,' Tara said suddenly.

Flattered, Anne touched her pink spikes. 'Thank you.' She turned her attention back to the bespectacled woman and watched her magnified eyes roll myopically behind the lenses of her glasses. Perplexed, Anne wished she could understand the paradox that was Tara. When the interview had first begun Tara had seemed uneasy in Lisa's presence. Her reserved nature made Anne think the woman would be a mute when it came to responses for her interview questions. But, after a couple of general exchanges about swinging, Anne had found Tara to be talkative and animated and anxious to brag about everything she had done since becoming a swinger. Anne had almost broken her pencil trying to scratch down the full and colourful answers Tara supplied, and she had repeatedly checked that her dictaphone was properly recording the conversation so she didn't miss a single word. All the time that Tara was speaking Anne caught herself thinking how quotable the woman was. She could imagine her article including a fascinating contrast between the description of Tara's plain and unremarkable appearance and her torrid revelations about a swinging lifestyle. Even though the copy wasn't even written, she knew it would make for a compelling read.

'The best swinging experience I ever had was when I was living with a master. I was his slave. I have a bit of a submissive streak. And he invited a friend of his to our flat to share me one night. Between them they tried to work out how best to use me. I didn't have a say in it because I was just the submissive and a submissive isn't allowed to say what should happen to her but I think I got to influence things anyway. My master was saying, "why don't we see if she can suck both our cocks at the same time?" And I was thinking, I could do that so easy, but there wouldn't be a lot in it for me. I mean, I don't mind sucking cock but it doesn't do a lot for a girl, does it?' She raised an eyebrow and waited for Anne to nod agreement before continuing. 'And I do enjoy being penetrated,' she went on. 'If I'd been allowed to say so, I would have told them that. But, because I was being submissive, I had to stay quiet. And, luckily for me, the other guy, my master's friend, he said, "If she can fit two cocks in her mouth, maybe she can fit two cocks inside her pussy?" My master thought this was a great idea, and I thought it would be sort of fun to try it. But, instead of just being a good

180

submissive, and allowing them to do whatever they wanted with me, I said, "Why don't you both fit your cocks into my arse?" I was gagged after that, which I didn't really mind, because being gagged stops me from saying dumb stuff like "Why don't you both fit your cocks into my arse?" ' She flashed a brief grin, snatched a breath and then hurried onto to complete her story.

'So then they spent an hour with one of them sucking my tits and eating my pussy while the other one of them squirted two tubes of KY Jelly up my bumhole. That stuff is so cold it's a wonder that didn't kill my appetite for getting fucked by them. But I was dripping when the first one of them slid inside me. They'd also spent a lot of their time stretching my ass – pushing their fingers inside and getting me ready – so I was easily able to take them both.' She paused, reflected on the last remark, and then said, 'Well, perhaps it wasn't that easy. I know, when the second one pushed himself inside, I would have screamed like a banshee if not for the gag. I was crying so much it looked like the lubricant was leaking from my eye-sockets. But I also remember it was the most intense sexual experience of my life. I've never known pleasure and pain like it. It was absolutely awesome. When I came I thought I'd died and gone to heaven. I don't think I'll ever beat that.'

Anne had tried to break into this monologue, anxious to ask for details and clarify one point or another, but Tara had blundered through the anecdote with a cheerful exuberance that defied interruption. She did supply details when Anne asked afterwards, chuckling wickedly as she described lengths and girths, laughing as she made salacious comments on the use of condoms, and grinning with proud embarrassment over the awkwardness of some of the more demanding positions that had been needed for the penetration.

At that point, Anne had thought Tara would prove herself a champion at giving too much information too

181

quickly without any consideration for the struggling interviewer. But, when Anne had asked what Tara expected from this evening's party, the woman had become taciturn. She clammed up as though the subject was upsetting, unpleasant or simply embarrassing. Anne supposed the fault lay within herself: she didn't understand the protocols of the swinging community sufficiently to know what questions could and couldn't be asked. Yet it seemed amazing that any woman could willingly recount every detail of having two cocks slide simultaneously into her anus, and then fall reticent when asked about a forthcoming party.

'Do you colour your hair yourself?' Tara asked, nodding at Anne's head.

'Yes,' Anne said. Her fingers returned to the freshly pinked tips of her hair. She widened her smile a notch and hoped the expression of forced cheerfulness would help to banish Tara's uncooperative mood.

'It looks like it's been done by a professional.'

'Thank you. I change the colour quite often, so I suppose I get a lot of practice. Thanks for saying it looks professional.'

'You're welcome,' Tara told her. In the same breath, and without altering her tone of voice she asked, 'Do you want to lick my pussy?'

Anne almost squealed with surprise. 'Excuse me?'

'Do you want to lick my pussy?' She spoke quickly, as though trying to clarify a matter before it could cause offence. Her gaze shifted from Anne's face to the crotch of her jeans. 'I was just sitting here, thinking how much I'd love to lick yours, and I wondered if you felt the same way. We could eat each other out, and you could tell your readers how good I am at licking cunt.'

Licking cunt! Anne blinked, half expecting Tara would next suggest those two words could be used for the title of her article. With her automatic responses failing to kick in she thought the words sounded like the name of a Native American lesbian. A shriek of defensive laughter bubbled at the back of her throat and she tried to stifle it before it blurted into the room and caused her to die from embarrassment. Mercifully, Lisa ran to her side with a placatory grin plastered across her lips. Anne had hoped Lisa might be listening and inwardly thanked her for her timely appearance.

'How's the interview going?' Lisa asked. She sounded as though she was making a genuine enquiry but the expression on her face suggested she already knew the answer. From Anne's perspective the interview had just entered the Twilight Zone.

Tara had flinched when Lisa appeared. Her large eyes turned towards the floor and she refused to lift her gaze. Her mood swings were so extreme Anne began to wonder if the poor creature was afflicted with some sort of mental illness or personality disorder.

'The interview is going fine,' Anne said easily. Confident that Tara wasn't looking at her, Anne glared at Lisa and mouthed 'Help me!'

Lisa nodded. Her lips were pursed into a barely suppressed smirk. Anne knew that, later, they would laugh about this moment, and it helped her to calm her rising hysteria and resume her role as a professional writer conducting an interview. She found her notepad and pencil and flicked the switch on her dictaphone.

'Did I mention that Tara is a natural submissive?' Lisa asked. She spoke to Anne but she was constantly trying to catch Tara's gaze. Her voice was rich with forced enthusiasm. 'If you ever want to dominate another woman, and you think I'll prove too feisty, Tara is the one you want to try. Isn't that right, Tara?'

'I guess.'

Tara continued studying the floor, allowing Lisa to pass Anne a questioning frown and Anne to respond with a bewildered shrug. Lisa knelt down beside Tara and placed a hand on her shoulder. It was obvious the bespectacled woman didn't want to suffer the contact but she didn't pull herself away. Instead she simply remained in her seat, trembling lightly.

Lisa asked, 'Is everything OK, sweetheart?'

Anne thought she could see tears swelling in Tara's eyes. She mentally backtracked over the interview and wondered if she had been too harsh with her questioning. She didn't think she had said anything particularly contentious but then she had never before interviewed a woman who was boasting about having two cocks penetrate her anus.

'PMT?' Lisa suggested.

'No.'

'Man problems? Woman problems? Or are you having a combination of both at the moment?'

'I just asked her if I could lick her pussy,' Tara snapped. She jerked her shoulder away from Lisa's hand. 'That's all I asked. You shouldn't be making such a big deal out of this.'

Lisa blinked and then glanced at Anne. 'Would you like Tara to lick your pussy?' In a matter-of-fact tone she added, 'Tara's pretty damned good. She found my G-spot at the last party where we were together.'

When Tara asked the question, Anne had been astounded that she was being propositioned with such an unexpected intimacy. But, when Lisa made the same offer, Anne considered it seriously. A small voice at the back of her mind insisted that what she was thinking about was absolute madness. But, intrigued by the idea of being so open with her body, and sure the small voice belonged to the same unwanted emotion that had caused so much upset the previous evening, she was sorely tempted to nod. 'If Tara's as good as you say she is, I'd love to have her lick my pussy.'

Tara wasn't looking at her.

Anne didn't know what she had said wrong, or why the situation seemed to be slipping away from her. 'But,' she added quickly, 'if she's genuinely submissive, I'd much prefer to find out what it's like dominating another woman.'

She looked toward Lisa who nodded understanding and rose from Tara's side. In a stern voice, the sort of disciplined tone Anne remembered her strictest school-teachers using, Lisa said, 'You are a submissive, aren't you, Tara?'

'I guess.'

'Then you'll be a submissive for us now.' Lisa grabbed the shoulder of Tara's jacket and shook until she had the woman's attention. She was no longer the caring individual who had tried to coax Tara from her melancholy fugue. She was acting like a ball-breaking bitch. 'Get out of that chair. Remove your jacket, and bend over ready to be spanked.'

Anne watched the scene with growing consternation. She could sense Lisa was grinning behind her authori-tarian mask and Anne trusted her friend enough to believe she knew what she was doing. But the situation was different from anything she had ever encountered and it took an enormous amount of faith to believe she was participating in acceptable behaviour. Tara had already admitted having a submissive streak but Anne did not feel confident enough to pinpoint the difference between consensual domination and unwarranted bullying. She was ready to raise her objections, tell Lisa it didn't matter about Tara proving her submissiveness, when the bespectacled woman pulled herself from the chair. She truculently shrugged off her jacket and then bent over the back of the chair with her bottom sticking high in the air. The rear of her jeans pulled tight against her buttocks and revealed an enviably slender behind.

'Take your jeans off, Tara,' Lisa barked. 'How are we expected to spank your bare bottom if you're still wearing jeans?'

Tara responded immediately.

185

Anne clutched Lisa's arm.

Lisa gave her a reassuring grin. 'I'm not normally into power games,' she whispered. Her breath was warm and moist against the edge of Anne's neck. Her breasts pressed against her arm as the two women huddled together to keep their whispered exchange private. 'I'm definitely not into being submissive,' Lisa confided. 'But, if you've ever wondered what it's like to spank another woman's backside, this is your ideal chance to find out.'

'Are you serious?'

Lisa glanced over at Tara. 'Take them off completely,' she called. 'And then remove your T-shirt. I want to see you naked, you little bitch.'

Anne noticed that Mark and Johnny were watching from their position behind the bar. Neither of them had made a show of shifting position but they had discreetly turned and the conversation between them had trailed to an end. She glanced at her husband and saw he was grinning at her with an expression of encouragement.

'I'm deadly serious,' Lisa hissed in Anne's ear. 'If you've ever wondered what it's like to spank another woman's bottom, this is your golden opportunity. Even if the idea has never crossed your mind, you should give it a shot now. Tara really does love to be punished.'

The words were enough to make Anne's decision for her. Stepping boldly behind Tara, drawing a deep breath, she glanced at Lisa to confirm she was doing things properly. Lisa joined her, and then winced when she cast a glance at Tara's backside. 'What the hell are all these marks, Tara? Who's been whipping you?'

Anne glanced down and was shocked by the sight of the red lines that striped the pale cheeks of the woman's buttocks. The injuries did not look particularly severe but it was obvious they were fading from the torment that they had once been. Anne couldn't bring herself to think how badly they must have stung when they were first inflicted.

'Who's been whipping you?' Lisa barked.

'I was punished earlier today.'

'I can see that,' Lisa agreed. She traced a finger against one of the red lines. Anne watched her follow the path of Tara's marked flesh and, before she realised she was doing it, her own hand was stroking one of the many welts. It was difficult to accept she was touching a submissive woman's bare backside and even harder to believe the pleasure it inspired. A tingle of excitement bristled through her loins and she realised the atmosphere in the house had grown thick with anticipation. The stripe cut across both cheeks and, as Anne traced along the line, her fingers brushed over the closed slit of Tara's shaved pussy. The contact was wickedly exciting, a thrill that she hadn't anticipated, and she was almost shocked enough to snatch her hand away. Deciding she liked the sensations of control and intimacy, she continued to stroke the woman's cleft.

Tara trembled.

'I can see you were punished earlier today,' Lisa repeated. 'I asked who did it. Will you tell me?'

'Do I have to?'

'No. You can just stand there and let Anne spank your backside. Would that suit you better?'

'Yes.'

'OK,' Lisa agreed. Speaking loud enough for Tara to hear, she told Anne, 'Slap her hard. I don't care for submissives who won't answer questions.'

Tara moaned.

Anne stared at the woman's buttocks, not sure how she was now meant to proceed, and glanced at Lisa for help. Obligingly, Lisa raised a hand in the air and mimed the action of driving it down swiftly. Anne shook her head, shocked by the idea of administering the punishment so brutally. Lisa rolled her eyes, grinned amicably and performed the same mime. She nodded as soon as she had finished, as though trying to show she was earnest about what was needed.

187

'That feels nice, mistress,' Tara murmured.

With a start of horror, Anne realised her hand had been resting against the submissive's backside. She hadn't consciously put her fingers there but, while she was silently communicating with Lisa, her hand had strayed as though it had its own agenda. A part of her wanted to snatch the fingers away and recoil from stroking Tara's backside. The instinct could not have been stronger if she had brushed against live electrical wires. But she resisted the impulse and allowed her fingers to linger against the woman's bare flesh. Daringly, she stroked towards the cleft of Tara's buttocks, her nails grazing the delicate skin of the neatly closed pussy lips. 'You've got a beautiful body,' Anne confided.

'Thank you, Mistress Anne.'

Anne came close to laughing when she was addressed with the title. Because Tara wasn't watching her, she was able to contain the mirth behind the back of one hand. She glanced in Mark's direction and could see he was also close to laughing. A part of her wondered if he would still be amused if she spanked Tara's backside. And then, before indecision could get the better of her and spawn enough arguments to make her back out, Anne raised her hand and brought it sharply down on Tara's rear.

The bespectacled woman flinched.

Mark, Johnny and Lisa regarded Anne with expressions of stunned amazement. But she knew that neither her husband nor her friends were as shocked as she had been. Not letting herself think about the actions, raising her hand swiftly and then clapping it down with a brisk and punishing force, she slapped Tara's other buttock and left a blazing red handprint on the cheek.

Tara whimpered.

Instinctively, Anne reached out to touch the woman's pussy. She could feel the smouldering heat that emanated from her sex. When her fingers went to the tightly

188

furled labia they slipped against a smear of dewy wetness. Anne wanted to believe she was only touching a film of perspiration but, when she caught the scent of the viscous fluid, she understood it was the musk of Tara's arousal. 'You're enjoying this,' she gasped. Without thinking, she slapped her hand across Tara's bottom again.

The submissive stiffened and apologised.

Anne glanced at her husband and saw he was no longer smiling in approval but staring in awe. Johnny and Lisa watched intently, their expressions too guarded for her to know whether her actions met with their approval. But, in that instant, Anne realised she didn't care about such minor matters. She was doing what she wanted and thoroughly enjoying the experience. Automatically, she lifted her hand and delivered another slap to Tara's rear.

The taut buttocks trembled beneath the force of the blow.

Anne glanced at the stinging palm of her hand and wondered how it was possible her excitement could grow when she had only slapped her hand against another woman's backside. She couldn't equate arousal with inflicting punishment and was trying to work through the quandary when she realised it didn't matter. The important thing was that she was enjoying herself. The only person suffering (if suffering was the right word) was a woman who got pleasure from pain. It was an aspect of swinging she had never contemplated and she embraced the discovery as though it was a vocation. 'I could have told you to lick my pussy,' she mumbled.

'I would have done it, Mistress Anne,' Tara assured her.

Anne drew a steadying breath. She was trying not to grow giddy on the thrill of power that came from being addressed with such reverence. 'I could have had you down on your knees in front of me, licking my pussy and making me come.'

189

'Yes, please, Mistress Anne,' Tara begged. 'Let me do that for you now. I promise, I'll do it better than anyone has ever done before.'

Anne slapped her hand down with all her force. The impact left a bright red weal on the woman's rear.

Tara gasped with surprise. Lisa stared at Anne with an astonishment that matched Tara's. Glancing over to the bar, Anne could see Mark and Johnny were considering her warily.

Anne ignored them all. 'You'd lick my pussy now if I told you, wouldn't you?' As she barked the question she pushed two fingers against the tight slit of Tara's sex. The lips yielded to her touch. It only took a little pressure and her fingers slipped inside the woman's sex. The tight muscles of Tara's hole squeezed around her. The sensation was exquisite and exhilarating.

'Yes, Mistress Anne. I'll do whatever you ask of me.'

Anne tore her hand away, suddenly frightened she was experiencing too much and too soon. The opportunity of dominating Tara had been an unexpected diversion for the afternoon and a marvellous revelation. But she knew she couldn't continue spanking and fingering the woman for the remainder of the day. Admittedly the party preparations were almost complete but Anne wanted to be a good friend to Lisa and make sure she didn't carry the burden of the party all by herself. Also – and she realised this was the thing that had really stopped her from carrying on – she wanted to know how Mark felt about her exploring a previously untapped dominant streak. She didn't think he would have any objections if it brought her satisfaction. But she wouldn't allow herself to take his opinion for granted. Straightening her shoulders, stepping away from the pert buttocks and marvelling that her blows had caused the blushes on those cheeks, she glanced at Lisa.

Her friend nodded as though she understood Anne's need to end this session of discovery. She stepped to

190

Anne's side, gave her a brief embrace, and then stroked Tara's punished backside.

The submissive stiffened, but she didn't flinch at the touch.

'OK,' Lisa said firmly. 'That was a fun way to get us all in the mood for the party. Thanks for the diversion, Tara. I knew we could count on you to keep us entertained.'

Tara said nothing.

Lisa glanced at Anne and asked, 'Had Tara answered all of the questions for your interview?'

Anne considered saying yes, and then remembered Tara's reticence when answering questions about the forthcoming party. To round the article off she had thought it would be prudent to record Tara's expectations of the party and then compare them to the reality during a second interview, after the event. 'No,' she said sharply. Placing her hand gently on the woman's buttocks, savouring the sensation and the warmth that radiated into her palm, she said, 'Tara, I'd really like to know how you feel about tonight's party.'

Tara moaned. This time she sounded genuinely pained.

Lisa and Anne exchanged a glance.

'Aren't you looking forward to the party?' Anne asked.

'There won't be a party,' Tara snapped viciously. She clapped a hand over her mouth. Glancing back over her shoulder she stared at them miserably. Her frightened eyes said she was horrified that she had just revealed too much.

'What do you mean?' Lisa asked, puzzled. 'You can see the place is ready for a party. All we're short of are the caterers and a few guests and then ...'

'All right!' Tara wailed. This time her cry was filled with distress. 'I admit it. I'm sorry. It was wrong of me. I just thought it was all part of a kinky sex game.'

191

'You admit what?' Anne asked carefully.

Tara stared at Lisa. Tears swelled behind her large glasses, making her eyes swim at the bottom of the huge lenses. She moved out of her submissive position and started to pull her clothes from the floor. 'Becky had Alec and me cancel your caterers,' she mumbled.

'What?'

'You're fucking kidding!' The exclamation came from Johnny as he and Mark raced from the bar. Johnny's face was purple. 'You and Alec did what?'

'And why?' Lisa exploded. 'What advantage could it possibly give any of you to cancel my caterers?'

'Not just the caterers,' Tara wailed. 'Becky had us call about three hundred potential guests and tell them the door charge would be double what you'd originally said.' She sniffed away further tears and shot her gaze from Lisa to Anne. 'I'm sorry.' She sniffed again. 'I wasn't doing it to hurt you. I thought it was just part of Becky's kinky sex game.'

'What does this mean?' Anne wasn't sure she'd followed Tara's revelation. Lisa looked distraught and Johnny's mood was positively thunderous. 'I've heard everything she's said but I don't understand. What is she telling us?'

Tara had stopped crying but Lisa looked set to release her own flood of tears. Lisa rubbed a hand against her forehead and said bitterly, 'It's fairly straightforward. She's telling us that tonight's party is going to be a disaster.'

15

Playroom

The four of them fell into action as though they had planned for just such a calamity. Johnny dialled the number of the caterers and, once they had finished apologising for being duped by the ruse, they contritely explained it was too late for them to cater the party. Hiding his frustration, Johnny ended the call before cursing.

Mark took hold of Lisa's arm. He tugged her to the door and told her to get her mobile phone from her handbag. 'Give it to Anne,' he said quickly. 'She can call all the contacts on your phone and try to rectify some of the damage that's been done.'

'Can't Anne do that from Johnny's phone?' Lisa asked.

'Johnny will be doing the same thing from his phone,' Mark said, glancing in Johnny's direction to confirm this was right. Johnny had already opened his mobile and started dialling. Turning back to Lisa, Mark added, 'Also, you're angry right now. You won't have the impartiality to deliver the simple message that's needed.'

Johnny nodded, pleased that he and Mark were tackling this problem in a similar fashion. He was aware that their collective mood had shifted pace. The relaxed atmosphere of the day was behind them and he felt as though they were now racing to meet an urgent and important deadline. The excitement coursed through his veins, thrilling him and making him want to meet the challenge.

Reluctantly, Lisa passed her phone to Anne. She glanced at Mark and asked, 'Where are we going?'

'You and I are going home. We'll sort out the catering.'

Lisa paused in the doorway, clearly reluctant to leave the party behind. 'Wouldn't you be better taking Anne?'

'I'll need to use your oven as well as my own.' He spoke quickly but with only a slight suggestion of impatience. 'Anne has difficulty finding her way around our kitchen. She'd be truly stuffed if she had to work her way around yours.' He gave a dry laugh and added, 'Johnny would be lost in either room unless he was searching the fridge for beer.'

Johnny grinned, pleased that Mark already knew him so well.

Lisa opened her mouth to raise another objection. Mark spoke quickly over her. 'You can use my mobile to call Johnny or Anne if anything else occurs to us while we're away. But we've got to leave here now if I'm to have half a chance of cooking enough food for this party.'

Lisa looked set to say something else, then her shoulders collapsed in deflated agreement. She blew Johnny a kiss, waved farewell to Anne, and the pair of them were gone. The others heard the roar of Mark's BMW as he gunned the engine, and the spit of gravel being churned as he sped down the path and away from the house. Johnny heard the sounds as a background to his first conversation with a name from the contact list of his mobile.

He was about to dial another number when Tara asked, 'What can I do?'

Anne raised her hand and Johnny had to grab her wrist to stop his neighbour slapping Tara across the face. She glared at him but he didn't let go until she had grudgingly ceased her silent threat. Reminding himself they were trying to control the damage that had been caused, forcing his voice to sound pleasant and non-judgemental, he asked Tara, 'Do you want to help?'

Tara nodded meekly. She stared at Anne with a mixture of reverence and fear.

Johnny guessed that either of those emotions would make her malleable and potentially useful. He supposed the combination could be used to their advantage. Her large eyes were watery behind the lenses of her spectacles. 'Have you got a mobile?' Johnny asked. When she nodded he said, 'Start phoning your swinging contacts. Call as many people as you can remember phoning this morning. Once you've run out of numbers tell me or Anne and we'll pool our resources. But start phoning now.'

'What do I say?'

He glared at her. 'It might be difficult for you, but this time I want you to tell the truth.'

She flinched at the words and looked as if she was about to start crying.

Johnny couldn't feel sympathy for her. But he understood she would be no use to their common cause if he reduced her to a quivering wreck of tears and sobs. Drawing a deep breath and quashing his anger, he said, 'Explain that some malicious twat has been phoning people and telling lies about the door charge for Lisa's party. Tell them you've just heard this scurrilous rumour, and you didn't want *that particular person* to miss *this particular party*. Make it sound as though as you're fizzing at the bung hole with the thought of seeing them here tonight.'

Tara backed away from him. As she retrieved the mobile from her jacket pocket a pack of cigarettes fell to the floor. Johnny picked them up and lit smokes for himself and Anne. To Tara's obvious dismay he put the packet in his own jacket pocket. And, as the three of them began to work their way through the numbers, he prayed there was a chance that they might be able to save the party. At some point the CD player fell silent and the main hall was filled with the sound of keypads being pressed and the chatter of three voices delivering the same script.

'. . . sorry to trouble you like this . . .'

'. . . I don't know if you were thinking of attending Lisa's party tonight . . .'

'. . . some wag has been calling round and saying . . .'

Johnny remained focused on his own words, not daring to listen to the others for fear that he would lose track of what he was saying. Occasionally he would pause between calls and remind Tara and Anne to keep their tone cheerful, and make sure they explained the situation without using vulgarities or accusations. Familiar with a lot of swingers, he understood they could do worse damage to their situation if potential guests thought anything was amiss.

An hour later, the last of the calls had been made.

Johnny had been surprised by the number of people who claimed they had been planning to come regardless of the price increase but, because he was rushing to inform as many people as possible, there was no opportunity to discuss the subject with each individual. Nevertheless, it crossed his mind that if Lisa ever organised another party it could be a lucrative venture. For now, though, the success of future events depended on the evening that lay ahead.

Thinking about Lisa, and remembering how upset she had been when Mark dragged her away, he instinctively dialled her mobile. When Anne, sitting next to him, answered the call, he muttered an embarrassed apology and then phoned Mark's number. 'I just wanted to make sure you were OK,' he told Lisa. 'You weren't the world's happiest bunny when you left here.'

'No time to talk,' Lisa gushed. Instead of sounding distressed or maudlin her voice brimmed with excitement. 'I'm doing things in the kitchen that I didn't know were possible.' She paused, and then giggled in response to something Mark had said in the background. The words were difficult to make out. Behind her the kitchen was deafening with the clank of pans, the sound of boiling water, a running tap and the metallic clatter of cutlery. Johnny grinned when he heard Lisa quietly promise Mark, 'Later.' Speaking to Johnny, still bursting with adrenalin-fuelled enthusiasm, she said, 'Did you know that Mark is an absolute genius?'

'I was the first to spot Mark was a genius,' Johnny snapped. 'Don't think you can take credit for that particular discovery.' Realising he was intruding on her time, and aware that she and Mark would be hard pressed to organise any catering in the limited time available to them, he decided to cut the call short. 'I'll let you two get on with saving the day,' he said firmly. 'Give Mark a kiss from Anne and tell him we all think he's a hero.' They concluded the call with an exchange of 'I love yous' and then he severed the connection.

'Did I just hear you tell your wife to kiss my husband?' Anne asked. She reached into his jacket pocket and retrieved Tara's cigarettes.

Aside from Lisa, Johnny didn't think he could have tolerated anyone invading his personal space without feeling angry or violated. Yet he had no problem with Anne taking the pack of Marlboros and then patting his pants pockets as she searched for a lighter.

'After the way Mark's stepped in to save the day I should have told her to suck his dick,' Johnny responded. They exchanged a glance and both knew that, if Lisa was no longer preoccupied with the fate of her party, there was a strong likelihood that she might already have sucked Mark's dick. When he saw Anne blush, Johnny asked, 'Are you still comfortable with this?'

197

She giggled as she lit her cigarette. 'It's a constant thrill, isn't it? It's nothing like what I expected. It's like opening a door.'

He shrugged, took the lighter from her and lit his own smoke. 'You lost me there,' he admitted. 'Unless you get really excited from the action of opening doors.'

She pushed at him, grinning. 'Mark and I made a conscious decision to try swinging. Our sex life was here . . .' – she lifted a hand so it was on the same level as her breasts – 'and we expected swinging might move it up to here.' She raised the hand to eye-level.

Johnny nodded. What she was saying made sense so far.

'But our expectations were wrong,' Anne explained excitedly. 'It's not a sliding scale where swinging makes things better by a couple of inches.'

Johnny considered making a joke about how a couple of inches could often make things better, and then realised the seriousness of the conversation didn't warrant such levity.

'Instead of this being a measurable scale, it's like opening a door to a whole new world.' She pressed her lips together and looked as if she was trying to find words to better express what she was saying. 'It's like when Dorothy opens the door in *The Wizard of Oz*, and the whole movie goes from black and white to glorious Technicolor.'

'I've a feeling we're not in Kansas anymore,' Johnny said with a grin.

Anne laughed. 'I'd never thought of dominating a woman until I got the chance to spank her.' She nodded in Tara's direction.

Tara tested a smile that they both ignored.

'Tonight's party, if it still happens, should be fun,' Anne continued. 'It should certainly add a few kinks to the learning curve. But it's not what either of us expected when we contemplated swinging. And, while

198

I'd always thought that Mark and I would do our swinging together, I don't mind that he's out of sight with your wife while you and I are here and alone together.' She looked genuinely bewildered as she added, 'This whole experience has turned out to be so much more than I thought it could be.'

In unison they tossed their cigarettes out of the open front door. Johnny reached for her hand and squeezed to offer companionable reassurance. Reminding her they had a change of clothes in one of the upstairs rooms he suggested they should get ready for the party. 'You can make yourself useful and mind the door,' he told Tara. 'If any of the guests arrive early, I want you to greet them pleasantly. Understand? If there are any problems I want you to find me or Anne. I don't trust you to make decisions for the good of the party.'

'I really am sorry for what I did,' Tara said earnestly.

Before Johnny could respond Anne said, 'Well, you're making amends right now, aren't you?'

'There are other ways I could make amends,' Tara said slyly.

Anne blushed and hurried out of the room with Johnny.

They were walking past the playroom when she pulled him to a halt and glanced inside. Ordinarily it would have appeared to be a large room. But the massive bed that now monopolised the floor space – six divans strapped together in a three by two formation and covered by a single sheet – made it look cramped. The décor was heavily accented with reds and oranges, one of the main reasons Lisa had selected it for use as the playroom. With a dim light bulb illuminating the room it looked like an abstract depiction of sexual anticipation. 'This place will be teeming with naked bodies in two hours, won't it?'

He considered his answer honestly. 'If we did a good enough job on the phones, then there's a fair chance that will happen, yes.' Raising an eyebrow, deciding it would not be inappropriate to tease her a little, he asked, 'Will you be one of those naked bodies?'

'I want to be one of them now,' she decided. She didn't wait for his reply. Instead, she simply ran into the room.

He hesitated for a moment and then followed.

Anne was sprawled in the centre of the bed, tossing her clothes aside as she grinned eagerly and expectantly for him. She had been dressed for work, and the underwear she removed was plain and far from glamorous. She peeled white cotton panties away from her hips, removed a plain white T-shirt bra, and then writhed against the bed's vast white sheet. She glanced at Johnny as he started to remove his clothes and asked, 'Lisa won't mind us doing this, will she?'

'Lisa and Mark are probably doing the same thing while they wait for the oven timer to go ping.' He plucked a condom from his pocket and pushed his jeans aside. Tossing the sealed prophylactic on the bed, he climbed towards Anne and took her in his embrace. Her body was filmed with a light sheen of perspiration. He inhaled the scent of clean sweat and fresh arousal. He savoured the way her slender body squirmed against the heat of his hard flesh.

'Will there really be twenty or thirty people on this bed?' Her voice was an incredulous whisper. 'It's hard to imagine so many people on one bed all with the same thing on their minds.'

Johnny lowered his mouth to her left breast, suckling the nipple and enjoying the way she pushed against him. Her thigh rubbed at his erection, then she placed her fingers around the thick, throbbing length. As their caresses grew more intimate he realised she was already quivering with anticipation and excitement.

'The party starts at eight,' he told her. He shaped the words between kisses pressed against her breasts. Pinning her to the bed, taking control of the situation, he drew his tongue down her narrow stomach towards the triangle of curls that concealed her sex. 'If people do come, then by nine o'clock this room will see a dozen couples fucking. By ten o'clock they'll be crammed on here two deep.'

She trembled against him. 'It's hard to imagine,' she whispered.

He agreed. Staring at the vast lake of white sheet surrounding them it was difficult to visualise the room when the bed was hidden beneath a melée of naked flesh. Johnny supposed it was only because he had visited enough playrooms to know what happened that he was able to speak so confidently. 'Will you be coming back here later, around the ten o'clock mark?'

'Christ! Yes,' she said with a laugh. 'I have to see this place when it's full.'

She shifted, pulling herself from beneath him before his mouth had a chance to connect with her sex. He had caught the scent of her pussy before she moved and realised her day had been filled with too much arousal. Aside from working alongside Lisa and preparing the house for the party, he remembered how excited she had looked when she had been spanking Tara. If not for the emergency situation that had necessitated their foursome splitting up, Johnny supposed Anne would have been on the playroom bed with Mark instead of him. If not for that unexpected deviation to their plans, Lisa and he would have probably joined them. The mental image of the four of them together made his erection swell. Anne's lips brushed a liquid kiss against the heat of his cock.

She had placed herself above him, thrusting her musky wetness in his face as she lowered her mouth to his shaft and balls. Her tongue stroked his cock and she repeatedly worked kisses along the sensitive flesh. In return he buried her nose in her scent and drew his tongue through the thatch of curls covering her labia. Because Lisa always kept her sex so smoothly shaved he never failed to take pleasure from the chance to lap at an unshaved cleft. The hairs tickled pleasantly at his nose and jaw, lightly reminding him he was with another woman. Anne was responsive, teasing him as she wriggled closer to his face while concentrating her efforts on licking his length.

He strained to push his face against her, and she tantalised him by constantly pulling herself out of his reach. The most he managed was a cursory brush against her oily labia, or a dry lap at her stiff curls. Eventually, when the torment proved too much, he grabbed her by the waist and forced her to lie down as he climbed above her. Not allowing Anne the chance to catch her breath or squirm away, he thrust his tongue against her hole and lapped at the mingled intoxicating flavours. Her flesh parted easily for him, surprising Johnny with its copious wetness. As he stroked his tongue against her clitoris, he was delighted to hear her groan.

'You're a brute,' she giggled. 'You shouldn't be pinning me to the bed like this.'

'You're a tease,' he returned. 'Dangling your pussy in front of my face and not letting me have a taste.'

'You're tasting it now, aren't you?'

He buried his face back against her, licking and drinking and greedily devouring. She fell briefly silent, stiff against the sheet as he hurried through the pleasurable chore of heightening her excitement. And then her mouth had moved around his shaft again and she was hurrying him to a peak of excitement.

Johnny pulled away gasping.

Anne followed, placing herself over him. She kissed him and the flavour of pre-come glossed her lips. His length twitched. Her fingers wrapped around him and he felt the familiar sensation of a sheath being stroked down his erection. He glanced down and saw she was guiding the end of his shaft to the centre of her sex.

'This will be the first time that you and I have . . .' His voice trailed off as she kissed him again. This time it was a passionate exchange of tongues. Her breasts crushed against his chest. They rolled together for a moment, turning over and over along the length of the vast bed. All the time his shaft rested on the lips of her pussy, never quite pushing inside.

'Yes,' she agreed. 'It's going to be our first time. But I don't think it will be the last, do you?'

Johnny found himself on top. He pushed his hips forward and, without ceremony, buried his length deep inside Anne's sex. It worried him that their use of the playroom might be a bad omen for the party. The beds had been strapped together for twenty or thirty couples to use. Instead it was just him and Anne. He forced the thought from his mind, determined to make Anne happy and find his own pleasure in her satisfaction. The day had been long and fraught with disappointments and upsets. He knew that Anne was experiencing her own learning curve and, while there were other problems they could both worry about, the distraction of discovering each other's bodies seemed far more important.

Anne wrapped her thighs around him and bucked her hips to meet each thrust.

They shifted positions as each tried to outdo the other. Johnny pumped between her legs until the muscles in his thighs grew weary. Anne took advantage of his fatigue and pushed him down on the bed so she could straddle him and ride him from on top. She squatted on her haunches, facing him but leaning back a little. He guessed the end of his cock was stroking the centre of her G-spot. They both moaned and groaned with mounting pleasure, neither of them able to break the spell of the moment by pulling away. Anne gasped her way through an occasional minor climax but, like Johnny, she seemed to be reserving her true energies for later in the evening.

'You're an animal,' he gasped eventually.

'A sloth?' she suggested. 'Or are you calling me a big fat pig?'

He chuckled, and realised it was the first time he had ever laughed with another woman whilst fucking. He and Lisa had attended dozens of parties during their swinging career, and they had been involved in hundreds of one-off encounters. But he was certain that he had never found himself laughing with any other women except Lisa. The mirth came close to making him lose his erection.

Anne squeezed her muscles tight around him as though she sensed he was in danger of slipping away. She pulled him into an affectionate embrace and asked, 'Are you going to come?'

'I was going to ask you the same question.'

She sniffed. 'My last three orgasms don't count for anything?'

'God, but I'm good, aren't I?'

'If not for the fact you're so conceited, you'd be perfect.'

They pulled away from each other with a comfortable camaraderie. Johnny removed his condom and retrieved their clothes while Anne straightened the rumpled sheet. They were both naked as they walked towards the en suite room where their party clothes waited. He felt relaxed and comfortable at her side. The conversation shifted easily to the forthcoming events of the night and, as Johnny quickly showered, Anne busied herself around the bathroom, shaving her legs and reading the labels on Lisa's makeup and perfume. They had just finished dressing for the party when Tara burst into the room.

'I think you'd better come downstairs,' she said quickly.

The urgency in her tone made them both start. They exchanged a panicked glance. 'Is there a problem?' Johnny asked.

Anne was already moving and he hastily followed the two women. He passed Tony Samuels, the elderly man admiring what had been done to his building with a reluctant smile. Debbie stood behind the bar. Looking more resplendent than ever, she served drinks to the handful of guests who were already in the room. She waved at Johnny and Anne when she saw them, her smile no longer frosty.

Johnny waved back, heading towards the door with a feeling of growing anxiety in his stomach. 'What's the problem?' he asked. 'What's happened, Tara?'

'Becky and Alec have just pulled up outside. I didn't know what to do.'

The news struck him like a punch to the stomach. After spending an afternoon trying to sort out the mess that Becky had deliberately made, he wasn't prepared for the woman to brazenly appear at the party. His first instinct was to scream at her and tell her she wasn't welcome. His second instinct was to turn Becky over to Lisa and Anne, although that seemed to be a crueller option than his original idea.

'Is Lisa back yet?' Anne asked.

'She's setting up the catering stuff in the dining room.'

Johnny asked, 'Is Mark with her?'

Tara shrugged and nodded.

He realised she hadn't been introduced to Mark and wouldn't know who he was. 'Tall guy. My height. Smiles too much. Everyone calls him a genius. He was the one who drove Lisa out of here two hours ago.'

'Him?' Tara nodded. 'He was carrying some of the stuff for Lisa.'

Anne nodded, pecked Johnny on the cheek and went to find her husband. Lisa came running back from the dining room, grinning elatedly. It only took a glance for

Johnny to know that his wife had been doing more than cooking with Mark and he flashed his approval with a broad smile. His gaze finally went to her dress and he quietly marvelled at the sexiness she exuded. They embraced, falling comfortably into each other's arms, and murmured soft words of adoration. 'Mark's been impressing you in the kitchen?'

She blushed, but didn't lower her gaze. 'Not just in the kitchen.'

She looked ready to say more when a redhead in a gold leather cat-suit brushed past them and screeched with surprise. 'Hi, Lisa darling!' Becky gestured at the room around them and said, 'This looks absolutely splendid. I'm so happy you finally settled on a place to host this soirée.'

Johnny placed a restraining hand on his wife's arm. He could feel the tension throbbing in her body and knew if Lisa got close to Becky, she would beat the redhead senseless. 'Restraint,' he hissed between clenched teeth. 'Show some restraint. And don't give her the satisfaction of thinking she's beaten you.'

Lisa forced a grin that looked like pure plastic. 'Becky. You look sensational this evening. It's amazing what makeup can cover nowadays, isn't it?'

Johnny gripped her arm more tightly.

Becky's smile faltered as she realised she had been insulted.

Lisa acted as though they were old friends and glanced around the busying hall. 'I'm glad you like this house.' She smiled dangerously. 'It's a far better venue for the party and I only happened on it because some meddling little trollop cancelled the Red Mill for me.'

'Really!' Becky either couldn't act or wasn't bothering to hide behind a façade. 'That's quite shocking,' she said with a smile. 'Any idea who it might have been? I can ostracise them from the party list if you think it will teach them a lesson.'

'I couldn't say who it was,' Lisa started carefully.

Johnny relaxed a little, but he didn't loosen his hold on her arm.

'I think it was the same interfering tart who cancelled my caterers and then called three hundred swingers and told them the door charge here would be extortionate. The bitch really is a nasty piece of work,' Lisa continued blithely. 'And she's going to be thoroughly fucked off when she sees my party has been a success despite her best efforts. She's going to be so fucked off it should add extra wrinkles to her cellulite.'

'It sounds like this has been a terrible time for you,' Becky said stiffly. 'But I'm sure tonight will prove who is able to organise the better party.' She paused, a sly smile spreading across her lips as she added, 'Have you organised entertainment?'

16

In the Mood

'In the Mood' began with a cheery reveille. On a PA system it would have reverberated through the building and echoed over the empty grounds surrounding the party house. Because this version was played on Anne's portable CD player the trumpet call only just managed to fill the hall. But it was still loud enough to capture everyone's attention.

The lights had been muted.

The crowd stood in expectant silence.

And Anne's bowels churned with dread. She tried not to think how she had managed to find herself alone and nearly naked in front of a crowd of strangers. She stood with her shoulders squared and thrown back, allowing the audience to admire her appearance. Her pink hair had been freshly spiked. She wore a long black jacket, one of a dozen identical ones found in the house's storage room. With the buttons open it revealed a glimpse of the naked body beneath. The hold-up stockings had been Lisa's idea, a last-minute accoutrement to which Anne had agreed in the spirit of friendship. The heels, not ideal for dancing, were the shoes she had planned to wear for the party. The thrill of anticipation, a raw sexual tingle that seared through her loins, was outweighed by her dread that things could go shamefully wrong.

She waited for the first strains of the melody itself.

Her cheeks burnt with blushes. Her heartbeat raced so fast and loud she feared she might suddenly collapse and die. It crossed her mind that, if she did die, it would save her the embarrassment of having to continue with the performance. And, as that cheery notion was going through her mind, the reveille began to spiral down with a jazzy flair.

She drew a deep breath and willed the tension to ease from her body.

Her skin was caressed by hundreds of gazes. She glanced around the room at a sea of unfamiliar faces. Expectation, smiles and casual assessments were visible wherever she looked and Anne prayed that she didn't appear half as nervous as she felt. She remained motionless until the first bars of the melody, and then began to dance. She took a daring step forward and allowed the lapels of the jacket to fall open. With the second step she was virtually exposing herself to the entire room.

A whisper of amazement flooded through the building as she revealed that, beneath the jacket, she only wore stockings. Not allowing herself to contemplate her actions, or the audience's response to her nudity, Anne threw herself into performing the jitterbug. It was easier to think about the reasons why she had agreed to dance.

Lisa's panic had seemed insurmountable.

Johnny had made a quick call to Rupert, Amber and Trish and, when there had been no response, drew the same conclusion as the rest of them: Becky had cancelled the entertainment.

'We're fucked,' Lisa snapped. As soon as she had said it, she turned towards the gathering crowd of swingers and hissed, 'I'm going to find Becky and rip her tits off.'

Johnny tried to grab her arm but Lisa shrugged him away. 'I'm serious this time,' she growled. 'I'm going to throttle the bitch.'

In a conciliatory tone Mark asked, 'Is there another way we can get everyone in the mood?'

And that was when Anne had heard herself say, 'I can jitterbug to "In the Mood".' As soon as she had spoken she had bitten her lower lip and tried to recant the exclamation. The memory of dancing for Johnny and Lisa, while it had been fun and led to an entertaining night, still made her feel like the most shameless exhibitionist in the world. The idea of performing that dance for this party of swingers – maybe a more daring version of the dance – left her cold with apprehension.

'You'd do that for me?' Lisa asked.

Anne considered her friend's expression of relief and knew there was no way now she could dash the woman's hopes. Cursing her own stupid mouth for making the suggestion, quietly hoping the world would end or some fortuitous nuclear catastrophe would wipe out mankind and save her the humiliation of having to go ahead, she kept her tone even and confident as she said, 'I'd be happy to.'

Mark studied her with a broad smirk. She was pleased to note her husband did not look as smug when she told him how she thought the dance should progress. Being honest, she thought his apprehension mirrored her own fears. And, at the time, it was a small consolation.

Lisa appeared by her side on the dance floor. They wore identical outfits: long-line jackets over nudity, stockings and heels.

Lisa's natural flair for dancing, and the little tuition that Anne had given her, allowed the two women to move with choreographed unity. Each time Lisa threw out a kick, Anne could see the hem of the jacket sliding back. The movement revealed the woman's long, shapely legs and exposed a fleeting glimpse of her pussy. Because they were performing the same steps, Anne knew that she must be displaying herself with equal abandon.

The thought made her pulse race.

As they performed a shoulder roll, wriggling their bottoms backward and supposedly offering a glimpse of cleavage, she understood there were no longer any secrets of her body that had not been seen by the audience. Arousal surged through her with the force of a lightning bolt. She almost faltered in her steps as the rush of excitement left her weak, trembling and in need of satisfaction.

Lisa blew her a kiss as they danced.

Anne caught the shine in the woman's eyes and for an instant she thought she could read Lisa's mind. She didn't know if it was possible to discern so much from a single glance, or if she was merely attributing thoughts that she hoped were there, but she felt sure her friend was thinking about that night less than a week ago when Anne had said, 'I've always wanted to do something bold like dancing near-naked in front of a group of strangers.' She grinned and made each movement that little bit more excessive. Each shoulder roll revealed a less ambiguous glint of cleavage. Every kick allowed the audience a moment longer to gaze at her legs, breasts and unshaved cleft. Aware that Lisa was following her lead, Anne watched her friend and realised that together they were providing a truly exhibitionist display.

Johnny and Mark appeared by their sides.

They had identical jackets to those that Lisa and Anne had found and, although they were shirtless, they wore dark pants and black shoes. Anne conceded that neither of them was a great dancer but she thought they went through the moves with enough confidence that no one would notice their steps were out of sequence. Lisa danced the middle eight with Johnny while Anne faced Mark for that portion of the music.

In her husband's loose embrace, with a crowd of strangers watching, she daringly kissed him. Mark responded eagerly, one hand falling to her bare breast. Because they had rehearsed this move, Anne knew that Johnny and Lisa would be enjoying the same moment's intimacy.

As the music reached another crescendo, they exchanged partners and Mark kissed Lisa while Johnny kissed Anne. As Mark had done, Johnny stroked his thumb over the stiff thrust of Anne's nipple. For some reason she couldn't fathom, Anne thought the caress was more exciting than when Mark had touched her. She supposed the added stimulus of the audience had been exciting but, now they knew she was not exclusively reserved for the hands of her husband, she was presenting a side of herself that no one had ever seen before.

The audience clapped hands and tapped feet in time to the music. Although she was trying to concentrate on her own performance, and willing herself not to worry about how the others were faring, Anne found that her observation skills had hit overdrive. She could see the way Mark and Lisa embraced, their movements a perfect blend of jitterbug and foreplay. Johnny held Anne with a similar degree of intimacy, swirling her around the makeshift dance floor to the approving cheers of the audience. Women in the front row were imitating Anne's dance steps and the simple moves were replicated and mutated into something more flagrant with each interpretation.

When the middle eight was finished, Tara and Debbie joined their foursome. They had also found matching jackets, making the six of them look like a professional troupe. Debbie's movements were stilted but Anne thought the woman's stunning appearance made up for her lack of skills as a dancer. Tara was a little more capable at performing the jitterbug and, because she showed off such a perfect body with each emboldened step, her moves generated spontaneous applause and wolf-whistles.

The six of them danced together for the final bars of the music. Debbie and Tara were enviably shameless in the way they revealed themselves to the audience. Although Anne knew she was centre stage she was grateful to have Lisa by her side because she felt that eased some of the pressure. She turned to face her friend and saw a questioning smile in the woman's gaze.

Again, as though they shared some form of telepathy, Anne understood exactly what the woman was thinking just by staring into her eyes. She almost shrank from the boldness of the suggestion but, knowing it would be the perfect conclusion to the number, she nodded agreement. She threw herself into the final bars with renewed vigour. Sweating from the rush of arousal, exertion and excitement, she listened as the tune spiralled up through one octave, into another and on to the next. The music raced towards a shrill crescendo, horns and woodwinds musically battling for the final word.

As the final sting was played Anne and Lisa removed their jackets.

They stood in front of a cheering crowd wearing only stockings, heels and satisfied grins. The CD was about to move to the next track, but mercifully Tara disconnected the player before another jive tune could force Anne to remain in the spotlight.

Lisa embraced her while Debbie slipped away from the dance floor and Mark went to turn on the house lights. Johnny stepped in front of his wife and waved his hands for the attention of the audience.

'Thank you, ladies and gentleman,' Johnny called.

He gestured for the applause to finish but without any real enthusiasm. Anne guessed that he was happy to have broken the ice of the party. She gave Lisa a kiss and then told her to get herself properly dressed. When her friend started to thank her, Anne silenced her with another kiss and said they would talk later. Lisa nodded agreement and disappeared.

'I hope that got you *in the mood*,' Johnny told his audience. He paused, waiting for laughter. When no one responded he carried on cheerfully. 'I know it's worked for me. I won't bore any of you with the rules for this evening, but that's mainly because there aren't any . . .'

The line got a small laugh.

'. . . I'll just let you know there's a swimming pool out the back. There are canapés in the dining room, and there's a bar in the corner over there.' He pointed towards the bar. Debbie and Tara were already in place serving drinks. They waved brightly back at him. 'We've got a playroom upstairs, as well as some private rooms for the more prudish . . .'

Another titter of laughter.

'. . . and I sincerely hope you'll all have a good time this evening. Anyone with any questions, just come and ask one of us who've been dancing here . . .'

His voice trailed away. Mark was taking Anne in his embrace, smothering her with kisses and telling her how much she had excited him with her dance. His hands slipped easily against her bare skin. She could feel the hardness of his erection pressing at her through his pants. And she knew they wanted each other with equal urgency. The excitement that raged in her loins was now so strong it seared like liquid fire. And she told him she needed to have him.

'You've come around to the idea of this swinging?' he grinned.

She remembered their conversation of the night before. A light blush coloured her cheeks as she admitted, 'I don't know if it's what I really want. But I'm prepared to give it a good try before I decide one way or the other.'

He kissed her again. His hand was upon her breast as Johnny continued to regale the audience with light banter. A crowd of onlookers watched Anne being fondled by her husband. And she understood, despite what she had just told her husband, she had already made up her mind how she felt about swinging.

17

Queen of the Party

Lisa wouldn't let herself think about Becky. After all that the woman had done to spoil her party, Lisa wasn't going to make the woman victorious by brooding on her wickedness. It took a strong effort of will – an effort she had to renew each time she heard the redhead's simpering laughter or caught sight of her gold leather cat-suit – but Lisa prided herself on having a strong will. And with so much going on around her the trick of distracting herself was comparatively easy.

Debbie had organised drinks for the dancers. Tara served them with another apology. Lisa accepted her bottle of lager and told Tara to shut up. She clung to Johnny, relieved to be back by his side and thankful that the evening had started with a successful opening. Couples milled around them, moving between the bar and the dining room, chattering easily together. When Lisa got round to putting the CD player back on, filling the room with a random selection of Elvis hits, she quietly prayed the evening would be a triumph.

There looked to be in excess of a hundred couples in the hall.

The makeshift dance floor remained empty, save for a handful of couples who smooched lovingly together. Hands roved eagerly over lightly clad bodies. There was

216

bare flesh everywhere. Lisa saw one woman dance with two men and, untroubled by the fact that there were so many others in attendance, step out of the dress she had been wearing. Naked save for a thong and heels, she continued to writhe and roll in time to 'All Shook Up'. Watching the other couples mould together, Lisa couldn't decide if they were genuinely dancing or casually fucking. Her chest momentarily tightened and she realised arousal had pinched her nipples hard. Unaware that she was doing it, she rolled the wedding band around her finger. The diamond-cut facets sparkled in the light from the great chandelier.

A shriek of hateful laughter made her turn. She saw the bitch in the gold cat-suit. Lisa's forehead wrinkled as she glowered in Becky's direction.

Johnny tightened his grip around her waist. 'Do you want me to throw her out?'

Lisa shook her head. 'That would look petty.'

He considered this for a moment. 'I could go outside and piss in her petrol tank.'

'That's a nice thought. I'm barely going to see you tonight, am I?'

He frowned. 'A good host and hostess would cover more ground if they split up.'

She nodded and squeezed a companionable embrace from him before letting him go. 'Take Tara to the side of the swimming pool,' she decided. 'Make an announcement here, in the centre of the room, before you go. Offer her up as a spanking girl for any woman who wants to try her hand at slapping bare buttocks. That sort of diversion always causes a stir. I'm going to see if I can get something kinky going in the dining room.'

Johnny nodded. He reached across the bar to take Tara's hand.

Debbie said, 'You can't have Tara. I need her here behind the bar with me.'

Lisa glared at her.

Debbie shrugged. 'It's a busy bar. It'll need two of us working it.'

Lisa started to speak, not sure if she was going to plead with Debbie to try and manage on her own or explain that the demand for drinks would die off within half an hour as the guests found other ways to entertain themselves. She didn't get the chance to say any words.

'May I help behind the bar?'

She turned to see Tony Samuels, looking surprisingly resplendent in a blazer and bow tie. Delighted, Lisa smiled and kissed his cheek. He embraced her lightly and told her the dance routine had been stunning. As soon as he repeated his offer, Lisa installed him behind the bar alongside Debbie. She pushed Tara into her husband's arms. 'Let's get the party started,' she suggested.

Anne knew she was going to come hard.

Doggie-style had always been her favourite position and, after Mark had pumped into her for twenty minutes in the centre of the playroom bed, she was no longer able to contain the explosion.

It had been an electrifying experience dancing in front of strangers. The knowledge that they were attending a swingers' party had fuelled a fantastic heat in her loins, and Mark's skill as a lover was indisputable. Each time he pushed into her, filling her tiny hole with his huge length, she crept closer to the moment of release. He rode her at a tempo that she always enjoyed and with constant consideration for her needs. His hands touched her hips, buttocks, waist and breasts. Every caress was designed to heighten her pleasure, and each time he murmured her name and his love, Anne's climax inched nearer.

But because they were in the playroom she realised other factors were exacerbating her arousal.

This was the room where she and Johnny had whiled away an hour before the party had properly begun. The fiery colours on the wall created a mood of hedonistic abandon that she felt honour-bound to emulate. The Lords of Acid music, loud, raucous and unmelodic, was the perfect backdrop to her escalating excitement. With every passing minute another couple joined them on the bed and began fucking by their side.

A blonde man and woman entered first, stepping casually out of their clothes and smiling a pleasant greeting in the direction of Anne and Mark. It seemed insane to be exchanging polite nods while her husband pounded in and out of her pussy. Anne wondered if it was that sense of unreality that made her pleasure so extreme. The pair continued to watch her and Mark until they were undressed. The woman's eyes, large dark orbs, were almost mesmerising.

Anne caught herself gazing at their unclothed bodies with too much intensity. The blonde had trimmed her pubic hair to a thin tuft just above the lips of her sex. Her partner was free from hair around his balls and cock, making his length seem even more imposing than it already was. Anne's eyes grew wider as she stared at the couple, and then she caught her breath in surprise as the woman went down on her partner and began to suck his erection.

Her sex was molten around Mark's shaft.

She basked in the glorious pleasure of Mark slipping in and out of her hole while watching a pretty blonde smooth her lips along a stranger's erection. The pair were close enough that she could have participated had she wanted. Without asking her husband to change position, Anne could have reached out and stroked the blonde's cheek or shoulder, or the man's thigh or cock. The idea of doing something so daring inspired another shiver to tremble through her loins.

Mark ploughed in and out of her with furious lunges that pushed her close to the brink of release. She was almost on the verge of screaming with ecstasy when another couple entered the room and joined them on the bed. Again she could feel herself under the scrutiny of strangers, unknown eyes voyeuristically enjoying her pleasure. The sensation was a paradox: she didn't want to be the centre of attention but was aroused by the interest.

Each time she moaned, she noticed one of the others would smile in response. Every time Mark touched her in a different way, approval glinted in the grins of those around her. Other couples joined them, filling the bed but always making space for the next couple that came along. And, as Mark continued riding her, Anne realised she was also watching the others.

The blonde woman continued to suck on the smooth length of her partner's shaved cock. Her ripe lips encircled him and worked their way lazily up and down his stiff flesh. Instead of considering her partner, or concentrating on the cock in her mouth, the blonde met Anne's gaze in a playful challenge. Her full lips tried hard to force a smile around the erection they held.

Another couple rolled close to Mark and Anne, already fucking, and gasping and grunting with every penetration. Anne wondered if there was anything theatrical about their sound effects, or if they were simply giving themselves to the passion of the moment. When she saw the thickness of the man's shaft as it squeezed into his partner's tight cleft, she realised the excessive sounds could very well be genuine.

The air was thickened with the scents of naked flesh and wet pussies.

Aside from the creaking of bedsprings, the moans, sighs and slurps of couples melding together filled the room. Mark became more vigorous and, as she realised they were now sandwiched between two couples, Anne could feel a blistering wave of arousal soar through her frame. She struggled to hold her climax back, not wanting to appear theatrical with her orgasm, and anxious to hold off from the pinnacle of pleasure until she was sure her body was ready for the release.

And then the orgasm was forced from her. He bucked his hips forward with a passionate thrust and Anne squealed as the pleasure trembled through her body. She tried to remain where she was, anxious not to interrupt anyone else on the playroom bed, but the strength of the climax made her pull away from her husband and collapse against a neighbouring couple.

The pair grinned down at her. Their smiles were approving.

Anne realised her face was close to a woman's pert buttocks and she could see a thick, sheathed cock sliding in and out of flushed labia. The pink lips were glossed with arousal. The scent was intoxicating. The sights and sounds were too much and an echo of the orgasm flooded through her loins. She pulled herself away from the pair and found herself being kissed, hugged and caressed by her husband.

'What did you think of the playroom?' Mark asked.

He sounded as breathless as she felt. Anne grinned at him, realised the playroom was a much more satisfying experience when it was busy and decided she would tell him as much when they got outside. But as they started trying to make their way off the bed, moving over and through a sea of bodies, the enormity of what she was seeing made her forget about conversation. They had been the first couple on the bed when the party started, but there were now at least thirty naked figures lying there. The majority were fucking as couples but she saw some triples intertwined, a pair of women in one corner and another *ménage à trois* where two females were gobbling the same man's cock. Fingers plundered pussies as cocks were licked and sucked. Kisses were exchanged between pairs and triples. Bare breasts were crushed against naked chests or suckled, kneaded and teased. Again the pungent scent of sex touched her

221

nostrils and she didn't know whether the smell was the most exciting thing she had ever inhaled or the most frightening.

'I think I need a drink,' she told Mark.

He found her jacket on the floor and draped it over her shoulders. 'I'll take you to the bar,' he promised.

Johnny had never considered himself to be any sort of public speaker, yet he found it easy to hold the attention of his audience on this occasion. Standing by the side of the pool, barking 'Step right up! Step right up!', he thought he had found the mood of the party.

The pool room was a vast and brightly lit conservatory. Dusk was starting to settle outside, an amber sun sizzling behind an ebony landscape of hills and trees. But the dramatic sight had faded to a pastel painting on the glass walls now that the sodium lights blazed down. The tart scent of chlorine was a tang in his nostrils. The lap of water echoed hollowly from the tiles and windows. Chairs and tables ran along both lengths of the Olympic-sized pool. And Johnny encouraged his audience to, 'Gather round and step right up!' as he urged Tara to remove her jacket and bend over.

She really did have the most amazing backside and he wondered if that might be part of the reason he had cultivated such interest. As she bent over, legs straight, hands grasping her ankles, she presented a truly exciting spectacle. The whip marks she had sported earlier had vanished. Anne's handprints no longer reddened her skin. She presented a pair of peachlike orbs split by the smoothest cleft he had ever seen. Her outer labia sat close together, completely hiding her inner lips and the true mysteries of her sex.

Johnny landed his hand firmly on her rump and called, 'Who's going to be the first lady to take a slap at this young woman's backside?' He tickled his finger against the centre of her pussy, forcing Tara to shiver.

The audience around him grinned but no one stepped forward to take up his offer. His hand continued to rove over Tara's flesh, teasing the centre of her sex. All the time he maintained a patter of encouragement as he scanned the audience for a familiar face or someone with an expression of obvious curiosity.

The movement of a gold leather cat-suit snatched his attention to Becky. His automatic anger was replaced by a sudden revelation of opportunity. Not sure what he could do, but only certain it was right, he called to her to join him at the side of the pool. 'Becky, sweetheart! Becky, queen of swingers' parties! Come here, show everyone how to properly spank a woman's backside.'

Heads whirled in Becky's direction and Johnny grinned when he saw he had put her in an uncomfortable position. He didn't consider himself a malicious person but, after the torment Becky had inflicted on Lisa, he figured she deserved a little discomfort.

'Come on up here, Becky!' he cried cheerfully.

'I . . . I can't,' she stammered.

Johnny acted as though he hadn't heard her demurral. The broadening crowd were already cheering her on, clapping hands and coaxing her towards Johnny's side. 'Come on up here, Becky, sweetheart,' he called. 'Show these people how you'd spank Tara's lovely pert bottom.'

'Not her,' Tara pleaded softly. 'She'll kill me if she finds out that I've told tales on her.'

Johnny soothed her to silence by patting her rump. With his other hand he gestured to Becky to join them. Unable to back away from the demonstration, urged on by the crowd and too conscious of her self-image to renege, Becky slipped to his side and flexed a tight smile. Her teeth were gritted so hard Johnny could almost hear the enamel being chipped away. 'This isn't funny,' she whispered.

Her lips didn't move and he quietly marvelled at her ventriloquism. Not trusting himself to be so adept,

Johnny lowered his face into the curls over her ear and whispered, 'It wasn't funny when you tried to spoil Lisa's party. Does Alec know how much of his money you spent cancelling the Red Mill?'

Becky glared at him so hotly there was no need for her to answer the question. His grin grew broader and more genial as hers became strained. He moved his face away from her ear, no longer worried if the closest members of the audience caught his words. 'I have the most efficient secretary,' he explained. 'And she has a very persuasive way about her when she sets her mind to discovering a particular detail.'

'Alec won't say a word to me, even if you tell him,' Becky hissed.

'No,' Johnny agreed. 'And he probably won't say anything if he finds out what you paid to cancel The Duelling Dildos.'

'You shouldn't have told her about that,' Tara mumbled.

Becky glowered at him, but this time she extended her glare to include Tara's backside.

Johnny laughed as he watched Becky's composure crumble. 'Tara told me about it earlier,' he explained cheerfully. 'She's helped us put together a picture of what you've been up to.'

'You little fuckwit,' Becky hissed.

A woman close to Johnny and Becky gasped.

A male voice behind her cried, 'Spank her, Becky! Show us how it's done!'

'Don't let her hit me, Johnny,' Tara whispered. 'She hurts when she's just playing. In this mood she'll tear me apart.'

Johnny stepped back from Tara's side and gestured at the inviting plain of her buttocks. Becky glared at him with so much vitriol he wondered if she might strike him instead of the submissive. Raising his voice so the large crowd could hear, he called, 'Watch this carefully, ladies

224

and gentlemen. Becky's a mistress in the art of domination. This is how you should spank a submissive's backside.'

'Please, Johnny,' Tara hissed. She let go of one of her ankles and reached out for him. 'I've said I'm sorry. I really meant it. Don't let Becky hurt me.'

He took the hand that reached for him and patted it reassuringly.

Becky took centre stage and waved for the audience. In her ventriloquist's whisper she said, 'I'm going to make her pay for this now. I'll deal with you and your wife later.' Raising her hand high in the air, grimacing with the effort she invested, Becky hurled her open palm down towards Tara's exposed backside.

Johnny waited until the last moment and then pulled Tara out of harm's way. She was close to the edge of the pool and, if his grip hadn't been strong, she would have fallen into the water.

Becky was not so fortunate.

Her hand continued to descend, smashing through the air where Tara's bottom had been and continuing downward. Becky's gold heels were designed to look good with the leather cat-suit but they offered little security for poolside use. As Becky's balance shifted they refused to support her. Someone in the audience saw what was going to happen before the redhead went face first into the water. They shrieked with surprise.

But, as the sound of Becky splashing into the deep end echoed through the pool room, it was a wave of mirth rather than horror that rippled through the crowd. By the time Becky had pushed herself to the surface, the conservatory windows rattled with the audience's cheers, applause and laughter.

'Man overboard!' Johnny shouted, earning another wave of laughter. He glanced down at Becky and cried, 'I hope that suit's not real gold. You'll go down like the bloody Titanic!' He could think of a dozen more quips, each one designed to ridicule her and all of them to be repeated at every party she threw in the future. *Is your pussy wet? You've made a big splash at this party! I had no idea you were into watersports! Is that how you properly spank a woman? The rest of us must have been doing it wrong!* But because he wanted people to remember her misfortune and not his vicious tongue, he forced himself to stay silent. Unable to suppress his grin, he hunkered down to his haunches and extended a hand to help Becky from the pool.

She slashed an angry palm through the water, splashing him with a harmless spray. He laughed and stood up again.

'That was Becky!' Johnny said loudly. He watched as she swam gracelessly to the opposite side of the pool. 'Can we have a big round of applause for her sportsmanship?' The ripple of handclaps was louder and stronger than he had expected and Johnny wondered if there were others in the audience who were equally happy to see the redhead suffer a public embarrassment. Knowing that he needed to keep the crowd entertained, Johnny wouldn't allow himself to dwell on the thought. 'Becky was showing you the wrong way to spank Tara's bottom,' he said quickly. 'Now can I please have someone up here to demonstrate the right way? Don't crowd me. We don't want any more slip-ups, do we?' He pointed to a brunette he recognised and said, 'Viv? Are you going to do the honours?'

And, as Viv took her place by his side, Tara squeezed past Johnny, kissed him on the cheek and whispered, 'Thank you.'

Mark stood in a corner of the dining room talking with Dawn and Kelly. Lisa had introduced him to the room as 'the man responsible for the evening's culinary delights', and the two women were ostensibly trying to get recipes and cooking tips from him.

Dawn was stocky and blessed with a pretty face. She wore a see-through blouse that revealed the stiff tips of her nipples and the shadows of her areolae. As she spoke with Mark her fingers constantly reached for the lapels of his jacket or the cuff of his sleeve. She rolled a carrot stick against her lower lip and asked him about his béarnaise sauce.

Kelly was more intrusive, pressing herself against Mark, stroking his cheek and taking every opportunity to show that her open jacket revealed nothing but bare flesh beneath. A slender brunette, she constantly fixed him with her most winsome smile and asked if he might be available to join her and her husband in one of the private rooms.

From the other side of the room, Anne watched her husband with an encouraging grin. Lisa was by her side and, remembering Johnny's quote from earlier in the day, she said, 'I've a feeling we're not in Kansas anymore.'

Lisa smiled despite herself. 'Don't try and cheer me up,' she complained. 'I'm still pissed at Johnny for throwing Becky in the pool.' She rolled her eyes with frustration, stamped her foot against the floor and said, 'Why couldn't he have waited until I was there to watch? That was so bloody typical of him. I really am angry with the bastard.'

'You would have held Becky's head under,' Anne said dryly.

'Only until the bubbles stopped rising,' Lisa admitted. She took a consoling swig at her bottle of beer and shook the bad mood away with a shiver. 'I'm taking solace from the fact her leather cat-suit is ruined.'

'You have a streak of kindness that you keep hidden from most of the world.'

Lisa shook her head. 'You sound like Johnny some-times. I don't know whether that's a good thing or a bad one.' Grinning she raised the bottle high so Mark could see her saluting him.

He looked more comfortable now, responding to the tactile intrusion of both women by placing an arm on the shoulder of each. Trapped between the pair he looked like some male model on a photo-shoot, caught between a pair of seductive temptresses. And while Anne saw that neither Dawn nor Kelly would ever be mistaken for a supermodel, she thought their lack of glamour made them seem more sexually arousing. Trembling a little, she sighed and glanced at Lisa. 'How long did it take you to get used to these parties?'

'I don't think you ever get used to the parties,' Lisa reflected. 'If you do, you move on to something more exciting. Like watching soap operas or collecting stamps.'

'But—' Anne paused, frowned and shook her head. 'Why aren't I jealous? At any other party I would scratch the faces of two near-naked women who were pushing themselves at my husband. Dawn and Kelly are both flirting with him, flaunting themselves for him and virtually offering it on a plate, and I'm waiting to see which one of them gets lucky.'

Lisa laughed and squeezed into her embrace.

Anne was surprised how good it felt to have the other woman in her arms. Lisa still wore the jacket she had used for the dance routine and, when it slipped open, Anne found her body being caressed by the woman's bare skin. It was instinctive to reach for her waist, stroke down to the curve of her hips and lower her fingers to the wet flesh between her legs. As their embrace became more intimate their legs intertwined and they rubbed stockings together.

'You do know he's going to fuck both of them, don't you?' Lisa whispered.

Anne thought the woman's words were an echo of her own thoughts. Yet, while she hadn't known how to respond to the notion when it bounced hollowly around her mind, Lisa's husky suggestion made her realise the prospect excited her. Mark would be sandwiched between the two women. The chances were good that he would lick the pussy of one while fucking the other. Both women would have their mouths around his lips, erection and balls. And the idea only fuelled liquid heat between her thighs. More arousing still was the knowledge that he would share every lurid detail with her when they were next alone together. The thought made her inner muscles tremble.

'There are plenty of people here who can wax lyrical about guilt and jealousy, and how they've risen above it,' Lisa gasped. 'And if you want your tits bored off, I'll find one of them and let them talk to you for the remainder of the night.' She stopped speaking and lowered her mouth to Anne's breast. Taking a nipple between her lips, she sucked and nibbled until Anne sobbed. Lisa broke the contact to move her lips close to Anne's ear. Her fingers stroked the wet flesh of the stiff nipple as she spoke. 'The truth is that you love Mark, just like I love Johnny. You love him without condition or reservation. If he's happy – you're happy. If you're happy – he's happy. You know your mutual love isn't affected by what goes in your pussy. Just like he knows it's not harmed by where he puts his cock. You're both big enough to understand that and smart enough to use it for your personal satisfaction.'

'Wow,' Anne mumbled. She didn't know if the exclamation came from Lisa's insight or the pleasure she was experiencing at her breast. A part of her was willing to describe either as being a revelatory experience. 'I wish I had my notepad and pen,' she murmured. 'I could have used that quote for my article.'

Lisa pulled Anne out of the dining room. 'Follow me,' she breathed huskily. 'If you're in a mood to thoroughly research your article, I've got something you have to take down.'

* * *

Johnny ambled easily through the party, enjoying the freedom of being one of the hosts. Ordinarily it was expected etiquette for a couple to remain in fairly close proximity while they partied. Exchanges were often made, but even then it was the done thing for a couple to remain as a couple. The last party he had attended – one of Becky's, he remembered coldly – had proved to be an exception because he had spent most of the night with Viv while Lisa had spent a happy evening catching up with some old acquaintances.

Yet this evening, now that Tara's punishment by the pool was finished, he was free to go wherever he wanted with whoever would have him. He saw Mark stumble up the stairs, trapped between a pair of women, and grinned at the way they were both caressing him. The two men exchanged cordial nods but Mark made no invitation for Johnny to join him and Johnny had no desire to intrude on their threesome.

'Mr West?'

He looked up from his reverie to see Tony Samuels standing before him. 'Call me Johnny. How can I help?'

'The young lady serving drinks,' Samuels began. 'Deborah.'

Johnny nodded, encouraging him to continue.

'I've asked her a question but she says I need to consult with you before she can say yes.'

Johnny frowned, not sure what Samuels was talking about but uncomfortable with the idea of suddenly being considered Debbie's guardian. He glanced down at the bar and saw the blonde grinning up at him. She waved, the gesture surprisingly impish for Debbie. His unease grew stronger. 'What's the question, Tony? I'll give it my fullest consideration.'

Samuels cleared his throat. 'Deborah's accepted an invitation to come and work for me. She knows your company expect her to give a month's notice but I've asked her if she can start work in my office on Monday morning. She says the final decision on that matter is yours.'

Johnny considered his answer for a full minute. He kept his emotions concealed behind a mask of contemplation, not sure if he was happy that Debbie had found alternative employment or sorry that she would no longer be working by his side. He listened to the shrieks of elation around him and eventually made up his mind. 'Debbie can start working for you on Monday,' he agreed. 'But would it be OK with you if she arrives at your office after lunch?'

Samuels shook Johnny's hand and, with the agreement confirmed, hurried down the stairs to tell Debbie the good news. Her face broke into a beautiful smile when Samuels passed the message on and she waggled a playful finger in Johnny's direction. He grinned at her and began patting his pockets for the pack of cigarettes he had stolen from Tara. From the galleried landing he saw couples lazily enjoying the freedom of the evening, chatting sociably, dancing erotically and fucking crazily. No one seemed troubled by what their neighbour was doing and the most outrageous acts of exhibitionism were greeted with little more than approving nods or discreet smiles of acknowledgement.

In short, he thought proudly, his wife's party was a success.

The realisation had barely finished lifting his spirits when he heard a scream from a room behind him. Although Elvis still sang downstairs, and the Lords of Acid continued to shriek in the playroom, he could hear enough of the cry to feel alarm. He also knew, instinctively and with a frisson of horror, that the woman in pain was his wife.

'They call him the donkey,' Lisa told Anne.

'They call me Trevor,' the donkey corrected. 'It's only nymphos like Lisa who call me the donkey.' The four of

231

them had retired to a private room on the first floor. If Lisa had thought the party would be this successful she would have organised more of the private rooms to be available. As she and Anne searched for Trevor, Lisa had seen that the playroom was a throng of sweating naked bodies. In all the parties she had ever attended, she had never seen so many gathered on one bed. The sight was astounding. Bare buttocks, breasts, balls and backsides were blatantly visible in the dim lighting. If it hadn't been for the wail of the Lords of Acid, she might have considered taking Anne there so they could experience the pleasure of having their bodies mauled by a couple of hundred naked strangers. The prospect filled her with conflicting sensations of disgust and excitement. But, before she had a chance to brood on which emotion won, she saw Trevor and his wife and realised the playroom was no longer a consideration.

Hastily, before they could escape, she pulled them into the sanctuary of an empty room. 'I need to introduce your husband to my friend,' Lisa explained.

'Introduce?' Trevor's wife queried. Her lips tilted into a thin smile. Her eyes sparkled with obvious enjoyment. 'How terribly formal of you, Lisa,' she breathed. Smiling at Anne, she added, 'I loved the way you jitterbugged. Old-fashioned dancing is so in vogue at the moment. Could you teach me how to do that, perchance?'

Lisa rolled her eyes. 'For fuck's sake, Victoria,' she snapped. 'We're both chomping at the bit to get our hands on your husband. Stop being such a pussy teaser and get him out of his clothes.'

'My, my!' Victoria chided. 'You're quite impatient this evening, Lisa. I'm almost sorry I defended you against the catcalls of that vicious little trollop Rebecca.'

Lisa's interest in the donkey vanished.

'What's that bitch saying now?'

232

'Nothing for you to worry your pretty little head about,' Victoria soothed. She patted Lisa's cheek and grinned. 'I met her when she was peeling that ghastly cat-suit from her body. Did you know the silly little bitch tripped and fell into the pool? Everyone's talking about it.' She paused, flashed a smile and amended, 'Well, everyone who isn't laughing about it is talking about it. Someone said it was nice to see her splashing out on a party. Isn't that the funniest thing you've ever heard?'

'Yes,' Lisa hissed. 'My sides are hurting from laughing so much. What's the bitch said about me?'

Victoria sniffed. 'Rebecca was whining about this party, telling anyone who would listen that it was a failure and a huge disappointment.'

Lisa's hands balled into fists. Before she could turn to the door Victoria had placed a hand on her arm.

'She had quite a crowd of people around while she was saying these scurrilous untruths. And she was looking at me as though she expected me to back her up. But I didn't. I waited until she'd fallen silent, and then I told her not to be so wet.' Victoria's smile blossomed again and she added, 'I'm surprised you didn't hear the roar of laughter.'

'If your husband's cock wasn't so appealing,' Lisa began, 'I think I could kiss you.'

Victoria considered her in silence for a beat. Glancing past Lisa she said, 'You might have to kiss me. It looks like your friend is already making use of my husband's cock.'

Dawn told Mark she had to fuck him.

Kelly had stayed with them for a while but, because she said she was ideally looking for a man who wanted to be with her and her husband, she thought it unfair to spoil Mark and Dawn's time together. They had exchanged mobile numbers and Mark had promised he would contact her with the recipe for his béarnaise sauce. Kelly had grinned and said that sounded like an appetising offer.

And then she left Mark and Dawn together in a private room. They weren't technically alone. Not only was the door open, allowing every passing guest to glance inside and see their bare bodies, there was also another couple sitting in the corner of the room, attentively watching. Dawn had described them as soft-swingers, explained to Mark that they liked to watch but never touched, and told him there were several couples like that at every swinging party.

Untroubled by the pair, Mark had begun to excite Dawn with a series of passionate kisses. He wanted to believe he was the world's most proficient lover but, analysing the situation honestly, he knew it was the atmosphere of the party that excited Dawn. She was an attractive woman, enjoying the attention of a comparative stranger, and she would undoubtedly share every lurid detail of this encounter with her partner when they were next together.

Her labia were soft to his tongue. As he kissed the sweet musk away from her hole he understood that she would later get more from this moment than he could ever give her. The thought didn't trouble him because he supposed the same thing could be said for himself and Anne. Whatever she was doing now – and he knew he couldn't allow himself to think about that for fear of prematurely ejaculating – it would all provide fuel for further intimate exchanges when he and Anne were next together.

Dawn rolled a condom down his shaft.

He gave her pussy lips a parting kiss and then changed position to thrust into her hole. His erection hovered against the gaping lips of her sex and she smiled eagerly up for him, silently pleading for his penetration. He marvelled that his third beautiful woman of the day was beneath him, anxious to experience his cock. Satisfaction welled in his chest and he stiffened himself, ready to plunge inside.

The sound of Lisa's nearby shriek trembled through the walls.

Apologising to Dawn, and not caring that he was naked save for a condom, Mark ran to his neighbour's assistance.

Anne lay shivering on the floor, unable to believe what she had just done. Her stomach ached, the orgasm had been extreme, and she still couldn't comprehend the size of the cock that she'd had between her legs. 'Enormous,' she gasped.

Victoria chuckled. 'And one never gets tired of it.'

'I want a turn,' Lisa told them.

Anne stared at her and shook her head. 'You can't be serious.'

'I've had him before,' Lisa argued.

Anne tried to think of an argument why Lisa shouldn't go with Trevor but there was nothing that came to her mind. He was not a particularly proficient lover but then, Anne did not think she had been given the opportunity to show off her own abilities with him either. His erection was huge. She guessed it was longer than twelve inches, a size that would have made it impressive on its own. But he was also thick. The girth was so large that her fingers couldn't completely encircle him. And, when she tried to take him her mouth, she couldn't stretch her lips around the swollen dome.

Victoria and Lisa had watched with obvious amusement. Anne got the impression that both of them had seen women faced with this dilemma time and again.

Licking at him, perplexed by his huge size, she repeatedly tried to take him in her mouth. Before the stretching could make her jaw muscles ache, she said, 'I want you in my pussy.'

Victoria had produced a condom – a larger one than Anne had ever seen before – and between them the three women had stroked the sheath over his length. Victoria had lapped at her husband's erection while Lisa had licked at Anne's pussy and helped her straddle the donkey. Their saliva offered a little lubrication, which Anne supposed was some help, but she didn't think there could be enough lubricants in the world to help her accept the mammoth organ as it wedged into her hole. A hot wave of agonised pleasure washed over her. She didn't think her sex had slipped halfway down his length before the climax had crushed her body. Her inner muscles tried to clamp around him but he was too large, she was too stretched, and there was no opportunity for the spasm to run its course.

She dragged herself away from him, panting with startled satisfaction and still marvelling at the massive breadth she had managed to accept between her legs. The eddies of pleasure were strong and exciting. She was repeatedly crippled by paroxysms of delight. Staggering from the bed, almost falling to the floor, Anne teetered on the brink of consciousness. 'Enormous,' she said again.

'I've got to have him,' Lisa insisted.

'He's yours if you want him,' Victoria told her. 'Just make sure you don't damage him.'

Anne climbed back on to the bed, licking at Lisa's pussy while Lisa lapped at Trevor's massive cock. Victoria changed the condom for him, smiling privately for her husband, and Anne watched her tongue occasionally brush against Lisa's mouth.

And then Lisa straddled him.

Anne watched her friend's eyes grow wide and her mouth fall agape. It was almost as though every orifice on Lisa's body was trying to open wider so she could accept the massive shaft.

Her pussy was stretched impossibly wide.

Anne trailed her tongue against Lisa's labia. She could feel the throbbing pulse of her friend's clitoris and, instinctively, she nibbled against its thrust.

Lisa screamed.

Losing her precarious balance as the orgasm rattled through her, sliding further on to Trevor's enormous cock, her eyes bulged as she took his entire length into her sex. Anne could see the woman's clitoris was more engorged than ever and, taking advantage of the opportunity, sucked hungrily at the pulsing bead of flesh. She was close enough to see Trevor's balls as they tightened and, miraculously, his fat cock grow even thicker as he ejaculated.

As Lisa opened her mouth to release a second scream, Johnny and Mark burst into the room. Their panicked expressions relaxed into grins when they saw Lisa pull herself from Trevor's shaft and collapse happily on the bed in the throes of another orgasm.

'Did you enjoy yourself, Becky?' Lisa asked. Her tone was cool to the point of innocence. If anyone had overheard the question it would have sounded like a simple enquiry, without any underscore of menace.

'I had a lovely time, thank you, Lisa,' Becky replied, her smile going no further than her lips. Her eyes were glassy with loathing. Her luxuriant titian curls lay lank against her scalp, their sheen stripped by chlorine from her time in the pool. Her cat-suit, clearly still soaked and ruined, was draped forlornly over her arm. Alec had given her his jacket and he looked awkward and out of place in only a shirt and pants. With obvious force Becky struggled to keep her voice saccharin-sweet. 'I hope you have just as much fun the next time you attend one of my parties.'

'I intend to,' Lisa said with a smile. She glanced at Johnny, Mark and Anne and said, 'We all intend to enjoy ourselves at your future parties, and we expect to be treated like guests of honour.'

A couple walked between them all, pushing their way to the door. Recognising Lisa they both turned to her with cheery smiles. 'It was a great party, Lisa. Thank you. The best we've ever been to.'

'Thank you,' she replied, grinning.

The couple seemed to notice Becky for the first time. The woman looked slightly tipsy but cuddled happily against her man. Smiling at Becky, she asked, 'Are you taking tips from the new queen of the party circuit?'

Becky bristled.

Lisa realised that of all the things she had seen this evening, Becky's response to that question was probably the most satisfying of all. She had watched her husband and her best friend fucking in the playroom, she had enjoyed another chance to experience Debbie and she had savoured contrite cunnilingus from the delectable Tara. There had been other encounters, casual compliments from strangers, and intimate greetings from those occasional swingers she and Johnny had met at other parties. But none of those events had given her the wholehearted pleasure of seeing Becky look so absolutely crushed. She turned away from the woman, knowing there was no further need to flaunt her victory. Dismissed, Becky fled to the car with Alec.

'Are we done?' Johnny asked.

'I think we've said good night to all the guests.'

'I've just done a circuit of the upstairs rooms,' Mark told her.

'I've checked the pool and downstairs,' Anne supplied. 'Everyone's gone.'

'So it's only us four?' Lisa asked, staring around the big empty hall. She was thinking that she and Johnny had never stayed so late at a party, and remembering it was one of their traditions to reaffirm their love on the journey home. It was a tradition that she didn't want to break. 'What are you two doing now?'

Mark's grin turned awkward. He glanced at Anne and then turned back to Lisa and Johnny. 'I don't know if this makes sense to you two, but I'm desperate to make love to my wife right now.' He held up a hand to stop any attempts at interruption and said, 'It's been a great party. We've done things we never imagined. But for the rest of this evening I just want to take Anne to bed and tell her how good she looks when she's fucking other people.'

They exchanged handshakes, hugs and kisses.

'I've set aside a couple of spare rooms upstairs,' Johnny told them. 'Lisa and I will be doing the same thing. The rooms are on different sides of the building so none of us should keep the others awake, unless the screaming is really loud.'

Silently – comfortably – the four of them climbed the stairs together. Lisa hadn't yet decided if she and Johnny were getting too close to their neighbours. But she suspected that in another week or so she might have come to a decision. And if that didn't help her to make up her mind, they could always throw another party.

nexus

The leading publisher of fetish and adult fiction

TELL US WHAT YOU THINK!

Readers' ideas and opinions matter to us so please take a few minutes to fill in the questionnaire below.

1. Sex: Are you male ☐   female ☐   a couple ☐?

2. Age: Under 21 ☐   21–30 ☐   31–40 ☐   41–50 ☐   51–60 ☐   over 60 ☐

3. Where do you buy your Nexus books from?

☐ A chain book shop. If so, which one(s)?
_____

☐ An independent book shop. If so, which one(s)?
_____

☐ A used book shop/charity shop
☐ Online book store. If so, which one(s)?
_____

4. How did you find out about Nexus books?

☐ Browsing in a book shop
☐ A review in a magazine
☐ Online
☐ Recommendation
☐ Other _____

5. In terms of settings, which do you prefer? (Tick as many as you like.)

☐ Down to earth and as realistic as possible
☐ Historical settings. If so, which period do you prefer?
_____

☐ Fantasy settings – barbarian worlds

- ☐ Completely escapist/surreal fantasy
- ☐ Institutional or secret academy
- ☐ Futuristic/sci fi
- ☐ Escapist but still believable
- ☐ Any settings you dislike?

_____

- ☐ Where would you like to see an adult novel set?

_____

6. In terms of storylines, would you prefer:

- ☐ Simple stories that concentrate on adult interests?
- ☐ More plot and character-driven stories with less explicit adult activity?
- ☐ We value your ideas, so give us your opinion of this book:

_____

_____

_____

7. In terms of your adult interests, what do you like to read about? (Tick as many as you like.)

- ☐ Traditional corporal punishment (CP)
- ☐ Modern corporal punishment
- ☐ Spanking
- ☐ Restraint/bondage
- ☐ Rope bondage
- ☐ Latex/rubber
- ☐ Leather
- ☐ Female domination and male submission
- ☐ Female domination and female submission
- ☐ Male domination and female submission
- ☐ Willing captivity
- ☐ Uniforms
- ☐ Lingerie/underwear/hosiery/footwear (boots and high heels)
- ☐ Sex rituals
- ☐ Vanilla sex
- ☐ Swinging

☐ Cross-dressing/TV
☐ Enforced feminisation
☐ Others – tell us what you don't see enough of in adult fiction:

_____

_____

_____

8. Would you prefer books with a more specialised approach to your interests, i.e. a novel specifically about uniforms? If so, which subject(s) would you like to read a Nexus novel about?

_____

_____

_____

9. Would you like to read true stories in Nexus books? For instance, the true story of a submissive woman, or a male slave? Tell us which true revelations you would most like to read about:

_____

_____

_____

10. What do you like best about Nexus books?

_____

_____

11. What do you like least about Nexus books?

_____

_____

12. Which are your favourite titles?

_____

_____

13. Who are your favourite authors?

_____

_____

14. **Which covers do you prefer? Those featuring:**
   (Tick as many as you like.)

   ☐ Fetish outfits
   ☐ More nudity
   ☐ Two models
   ☐ Unusual models or settings
   ☐ Classic erotic photography
   ☐ More contemporary images and poses
   ☐ A blank/non-erotic cover
   ☐ What would your ideal cover look like?

   _____

15. **Describe your ideal Nexus novel in the space provided:**

   _____
   _____
   _____
   _____

16. **Which celebrity would feature in one of your Nexus-style fantasies? We'll post the best suggestions on our website – anonymously!**

   _____

THANKS FOR YOUR TIME

Now simply write the title of this book in the space below and cut out the questionnaire pages. Post to: Nexus, Marketing Dept., Thames Wharf Studios, Rainville Rd, London W6 9HA

Book title: _____

NEXUS NEW BOOKS

To he published in February 2007

SLIPPERY WHEN WET
Penny Birch

Penny Birch assembles her famous cast of naughty girls for a slippery and messy week of fun. Gabrielle, the mischievous Poppy, and their nurse Sabina (from *Naughty, Naughty*) receive a gift from Monty Hartle of one week at an SM boot camp in Wales. Gabrielle is doubtful, but Poppy and Sabrina are keen, so they go. The camp turns out to be a converted home hired for the purpose, and is run by Mistress Kimiko, a poisonous individual with a serious uniform fetish. According to the rules Mistress Kimiko has absolute authority, save for the mysterious Master. The girls are assigned to the kitchens, which is asking for trouble . . .

£6.99   ISBN 978 0 352 34091 7

THE ROAD TO DEPRAVITY
Ray Gordon

Helen's husband, Alan, has walked out on her yet again. But this time she won't take him back. Thirty years old and extremely attractive with long black hair, Helen is enjoying her freedom and she has no shortage of men after her. But Alan won't leave her in peace. When she discovers that he's spying on her through the lounge window, watching her having sex with a male friend, she's initially shocked. But she soon realises that his voyeurism is a great turn-on.

Knowing that Alan is watching, she enjoys one sexual encounter after another. Taking things further in order to shock Alan, she experiments sexually with Mary, a young blonde lesbian. And Helen's sexual conquests plunge her deeper into the pit of depravity to the point where she enjoys group sex.

Alan takes his voyeurism to the extreme by hiding in the house and watching Helen with her sexual partners. Unsure what his long-term goal is, Helen again tries to shock him. Indulging in bondage and spanking, she's not sure whether she wants to be rid of Alan or continue to enjoy his spying. Until . . .

£6.99   ISBN 978 0 352 34092 4

NEXUS CONFESSIONS: VOLUME I
Various

Swinging, dogging, group sex, cross-dressing, spanking, female domination, corporal punishment, and extreme fetishes ... *Nexus Confessions*
explores the length and breadth of erotic obsession, real experience and
sexual fantasy. An encyclopaedic collection of the bizarre, the extreme,
the utterly inappropriate, the daring and the shocking experiences of
ordinary men and women driven by their extraordinary desires. Collected
by the world's leading publisher of fetish fiction, this is the first in a series
of six volumes of true stories and shameful confessions, never-before-told
or published.

£6.99   ISBN 978 0 352 34093 1

If you would like more information about Nexus titles, please visit our
website at www.nexus-books.co.uk, or send a large stamped addressed
envelope to:
  Nexus, Thames Wharf Studios,
  Rainville Road, London W6 9HA

NEXUS BOOKLIST

Information is correct at time of printing. To avoid disappointment, check availability before ordering. Go to www.nexus-books.co.uk.

All books are priced at £6.99 unless another price is given.

NEXUS

☐ ABANDONED ALICE Adriana Arden ISBN 978 0 352 33969 0
☐ ALICE IN CHAINS Adriana Arden ISBN 978 0 352 33908 9
☐ AQUA DOMINATION William Doughty ISBN 978 0 352 34020 7
☐ THE ART OF CORRECTION Tara Black ISBN 978 0 352 33895 2
☐ THE ART OF SURRENDER Madeline Bastinado ISBN 978 0 352 34013 9
☐ BELINDA BARES UP Yolanda Celbridge ISBN 978 0 352 33926 3
☐ BENCH-MARKS Tara Black ISBN 978 0 352 33797 9
☐ BIDDING TO SIN Rosita Varón ISBN 978 0 352 34063 4
☐ BINDING PROMISES G.C. Scott ISBN 978 0 352 34014 6
☐ THE BOOK OF PUNISHMENT Cat Scarlett ISBN 978 0 352 33975 1
☐ BRUSH STROKES Penny Birch ISBN 978 0 352 34072 6
☐ CALLED TO THE WILD Angel Blake ISBN 978 0 352 34067 2
☐ CAPTIVES OF CHEYNER CLOSE Adriana Arden ISBN 978 0 352 34028 3
☐ CARNAL POSSESSION Yvonne Strickland ISBN 978 0 352 34062 7
☐ COLLEGE GIRLS Cat Scarlett ISBN 978 0 352 33942 3
☐ COMPANY OF SLAVES Christina Shelly ISBN 978 0 352 33887 7
☐ CONCEIT AND CONSEQUENCE Aishling Morgan ISBN 978 0 352 33965 2
☐ CORRECTIVE THERAPY Jacqueline Masterson ISBN 978 0 352 33917 1

□ CORRUPTION	Virginia Crowley	ISBN 978 0 352 34073 3
□ CRUEL SHADOW	Aishling Morgan	ISBN 978 0 352 33886 0
□ DARK MISCHIEF	Lady Alice McCloud	ISBN 978 0 352 33998 0
□ DEPTHS OF DEPRAVATION	Ray Gordon	ISBN 978 0 352 33995 9
□ DICE WITH DOMINATION	P.S. Brett	ISBN 978 0 352 34023 8
□ DOMINANT	Felix Baron	ISBN 978 0 352 34044 3
□ DOMINATION DOLLS	Lindsay Gordon	ISBN 978 0 352 33891 4
□ EXPOSÉ	Laura Bowen	ISBN 978 0 352 34035 1
□ FORBIDDEN READING	Lisette Ashton	ISBN 978 0 352 34022 1
□ FRESH FLESH	Wendy Swanscombe	ISBN 978 0 352 34041 2
□ HOT PURSUIT	Lisette Ashton	ISBN 978 0 352 33878 5
□ THE INDECENCIES OF ISABELLE	Penny Birch (writing as Cruella)	ISBN 978 0 352 33989 8
□ THE INDISCRETIONS OF ISABELLE	Penny Birch (writing as Cruella)	ISBN 978 0 352 33882 2
□ IN DISGRACE	Penny Birch	ISBN 978 0 352 33922 5
□ IN HER SERVICE	Lindsay Gordon	ISBN 978 0 352 33968 3
□ INSTRUMENTS OF PLEASURE	Nicole Dere	ISBN 978 0 352 34098 6
□ JULIA C	Laura Bowen	ISBN 978 0 352 33852 5
□ LACING LISBETH	Yolanda Celbridge	ISBN 978 0 352 33912 6
□ LICKED CLEAN	Yolanda Celbridge	ISBN 978 0 352 33999 7
□ LOVE JUICE	Donna Exeter	ISBN 978 0 352 33913 3
□ MANSLAVE	J.D. Jensen	ISBN 978 0 352 34040 5
□ THE MASTER OF CASTLELEIGH	Jacqueline Bellevois	ISBN 978 0 352 33644 6 £5.99
□ NAUGHTY, NAUGHTY	Penny Birch	ISBN 978 0 352 33976 8
□ NIGHTS IN WHITE COTTON	Penny Birch	ISBN 978 0 352 34008 5
□ NO PAIN, NO GAIN	James Baron	ISBN 978 0 352 33966 9
□ THE OLD PERVERSITY SHOP	Aishling Morgan	ISBN 978 0 352 34007 8

☐ ORIGINAL SINS	Lisette Ashton	ISBN 978 0 352 33804 4
☐ THE PALACE OF PLEASURES	Christobel Coleridge	ISBN 978 0 352 33801 3
☐ PALE PLEASURES	Wendy Swanscombe	ISBN 978 0 352 33702 3
☐ PENNY PIECES	Penny Birch	ISBN 978 0 352 33631 6 £5.99
☐ PETTING GIRLS	Penny Birch	ISBN 978 0 352 33957 7
☐ PET TRAINING IN THE PRIVATE HOUSE	Esme Ombreux	ISBN 978 0 352 33655 2 £5.99
☐ THE PLAYER	Cat Scarlett	ISBN 978 0 352 33894 5
☐ THE PRIESTESS	Jacqueline Bellevois	ISBN 978 0 352 33905 8
☐ PRIZE OF PAIN	Wendy Swanscombe	ISBN 978 0 352 33890 7
☐ PUNISHED IN PINK	Yolanda Celbridge	ISBN 978 0 352 34003 0
☐ THE PUNISHMENT CAMP	Jacqueline Masterson	ISBN 978 0 352 33940 9
☐ THE PUNISHMENT CLUB	Jacqueline Masterson	ISBN 978 0 352 33862 4
☐ SCARLET VICE	Aishling Morgan	ISBN 978 0 352 33988 1
☐ SCHOOLED FOR SERVICE	Lady Alice McCloud	ISBN 978 0 352 33918 8
☐ SCHOOL FOR STINGERS	Yolanda Celbridge	ISBN 978 0 352 33994 2
☐ SEXUAL HEELING	Wendy Swanscombe	ISBN 978 0 352 33921 8
☐ SILKEN EMBRACE	Christina Shelly	ISBN 978 0 352 34081 8
☐ SILKEN SERVITUDE	Christina Shelly	ISBN 978 0 352 34004 7
☐ SINS APPRENTICE	Aishling Morgan	ISBN 978 0 352 33909 6
☐ SLAVE GENESIS	Jennifer Jane Pope	ISBN 978 0 352 33503 6 £5.99
☐ SLAVE OF THE SPARTANS	Yolanda Celbridge	ISBN 978 0 352 34078 8
☐ THE SMARTING OF SELINA	Yolanda Celbridge	ISBN 978 0 352 33872 3
☐ STRIP GIRL	Aishling Morgan	ISBN 978 0 352 34077 1
☐ STRIPING KAYLA	Yolanda Marshall	ISBN 978 0 352 33881 5
☐ STRIPPED BARE	Angel Blake	ISBN 978 0 352 33971 3
☐ TASTING CANDY	Ray Gordon	ISBN 978 0 352 33925 6
☐ TEMPTING THE GODDESS	Aishling Morgan	ISBN 978 0 352 33972 0
☐ THAI HONEY	Kit McCann	ISBN 978 0 352 34068 9
☐ TICKLE TORTURE	Penny Birch	ISBN 978 0 352 33904 1

☐ TOKYO BOUND	Sachi	ISBN 978 0 352 34019 1
☐ TORMENT INCORPORATED	Murilee Martin	ISBN 978 0 352 33943 0
☐ UNEARTHLY DESIRES	Ray Gordon	ISBN 978 0 352 34036 8
☐ UNIFORM DOLL	Penny Birch	ISBN 978 0 352 33698 9
☐ VELVET SKIN	Aishling Morgan	ISBN 978 0 352 33660 6 £5.99
☐ WENCHES, WITCHES AND STRUMPETS	Aishling Morgan	ISBN 978 0 352 33733 7
☐ WHALEBONE STRICT	Lady Alice McCloud	ISBN 978 0 352 34082 5
☐ WHAT HAPPENS TO BAD GIRLS	Penny Birch	ISBN 978 0 352 34031 3
☐ WHAT SUKI WANTS	Cat Scarlett	ISBN 978 0 352 34027 6
☐ WHEN SHE WAS BAD	Penny Birch	ISBN 978 0 352 33859 4
☐ WHIP HAND	G.C. Scott	ISBN 978 0 352 33694 1
☐ WHIPPING GIRL	Aishling Morgan	ISBN 978 0 352 33789 4
☐ WHIPPING TRIANGLE	G.C. Scott	ISBN 978 0 352 34086 3

NEXUS CLASSIC

☐ AMAZON SLAVE	Lisette Ashton	ISBN 978 0 352 33916 4
☐ ANGEL	Lindsay Gordon	ISBN 978 0 352 34009 2
☐ THE BLACK GARTER	Lisette Ashton	ISBN 978 0 352 33919 5
☐ THE BLACK MASQUE	Lisette Ashton	ISBN 978 0 352 33977 5
☐ THE BLACK ROOM	Lisette Ashton	ISBN 978 0 352 33914 0
☐ THE BLACK WIDOW	Lisette Ashton	ISBN 978 0 352 33973 7
☐ THE BOND	Lindsay Gordon	ISBN 978 0 352 33996 6
☐ DISCIPLINE OF THE PRIVATE HOUSE	Esme Ombreux	ISBN 978 0 352 33709 2
☐ THE DOMINO ENIGMA	Cyrian Amberlake	ISBN 978 0 352 34064 1
☐ THE DOMINO QUEEN	Cyrian Amberlake	ISBN 978 0 352 34074 0
☐ THE DOMINO TATTOO	Cyrian Amberlake	ISBN 978 0 352 34037 5
☐ EMMA ENSLAVED	Hilary James	ISBN 978 0 352 33883 9
☐ EMMA'S HUMILIATION	Hilary James	ISBN 978 0 352 33910 2
☐ EMMA'S SECRET DOMINATION	Hilary James	ISBN 978 0 352 34000 9

☐ EMMA'S SUBMISSION	Hilary James	ISBN 978 0 352 33906 5
☐ FAIRGROUND ATTRACTION	Lisette Ashton	ISBN 978 0 352 33927 0
☐ IN FOR A PENNY	Penny Birch	ISBN 978 0 352 34083 2
☐ THE INSTITUTE	Maria Del Rey	ISBN 978 0 352 33352 0
☐ MISS RATANS LESSON	Yolanda Celbridge	ISBN 978 0 352 33791 7
☐ NEW EROTICA 5	Various	ISBN 978 0 352 33956 0
☐ THE NEXUS LETTERS	Various	ISBN 978 0 352 33955 3
☐ ONE WEEK IN THE PRIVATE HOUSE	Esme Ombreux	ISBN 978 0 352 33706 1
☐ PLAYTHING	Penny Birch	ISBN 978 0 352 33967 6
☐ PLEASING THEM	William Doughty	ISBN 978 0 352 34015 3
☐ RITES OF OBEDIENCE	Lindsay Gordon	ISBN 978 0 352 34005 4
☐ SERVING TIME	Sarah Veitch	ISBN 978 0 352 33509 8
☐ THE SUBMISSION GALLERY	Lindsay Gordon	ISBN 978 0 352 34026 9
☐ TIE AND TEASE	Penny Birch	ISBN 978 0 352 33987 4
☐ TIGHT WHITE COTTON	Penny Birch	ISBN 978 0 352 33970 6

NEXUS ENTHUSIAST

☐ BUSTY	Tom King	ISBN 978 0 352 34032 0
☐ DERRIÈRE	Julius Culdrose	ISBN 978 0 352 34024 5
☐ LEG LOVER	L. G. Denier	ISBN 978 0 352 34016 0
☐ OVER THE KNEE	Fiona Locke	ISBN 978 0 352 34079 5
☐ THE SECRET SELF	Christina Shelly	ISBN 978 0 352 34069 6
☐ UNDER MY MASTER'S WINGS	Lauren Wissot	ISBN 978 0 352 34042 9
☐ WIFE SWAP	Amber Leigh	ISBN 978 0 352 34097 9

NEXUS NON FICTION

| ☐ LESBIAN SEX SECRETS FOR MEN | Jamie Goddard and Kurt Brungard | ISBN 978 0 352 33724 5 |

------ ✂ ------------------------------

Please send me the books I have ticked above.

Name ....

Address ....

....

....

.... Post code ....

Send to: **Virgin Books Cash Sales, Thames Wharf Studios, Rainville Road, London W6 9HA**

US customers: for prices and details of how to order books for delivery by mail, call 888-330-8477.

Please enclose a cheque or postal order, made payable to **Nexus Books Ltd**, to the value of the books you have ordered plus postage and packing costs as follows:

UK and BFPO – £1.00 for the first book, 50p for each subsequent book.

Overseas (including Republic of Ireland) – £2.00 for the first book, £1.00 for each subsequent book.

If you would prefer to pay by VISA, ACCESS/MASTERCARD, AMEX, DINERS CLUB or SWITCH, please write your card number and expiry date here:

....

Please allow up to 28 days for delivery.

Signature ....

Our privacy policy

We will not disclose information you supply us to any other parties. We will not disclose any information which identifies you personally to any person without your express consent.

From time to time we may send out information about Nexus books and special offers. Please tick here if you do *not* wish to receive Nexus information.   ☐

------ ✂ ------------------------------